T0357722

BY SWATI HEGDE

Can't Help Faking in Love

Match Me If You Can

Can't Help
Faking
in Love

Can't Help Faking in Love

a novel

SWATI HEGDE

DELL
NEW YORK

A Dell Trade Paperback Original

Published in the United States by Dell,
an imprint of Random House, a division of
Penguin Random House LLC, New York.

DELL and the D colophon are registered trademarks
of Penguin Random House LLC.

ISBN 978-0-593-72293-0
Ebook ISBN 978-0-593-72294-7

Printed in the United States of America on acid-free paper

randomhousebooks.com

2 4 6 8 9 7 5 3 1

Book design by Alexis Flynn
Title page illustration: stock.adobe.com/mchlabs
Chapter illustration: stock.adobe.com/merfin

For Rachel—my agent, publishing soulmate,
and the balm to my anxiety.
None of this would be possible without you.

Can't Help
Faking
in Love

Chapter

ONE

"Welcome to the real world. It sucks.
You're gonna love it!"
—Monica Geller, *Friends*

Harsha Godbole had never been dumped like this before.

She sat across from her now ex-boyfriend during their lunch date, a forkful of spaghetti midway to her mouth, as he explained that he was ending their three-month relationship to marry a complete stranger.

"I really like you, I do," Shashank insisted, sipping his iced americano. "But I was just introduced to a prospective match, and with all of my parents' life experience, they probably know enough to make the right choice for me, don't you think?"

"Uh-huh." Harsha set her fork down and wiped her mouth with a napkin, her lips pressed together. The men she'd dated in the past had given her far simpler reasons—*There's no spark; I'm not ready for a serious relationship; Your family is too much to handle*—but to be rejected by a thirty-year-old man because he was letting his parents choose his bride? What decade was he stuck in, the 1980s? And now that she thought about it, why was he meeting prospective brides while still dating her?

Shashank looked at his wristwatch and did a double take. "Shit, I have a meeting in ten. I hope we're good? No hard feelings?"

It would have been funny if it weren't for the dread slowly sinking into the pit of her stomach.

Harsha forced herself to smile. "Of course. Thanks for lunch." She grabbed her purse and laptop bag and strode out of the Italian restaurant, refusing to turn around and check if he was looking her way. She didn't need any more disappointment.

She tugged on a stray coil of her curly black hair as she walked through the traffic-filled streets of Bangalore while cars honked and auto rickshaw drivers cursed at each other. If only the noise would drown out the fearful thoughts crowding her mind. Maybe moving here had been a mistake. Sure, it was cheaper than living in California, and there was no way she would move back home to Mumbai, but now she was not only friendless in this strange new city but also single. Alone. And—to top it all off—unemployed.

Her best friend from college, Sasha, would say she was being hard on herself. After all, Harsha was getting through life as a struggling freelance photographer, armed with just her camera, a steady hand, and an eye for beauty. Her double degree in sociology and photography from Berkeley had proved useless in getting a job in Bangalore, the city of software engineers, so she was relying on her camera to make her some money until she could figure something out. Research online promised her that Bangalore's urban, cosmopolitan vibes would feel familiar to her Mumbai roots, but with better weather and cheaper rent. Though the cool breeze was a constant, freelance jobs were few and far between. She had landed her last gig at a college graduation only because her aunt knew a professor there. That was two weeks ago, and her bank account was depleting by the minute. Her coffee addiction didn't help.

Sighing, Harsha pushed open the glass door to Sunstag Café, the only place that felt anywhere close to safe right now. She ignored the tinkling of the wind chimes and the "Welcome to Sunstag!" greetings of the baristas she saw every day and stormed upstairs to her usual spot by the wall.

"Well, you don't look happy. All good?" Veer, her favorite barista, said, quirking an eyebrow as he passed by her table with an empty tray.

"Yeah, I just—" Harsha's shoulders slumped, but she stopped herself from saying more. He was a barista, not a bartender. He wasn't going to listen to her sob story and offer sage words of advice. "Never mind."

Besides, the only thing he knew about her was her coffee order, although he teased her every day, acting like he didn't.

Veer shrugged, brown eyes bright and that goofy smile on his face like always. Maybe he was in a happy relationship, unlike Harsha. Maybe he didn't just get dumped by a man worthy of being the Indian Bachelor. *Not everyone can be so lucky,* Harsha mused.

"The usual?" he asked.

"Yeah, thanks." She lowered her eyes and handed him her Sunstag loyalty card. The tears were going to come any minute now, and she didn't want his sympathy.

"Blended mocha with whole milk and caramel syrup," he said as he headed downstairs. "Coming right up!"

She half-smiled at his retreating back, not even bothering to correct him. The familiar joke didn't make her laugh like it usually did. Harsha had only failure on her mind.

Sighing, she hunched in her seat and idly scratched her knee. At least she always had Sunstag to return to, where her favorite baristas made the best coffee and brought it right to her seat. At least she didn't have to carry her own coffee up one flight of stairs every morning and afternoon. *Gotta be grateful for the little blessings in life, right?*

Her phone chimed, and she dug her hand into her bag eagerly. Maybe Shashank had seen the error of his ways and was ready to reconcile. After all, who gave up three months of almost-love for a parent-recommended bride they barely knew?

Shashank had been her perfect match on paper. Her family would have approved of his career, status, and upbringing; society would have gone gaga over how good he and Harsha looked together . . . and sure, maybe their relationship wasn't all rainbows and sunshine in the real world, but was any relationship? They had had a good thing together—potential. Didn't that matter?

Harsha unlocked her phone screen, then exhaled. It was a text from the second-last person she wanted to hear from—the first being her father.

Maa:

Are u free? Need to talk to u

She scowled and put her phone face down on the table. What was it this time? More nagging about how Harsha's lack of marital status was bringing shame to the entire Godbole family? Or that capturing people on the best days of their lives wasn't a respectable enough way to make money? Or that she needed to come back home after three months of being away and put on a happy front for the sake of their extended family? She didn't need that toxic energy in her life.

Which was exactly why, a month before she had graduated from college, Harsha made the decision to separate herself from the Godbole family—and their money.

Before moving to America, Harsha wouldn't have had to think twice about doing as her parents said. Having your cake and eating it too—that was life with the Godboles in a high-rise penthouse apartment. The full-time housekeeper ready to do all the cooking and cleaning. The driver taking Harsha to and from the places she visited. Her parents willing to find her a handsome groom.

It was chocolate cake with the most delectable icing. No wonder most of the girls from her private school had opted for that kind of lifestyle.

The only thing missing was the cherry on top of the cake: freedom and unconditional love. And, unfortunately, Harsha would rather have the cherry than the actual cake.

She exhaled and took out her laptop, deciding to scour the internet for anyone looking to hire a photographer, when Veer appeared with a foaming hot latte. The smell of vanilla wafted into her nostrils, and she smiled contentedly. Her post-lunch coffee always cheered her up, no questions asked. "One triple-shot espresso with peppermint syrup," Veer said with a wink.

She smiled weakly. "I already know you've brought me the right order. I can smell the vanilla."

"I'm a barista. It's not the most exciting job on the planet." Veer let out a huff, scratching his stubbly beard. "This is the only fun I get to have."

"Fine, I'll play," she said. "Oat milk?"

"Yes."

"Half a shot of coffee?"

"Yes."

"Extra whipped cream?"

"Yeah."

"Five pumps of vanilla?"

"How have you not died of a sugar overdose yet?" he asked.

"I have good genes," she said primly.

Veer gave her a once-over, then looked away, smirking. "Yeah, I can see that. Enjoy."

Her lips turned up the slightest amount. "Thanks."

"Are you sure you're doing okay?" Veer's forehead creased. "That smile looks a little too small for how great my sense of humor is."

Harsha made a big show of rolling her eyes. "Maybe you're just not as funny as you think."

"Impossible. See you." Chuckling, he went downstairs, probably back to the counter, and Harsha took a sip of her overly complicated coffee, leaving a red lipstick stain on the cup.

The coffee almost felt off-putting today, though. Harsha set it down and tugged on her lower lip with her teeth, thinking of Shashank. She was going to miss resting her head on his muscular chest and sleeping contentedly three nights a week, when she'd visit his sprawling apartment instead of staying cooped up in her tiny one-bedroom.

When her phone rang, jolting her back to reality, she jumped. Her mother was video calling her. Harsha hesitated, her eyes on Maa's profile photo: a selfie atop the Burj Khalifa taken during the extended family's recent vacation to Dubai. Harsha hadn't been invited to that one, owing to their big fight four months ago. Maybe Maa was calling to apologize, finally.

She put on her AirPods and hit the green icon. Maa popped up on the screen, her gray eyes slightly widening as though she, too, couldn't believe Harsha had picked up. "Hi, beta," Maa said, smiling tightly, or maybe that was the result of her Botox. "How are you?"

Harsha shifted in place. "Fine. Just getting some work done."

"You got a job?!"

"I meant for my photography business."

Maa cleared her throat, clearly unimpressed. "All right. And how's your boyfriend? Neha saw your three-month-iversary dinner photos on your story last weekend at that gourmet restaurant. Her fiancé takes her there all the time."

Shit. Harsha had never posted Shashank's face on her Instagram or even tagged him, given that he refused to use social media, but showing off snippets from their fancy date nights was her way of hinting to her parents—and her snobby cousin—that she could find herself a perfectly suitable match without their help.

She widened her lips into a fake smile. "He's great. We just had lunch together."

"Wonderful." Maa scratched the side of her eyebrow. "I'm glad you've found a nice boy for yourself. A nice Indian boy who meets all of our standards."

"Thanks." Harsha's throat tightened, and she pretended to look sideways at her laptop. "I have a lot of photos to edit, Maa. Is there anything else?"

Maa nodded, looking smug. "It's your Uncle Madhu and Aunt

Pinky's twenty-fifth anniversary party next month, here in Mumbai. I've already told everyone you're bringing your boyfriend."

Harsha's mouth fell open, the phone nearly slipping from her grasp. "Maa! How could you do that without asking—"

"Shush." Maa put out her free hand, her diamond-studded wedding ring glinting. "We've given you plenty of space. The least you can do is make an appearance at family gatherings every now and then. You chose to move away from us with no warning. People talk."

Harsha licked her lips. "Okay," she said, if only to be done with this conversation. "I'll be there." She hit End Call and groaned. Uncle Madhu and Aunt Pinky's twenty-fifth wedding anniversary, bound to be a lavish affair at some five-star Mumbai hotel. That meant her entire family would be there: parents, uncles, aunts, grandparents, cousins, their spouses, their kids—everyone. And of course, that included Neha Godbole, her beautiful, successful cousin who worked for the UN and was engaged to a surgeon. Arranged marriage, obviously.

Aunt Pinky, Neha's mother, was the only sensible person in their family, the one ally Harsha still had among the Godboles. She was the aunt who had set Harsha up with her last freelance job. But she was probably busy planning the anniversary party; there was no point taking up more of her time and asking her for help.

It was fine. Harsha would figure something out; she always did when it came to her family, especially seeing how much drama being a Godbole entailed, given her dad's industrial business and her uncle's Bollywood movies. When she was younger, she used to have to meet her real friends in secret because they weren't "society-approved," or avoid the paparazzi during a terrible bout of teenage acne when visiting her aunt and uncle.

Harsha whipped out her phone and rested her finger on Shashank's contact. She could call him and ask him to play along, just for the anniversary party. But after the nonchalant way in which he'd dumped her, as though it were merely something he was checking off his daily to-do list, calling him was *not* an option. There was nobody to take her side, reassure her that she wasn't a complete failure, or tell her she was loved even if her parents didn't approve of her decisions. She was on her own again.

To top it all off, Harsha didn't have anything to wear to the anniversary party. She'd left most of her wardrobe at her parents' penthouse in Mumbai, and quality sarees were expensive.

Financially speaking, she had one decent backup plan, though her ego would be seriously bruised if she took it. Her dad had transferred a good sum of money from the family trust fund into a secondary account when she turned eighteen. She hadn't touched the money since moving back to India, but her father had encouraged her to use it, "just in case"—of course, he didn't believe she could make it on her own. There were probably still five million rupees in the account.

If she needed to make ends meet, she could always dip into the secondary account, and her father wouldn't even know. But it would mean breaking the promise she had made to herself . . .

First, she would breathe. She would send out a bunch of cold emails. And then she would head to a bar and find solace in a vodka soda, or three.

Until then, Veer's delicious coffee—and his silly jokes—would keep her company.

"THE COLLEGE CANCELED YOUR SCHOLARSHIP?" Veer Kannan paused in front of his locker, his apron still half-tied around his back, and tried to make sense of what his brother had just told him. "How can they do that?"

"I don't know," Arjun said. "They said there was some sort of technical error, and I was never even allotted the scholarship. I don't know why this is happening. I'm so sorry."

"No, look, we need to call them," Veer urged.

"But I already tried. I called so many times. I think they had to move money around, and maybe it went to someone else. You know how these things go." Arjun's voice was defeated and small. It tore at Veer to hear his brother sound so broken when just yesterday, at breakfast, he had been so giddy about the courses he'd signed up for, wondering which professors he would be assigned. Veer had nearly felt excited himself for that economics lecture, which ought to have been an impossible feat. Now, as Veer reflected in the dead air of the phone call, it made sense why the financial offices had delayed the scholarship for so long. They had known that certain strings were getting pulled, and people like them were never the ones with the power to yank back.

"When's the last date to pay the tuition?" he asked finally.

Arjun gulped, loud enough for him to hear it. "Monday."

Fuck. That was three days away. "I just got done with my shift. Let's talk about this at home," Veer said, biting his lip. "We'll figure it out, Arjun, I promise." He hung up and ran a hand through his hair.

Okay, all right. Veer had three days to make half a million rupees.

Well, probably not *make*. He didn't make that much money in a year, never mind in three days. The initial deposit money had been only a drop of the total, and even that had been painful to pull together by the deadline. The Business Institute of India, Delhi, was one of the top management schools in the country, and a well-paying corporate job was just about guaranteed after graduation. So he'd have to get his hands on the money somehow. If he didn't, Arjun would lose his admission to BII, he wouldn't get his MBA, and he wouldn't have the best future possible—one he had already worked so hard for.

And Veer couldn't let that happen to his little brother.

He took off his apron and folded it neatly, stowing it back in his locker, then sighed. Half a million rupees. He had less than ninety thousand sitting in his bank account right now, having spent a considerable amount last week fixing up his secondhand car after some asshole rammed into it in broad daylight. And as the sole breadwinner in their family, Veer was responsible for taking care of his mother's living expenses as well.

Maybe they could apply for an education loan? But it was Friday. There was no way a bank could process an application and grant the necessary funds by Monday night. Still, he could try.

He rolled his eyes as he slammed the locker shut. Colleges couldn't just offer you a full-ride scholarship on a platter and then claim there had been a department error. How could anybody pay up half a million rupees in tuition over one weekend? Were people really that rich?

Maybe if that sitcom pilot episode had been green-lit instead of getting scrapped . . . Veer still remembered the rush of adrenaline he'd felt when he walked into the small Mumbai studio on his first day of filming, and the bounce in his step after the daily shoot. He—and everyone else on set—had been so sure the sitcom, a hilarious show following a class of law school students, would be a hit. Veer had even bought legal textbooks, as boring as they were, to prep for his role as the underdog main character from the wrong side of town.

But then it went nowhere. It was the director's debut, Veer and the other actors were unknown names in the industry, and the market was "saturated" with both college shows and legal dramas. Nobody had faith in them. Or, as it turned out, in Veer. His film agent dumped him shortly after that.

It's pointless to think about that, he reminded himself. He grabbed his things and headed out into the store from the employees' room.

"Wanna get drinks later, Veer?" Deepika, his girl best friend and fellow barista, asked as she waved from the counter. Raunak, his other barista buddy, raised his eyebrows.

"Maybe tomorrow, I'm beat." He put on a smile and headed to the door, his mind on the astronomical sum of money.

Five hundred thousand rupees. *Fuck.*

He bit his lip. There was no way out of this, so Veer did the only thing he could think of: distract himself.

Turning back to his friends, he said, "On second thought, drinks sound like exactly what I need."

Raunak pumped his fist in the air, startling a customer at the counter, then apologized when Deepika side-eyed him. "See you tonight," she said, and Veer cracked the smallest of smiles before making his way out.

Chapter TWO

"What a week, huh?"
—Liz Lemon, *30 Rock*

Drinking alone was the worst. The main character in rom-coms could always pull it off, casually sitting on a barstool dressed to the nines, ordering a martini and waiting for the love of her life to walk up to her. But as Harsha sat there, hunched over in a too-short-for-comfort red dress, trying to get a piece of nacho out of her teeth, she could only think about her mother's phone call and the walk of shame she would have to do at the anniversary party, dumped and dateless.

She finished her cocktail and looked around the bar, sighing. This never would have happened to her in college, over eight thousand miles away from her Mumbai home. In California, she was confident in herself and didn't have such unrealistic expectations to uphold for her family's sake.

She'd made friends—real friends—without a second thought about what Maa or Papa would think of their family background. She had fond memories of going hiking with them, asking them to pose for her against the breathtaking views of Oakland Hills.

Although she'd still relied on her trust fund money for some expenses—California wasn't a cheap place to live, after all—her life was a breath of fresh air, and, away from the prying eyes of the Godboles and the media circus that tended to follow them, she no longer had to hold herself back from being her fun-loving, carefree self. It was fascinating how joyful life could be when Harsha wasn't constantly looking over her shoulder or apologizing for a social misstep.

Realizing that, Harsha told her parents, a month before graduation, that she wouldn't be returning to Mumbai—she wanted to make a name for herself instead of living in Papa's shadow forever.

Harsha wasn't surprised when her parents didn't show up to her graduation ceremony because of conveniently timed "work conflicts." It was all the proof she needed to distance herself from them—and their money—and decide that she didn't need their approval anymore.

And yet, the Universe wasn't done playing cruel jokes. Because the second she got on the plane to Bangalore a week later, ready to prove herself to the world, there Shashank Kapoor was, sitting in the seat next to hers. The perfect parent-approved gentleman. The handsome rich guy in a suit who was happy to listen to her talk about how she wanted to be her own independent self now that she'd graduated.

Maybe Harsha didn't have to face her family at the party at all. She could simply fake her death, move to Paris, and get a fresh start. Meet a nice Frenchman who'd buy her croissants and kiss her in front of the Eiffel Tower.

Except moving back to India was supposed to be her fresh start. Harsha snorted and ordered another vodka soda. Where was a good man when you needed him?

"Harsha?"

She looked to the left and smiled at Veer, who'd just joined her at the bar. He looked surprisingly different out of his black-and-yellow barista uniform, now dressed in a plain red T-shirt and fitted blue jeans. Without the Sunstag cap, his hair was smooth and wavy, slightly curling at the base of his neck. "Hey," she said. "What are you doing here?"

He hooked a thumb behind him. "Getting another round of beers for us."

Harsha leaned back in her seat to spot a booth where two of the other baristas she saw every day were sitting. Maybe they were all close friends. "Isn't Friday night about getting a break from the people you work with during the entire week?" she joked.

"It is." He grinned. "Why do you think I'm standing here with you?"

She laughed. "You see me at Sunstag every day, too, so I don't count."

Veer's eyes glinted. "I think I'll be the judge of that."

Harsha usually would have enjoyed this interaction a lot more, but right now, she was too mad at men—and humanity—to appreciate Veer's flirting skills. The bartender slid Harsha's third vodka soda in front of her, and she took a sip before easing into the itchy barstool that was rough against her bare legs. Then she said, "Hey, can I ask you something?"

"Sure, what is it?"

She took a deep breath, then spoke. "Why do Indian men care so much about what their parents think?"

Veer paused, just as he was about to signal to the bartender. "What?"

"For example"—she sipped her drink—"why do they bother dating modern women, telling them sweet nothings, making them feel wanted and chosen, only to turn right back around and decide to have an arranged marriage?"

"I . . . don't know?" Veer scratched the back of his neck, that very spot where his hair curled. "I've never been a fan of arranged marriages." His scruffy jaw gritted for a second before he quirked an eyebrow at her. "Why do you ask?"

She drank deeply and turned so she was facing him completely. "You know, just asking for a . . . friend."

Veer leaned both his arms against the bar counter and scrutinized her. His forearms were thick and dusted with dark hair, the muscles straining from his movement. Harsha looked away just as he said, "Is that why you looked so upset at Sunstag this afternoon? Someone broke up with you?"

Harsha bit her lip. A small instinct made her shift her barstool just a few inches closer to him. "I'm surprised you noti—"

"Harsha? Harsha, oh my gosh! Hi!"

No. No, no, no. Harsha slid off the barstool, having recognized that voice. That noisy, whiny voice. The voice of her cousin, who was now flashing her expensive diamond ring as a faux hello.

"Hey," mustered Harsha with a weak smile.

Neha was her only family member who lived in Bangalore, unlike the rest of the Godboles, who occupied Mumbai—the one downside to moving here. Luckily, she hadn't run into her until now. Neha pulled Harsha in for a hug, which Harsha did not return, and then added, "Oh, you haven't met my fiancé, have you?"

The engagement had happened while Harsha was still in California, so she thankfully never had the pleasure. "Nope," Harsha said, raising her eyebrows at Neha's future husband. *Hmm.* Tall, handsome, rich, and probably obnoxious, given that Neha had decided to marry him.

"Rohan, Harsha. Harsha, this is Dr. Rohan Jha. He's a neurosurgeon. Congrats on graduating—sociology, was it?"

"And photography," Harsha clarified.

"Right, congrats, tough field," Rohan said, shaking her hand stiffly, then looked at his wristwatch as though greeting her was a waste of his time. Yep. Neha's type, for sure.

Neha's gaze fell on Veer, and the very slight gap between his and Harsha's barstools, and she held her hand out. "Oh, hello. I'm Neha Godbole, Harsha's cousin."

"Hi," he greeted her back. "I'm Veer—"

"Oh, I know who you are." She simpered, then turned to Harsha. "Harsha, good to see you being serious about dating. After all those *flings* you had in America"—Neha let out an exhale—"it's nice that you've finally moved on from boring white boys."

Harsha's eyes widened, and she stared from her cousin to Veer, who had stood up from his barstool, looking just as confused as she was. "Neha, Veer is—"

Neha went on, clapping her hands. "And you're coming to my parents' anniversary party! Your first family event in nearly six months, with a boyfriend this time. How exciting! Rohan, isn't it exciting?" She turned to her fiancé, who stifled a yawn in response.

Harsha's palms went clammy with sweat, and she wiped them on her short dress. "Did Maa tell you about that?"

Her cousin beamed at her. "She gushed to everyone in my wedding prep group chat about how well things are going in your new relationship." Her eyes went to Veer again, and Harsha realized, with a deathly lurch, that Neha thought the man standing next to her at the bar was her boyfriend. The boyfriend who no longer existed. The Universe obviously hated her.

Veer sat back on the barstool, frowning. "I'm sorry, but Harsha and I—"

"—are so excited about the anniversary party," Harsha said, speaking over him before she could stop herself. She wound a hand around Veer's own and ran her other palm along his warm, muscley forearm. "And your wedding, of course."

"Your first plus one! I'll have to go in and update your RSVP—it must have gotten lost in the mail?" Neha added with a smile, though her eyes narrowed.

"Sorry about that," Harsha said. She rested her head on Veer's shoulder and forced out a sigh of pleasure. "We've been busy." She could feel his dark eyes on her, a searing gaze that made her want to disappear into the crevices of the earth and never surface, but she ignored him and held on tighter.

"So what do you do, Veer?" Neha asked, cocking her head.

"He works at Sunstag Café," Harsha said, then held back a wince. *Oh, fuck.* She knew without a doubt what Neha, with her classist, uber-rich upbringing, was going to say next.

"A barista?" said Neha, with a split-second wrinkle of the nose. "That's . . . cute."

"He works *for* Sunstag as the district manager." The lie fell out of Harsha's mouth, although she knew it was wrong to say it, and Veer stiffened next to her. She tried to ignore the churning in her belly. Ordering all those vodka sodas—and nachos—might not have been the best idea.

"I *guess* that's an upgrade." Neha frowned. "Well, it's been great catching up, Harsha, but I have got to get out of this dingy bar. The things we do for our friends, right? We'll see you both soon!" After giving Harsha a painful kiss on the cheek and shaking Veer's hand the couple walked away, whispering together.

The second they were out of sight, Veer pushed away from Harsha, scowling. "What the hell was that about?"

"Oh, thank you, thank you, thank you," whispered Harsha, letting go of his hand and running her fingers through her hair. "She'd never have let me hear the end of it if she found out Shashank and I broke up."

Veer's eyes narrowed. "Why would she care?"

"Because she's two years younger than I am, she works for the goddamn UN, and she's marrying McDreamy in less than two months."

"Well, sorry that being with a barista would be so embarrassing." Veer took a step back and folded his arms.

"You don't know her," Harsha said, pleading. "She'd have said something rude to you. I was just trying to—"

"She didn't need to. *You* did, on her behalf." Veer shook his head at her, sighed, and went back into the crowd.

Despite the guilt and embarrassment she felt, Harsha watched him walk up to the other baristas, considering the idea that was starting to form in her head—and it was a good one. Veer was handsome, now that she thought about it. Cute smile. A good physique. He wasn't an actor, but he could be with some training.

The anniversary party was in one month, and every single one of the Godboles was expecting Harsha to bring her perfect boyfriend, including her cousin. Maybe she could still make that happen . . .

VEER STORMED INTO THE BOOTH where his friends were waiting. Raunak frowned when he saw Veer's empty hands, and Deepika let out an *ugh*. "I thought you were bringing the next round of beers."

"You won't believe what just happened," he fumed, slamming his butt into the couch.

Raunak raised his brows. "Are you okay?"

"No." Veer put his head in his hands and whisper-yelled, "I saw Harsha here."

"Your Sunstag crush, here in real life?" Raunak teased. "Did you finally ask her out?"

"No, and I don't have a crush. Her cousin showed up at the bar and assumed I was her boyfriend," Veer explained. "Harsha went along with it and said we'd go to the cousin's wedding together. Then she insulted me by lying about what I do for a living."

Deepika's mouth fell open, while Raunak just stared mutely.

Veer groaned. "I'm so angry. You bet your ass I'm going to spit in her coffee tomorrow."

"I don't blame you," Raunak said. "We may be baristas, but we're the best damn baristas the world has ever seen." He slammed his fist on the table. "Now, let's get wasted!"

They cheered, raising their glasses of water as a toast.

Veer headed back to the counter to get their drinks, Deepika in tow this time, and as they placed an order for more beers, he bit back a sigh and flexed his hand, which still tingled from Harsha's soft, cool touch. And the way she'd grazed his forearm with her fingers . . .

"How are things at home?" Deepika asked, and he turned to her. "Is Arjun excited about going to BII?"

"Uh, yeah." Veer shuffled his feet and planted a smile on his face. "We're all excited."

"As you should be. This is such a huge deal!" She must have noticed the split-second frown on Veer's face, because her forehead wrinkled. "Hey. Arjun's getting his big break. You will too. You don't have to be a barista forever, unless you want to."

Veer tried not to roll his eyes. "Let's not go there again—"

"Shut up." Deepika stuck her hand out. "I'm older and wiser than you, and I know acting is gonna work out for you, if you would just let it."

He snorted. "You're only eighteen months older than me."

"That's not the point. Think about it, okay?" She grabbed two foaming mugs of beer and started back toward their booth. "Come on."

Veer grabbed the third mug and followed her, knowing this wasn't the time to think about his own dreams. Before meeting them for drinks, he had spent all evening filling out multiple applications for bank loans and emailing the BII administration asking for more time. But he hadn't heard anything from the banks or the college yet. Maybe he'd place his trust in the Universe and see what tomorrow would bring. Until then, he had beer and his two best friends to distract him.

"Look at those two hot girls there," Raunak said, jutting his head toward a nearby table as they sat back down. "Veer, be my wingman?"

Veer sighed. He didn't even bother to look. "Not tonight."

Deepika tutted, taking a sip of her beer. "Harsha's really got you feeling down, huh?"

He swallowed back the truth and decided to play along. "Yeah, she hurt my feelings. Anyway, enough about me. How's your mom's store doing?"

"Business has been slow." She set the mug down. "Hopefully it picks back up now that wedding season is here."

"Is she still bugging you about quitting Sunstag?" he asked. Deepika's mom owned a wedding boutique and had always wanted her to help out, but Deepika had other, bigger dreams—someday, she wanted to run her own café, and moving up the ranks at Sunstag was one step to getting there.

"Yeah, she is." Deepika's shoulders slumped. "She thinks it's silly that I prefer brewing coffee to designing clothes."

Raunak drank his beer, chuckling. "I bet you'll get that store manager promotion soon, then she'll have to understand."

"It'll happen," Veer agreed, and Deepika let out a grin.

Midway through their next round of drinks, Veer's phone dinged with a notification from Google. He still had alerts for Bollywood as well as the local Kannada film industry flagged in his settings. So far, none of the alerts had been useful, just depressing. But after that talk with Deepika, he figured he might as well take a look.

This particular alert was about Madhusudan Godbole's next rom-com going into production, inspired by his own daughter's arranged-turned-love marriage story.

Veer scoffed. That man's films were always the same—a "pick me" heroine falling for a "you owe me your love" hero—but they made millions at the box office, quality be damned. He was about to swipe away from the article when he saw the image underneath the headline. The famous director was hugging his wife and daughter, and the caption read: MADHUSUDAN GODBOLE WITH WIFE, PINKY [LEFT], AND DAUGHTER, NEHA [RIGHT].

His eyes widened. It was the same Neha he'd met minutes ago. Which meant that Harsha, the girl who had royally offended him, was the niece of one of Bollywood's biggest directors.

Chapter THREE

"People don't turn down money!
It's what separates us from the animals."
—Jerry Seinfeld, *Seinfeld*

The next morning, Harsha paced around in the living room of her cramped one-bedroom apartment, thankful for the music blasting from her phone that mostly hid the sounds of her upstairs neighbors having louder-than-porn morning sex.

Amid thoughts of last night and the white lie she'd taken one step too far, she sighed at the crumbling yellow paint and the smell of mold that never went away. Every inch of her wall was crammed with photographs she'd clicked of her friends, her life in Berkeley, and her trips to Europe. But even the wave of nostalgia from those pictures couldn't make up for the colossal downgrade in lifestyle she was now experiencing.

Harsha had grown up in a luxury gated community with a gym, spa, and temperature-controlled swimming pool, then moved to a simple one-bedroom apartment in Berkeley that had felt like a safe space, if not home. India would always be home, and she'd known as much.

However, going from that safe space to living in a building with leaky ceilings and paper-thin walls was . . . a weird transition, to say the least.

Deciding to be independent and not take her millionaire father's money, despite his insistence that she wouldn't make it on her own, might have been the wrong choice. One she was majorly regretting now. She'd spent two years after high school traveling across Europe with Aunt Pinky whenever her uncle headed there for different shoots, and that was where she had fallen in love with photography and bought her first camera. Once her parents had had enough of her globe-trotting lifestyle, they'd pushed college on her, so she picked California—the farthest place from them—and chose photography as her second major. The goal had always been to move back to India in the future, armed with independence, more maturity, and life experience. India was home.

If there was only one thing she had in common with her father, it was being stubborn. No way would she let him control her life anymore. She decided she would move back and find her footing in a new city, completely unknown to her, a good distance away from her parents. She would prove that she was capable and successful.

But she hadn't expected to start dating a rich man like Shashank, find comfort in the world of luxury again, and then get dumped with no warning, leaving her alone to fend off her family's expectations once more.

Harsha paused in front of a framed picture she'd taken of two swans whose necks made a heart, and she thought back to last night. The wisp of that idea had started to take proper shape inside her head since Veer walked away from her at the bar, and she wasn't sure if coming up with this fake-boyfriend proposition made her crazy or a bloody genius.

Neha's vicious smile flashed before Harsha's eyes along with the stinging words she'd said last night: "Your first plus one! It's nice that you've finally moved on from boring white boys."

Bloody genius it is.

She slid her laptop into her Gucci tote bag—a birthday present from Maa she couldn't bring herself to part with—and booked an Uber, which were thankfully so much cheaper in India than California. Harsha would apologize to Veer, convince him to be her fake boyfriend, and if worse came to worst, she'd pay him to play along, maybe fifty thousand rupees or so. She couldn't make a payment like that from her own bank account anytime soon, but that was fine. Papa's money from the trust fund was right there, dangling in front of her nose like a carrot. After returning from California, she had vowed never to touch that money, but breaking that vow would still be an easier hit to her pride than going to the anniversary party or Neha's wedding stag. Harsha didn't even want to imagine what faux consoling line Neha would come up with as she conveniently worked the breakup into every conversation. It would be the bridezilla nightmare that never ended.

So that settled it. Harsha had been put in this precarious situation because of her parents' interference in her personal life, so why couldn't she make *them* pay for it?

"Hi, welcome to Sunstag!" Deepika's cheery barista voice hit Harsha's eardrums as she walked through the doors, looking around for Veer in his black-and-yellow barista uniform. Damn it, he wasn't at the counter yet.

She held back a sigh. Hopefully, it wasn't his weekly day off. "Hi," she finally said, handing over her loyalty card. "I'll have the usual latte."

Deepika nodded, grabbing a tall mug, black marker, and label. "Do you want your extra whipped cream on the side or—"

"Just put it all on top of the coffee, thanks," she said impatiently. She craned her neck to look toward the kitchen. Two male voices sounded from inside, but not Veer's. "Um"—she rubbed the back of her neck—"is Veer around?"

"He is." Deepika's eyes narrowed, then her polite smile returned. "I'll ask him to bring your order upstairs."

"Thanks." Harsha took her card as well as the wooden table

number sign and headed upstairs, setting her tote bag and laptop at her favorite workspace by the staircase with yellow lightbulbs hanging over her head. The mural gracing the wall next to her depicted coffee bean plantations in all their glory. On the other side of the café was a floor-to-ceiling window overlooking Vittal Mallya Road, one of the priciest and prettiest neighborhoods in all of Bangalore. Sometimes, when she didn't have much work, she liked to sit by the glass and take photographs of the luxury cars that drove by.

"One vanilla latte with oat milk." Veer's stiff voice brought her back to the present moment. Her heart dropped to her stomach when he correctly stated her order. *Shit.* He must really be mad at her.

"Thanks. Veer, can we talk?" She nodded at the chair across from her.

He set the coffee mug down and glared. "I'm not done with my shift yet."

"There's nobody here." Harsha gestured toward the café, empty during the early morning hour. "Please, sit. Let me explain. *Please.*"

"Fine." He fumed, pulling out a chair and sitting. "What do you want?"

"I want to apologize," she said. "I shouldn't have disrespected you like that. It's just, my cousin has this air of superiority when it comes to people who aren't—" She paused at the tick in Veer's jaw. "I'm sorry. I shouldn't have disrespected you or your job, regardless."

Veer scratched his beard, but his teeth were still clenched. "It's all right."

As he stood, Harsha added, biting her lip, "Also, I need a favor."

"A favor." He let out a whoosh of breath, one hand on the back of the chair. "Let me guess, you once again want me to pretend to be Veer the Sunstag district manager *and* your boyfriend for the sake of your overinflated ego?"

She winced and took a sip of her latte. "Yes?"

Harsha knew how weird and unfathomable this proposition sounded, so she wasn't surprised when Veer's eyes bulged out. "You've got to be kidding."

"Look, you've met Neha. The rest of the Godboles are exactly the same. Judgmental, invasive, and—"

"Rich," he finished for her.

Harsha averted her gaze, cheeks flushed. "I haven't been on good terms with my parents in months. They think I'm an ungrateful embarrassment to the family name, that I'm helpless without them. I can't go to those events alone and prove them right. I—I can't." Her voice broke at that last word.

Veer's lips turned downward. "That sounds like a big problem," he agreed, pushing the chair back into the table. "Lucky for you, I studied acting in college."

Harsha's breath caught in her throat. She was seconds away from squealing and thanking him when he held up a finger. "*Unlucky* for you, I'm not interested. Have a good day."

Okay, this was it. Her one last shot. Time to pull the money card.

VEER TURNED TO LEAVE, UNABLE to believe Harsha's audacity—were all rich people this entitled? Then she yelled, "I'll pay you!"

He paused sharply and glanced back at her. Did he . . . did he hear that right? "*What?*"

Harsha's lips twitched. "I'll pay you, Veer."

Slowly, he sat back down, his heart racing. "How much?"

"Name the amount, and I'll do my best."

Veer's stomach twisted itself in knots. Half a million rupees was a lot to ask for from a woman he barely knew. But then again, the woman in question was crazy rich—she was Madhusudan Godbole's niece, after all—and Arjun's tuition had to be paid by Monday night. He looked from her flushed, eager face to her red tote bag with the Gucci logo, and decided to do it.

"Half a million," he said finally.

Harsha's jaw dropped open. "Half . . . a . . . million?" she repeated.

"That's what I said." Veer put his hands in his lap, hoping she wouldn't notice the trembling of his fingers.

She burst out laughing. "Are you kidding? I was thinking, like, fifty thousand rupees."

Veer scoffed exaggeratedly, as if Harsha were making the biggest mistake of her life turning down his offer. He got up from the chair. "Good luck with your family."

Please don't let me leave, please don't let me leave, he thought to himself as he turned to go. *Please don't let me—*

"Wait!" Harsha said.

Veer sighed with relief internally, but when he turned to Harsha, all he did was quirk an eyebrow at her. The things he'd learned in acting school were finally coming in handy.

"I have three conditions," she said.

"I'm listening."

"One"—she counted them down by hand—"you're Veer Kannan, a district manager for Sunstag Café and my head-over-heels-in-love boyfriend. Two, you'll pretend to be him for my uncle and aunt's anniversary party *and* Neha's wedding. And three"—she gulped—"you will never tell anyone about this. Not your friends, not your family, not even your diary."

Veer nodded and held his hand out. "Deal. But you'll pay me in full by Monday."

"I'll pay you in three installments over the next six weeks," she said slowly. "One up front, and the final two after each event."

His hand twitched. *Fuck.* That wouldn't work for the tuition deadline. But even the first installment was more than he could manage on his own . . . Veer held her gaze for ten seconds that felt like an eternity, weighing his options, before giving a slight nod. "Okay."

Harsha jumped up and shook his hand, her excitement palpable. "Yes! Deal. Give me your number, and we'll meet tomorrow to discuss everything. And sign a contract. Thank you, thank you, thank you!"

He let go of her hand and smiled softly. On the inside, he was dancing with joy, but he couldn't let that show. At least, not yet. "I should get to work. Deepika's probably wondering where I am." He texted Harsha his bank account details and went downstairs to the counter.

"What did she want?" Deepika mumbled under her breath as Veer sidled up beside her.

"Just to apologize."

"Oh. Well, she's got some nerve. Hi, welcome to Sunstag!" She directed her attention to one of the regulars walking in, and Veer went ahead and prepared some pending drink orders.

Veer had always dreamed of being paid hundreds of thousands of rupees to play a major role onscreen. But never in all his acting days had he expected to be the lead in a fake dating scheme, all so his favorite customer could one-up her equally shallow cousin.

Talk about dramatic.

He could do this; the three installments were substantial enough that he could figure something out with the college admissions department. He'd call them this afternoon and negotiate something, since they hadn't replied to his email yet.

As far as he knew, BII did *not* offer payment plans, perhaps not even to their financially underprivileged students. But he wasn't going to ask them for a whole year to make the payments—this was about six fucking weeks. Less than a quarter of a year. They'd agree. They would.

They *had* to.

Not to mention, Harsha's uncle was a direct line to Bollywood. Veer hadn't seriously thought about acting in two years apart from going for the occasional audition for advertisements and radio commercials. Thanks to the canceled sitcom, the roles he missed out on after his agent left him, and the financial responsibilities he had toward his family, he'd given up hope. But now? Veer could convince Madhusudan Godbole to like him enough to offer him a role. Mom could afford to buy any Kanjivaram silk saree she wanted from the market. Veer could pay Arjun's tuition in full next year, long before the deadline. Sure, he hated the subtle undertones of misogyny in Madhusudan Godbole's rom-coms, but beggars couldn't be choosers.

Veer let out a short breath and went over to a table with a tray of drinks. When his phone vibrated thrice to indicate a notification from his bank, he grinned more than usual at the customers, even wishing them a "happy day," because why the hell not? He was rich now.

Chapter

FOUR

"If we needed to talk about feelings,
they would be called 'talkings.'"
—Nick Miller, *New Girl*

Veer's mom didn't miss the wide smile on his face at the dinner table. As she ladled chicken curry onto his plate, she asked, "Kanna, you look happy. Had a good day at work?"

He nodded and tried to tone down his excitement by biting the inside of his cheek. "Yeah, I did."

"This can't be about work," Arjun piped up, waving his stubby finger in the air. "Nobody gets so happy about work. This has to be about someone special."

Mom let out a loud gasp and set the bowl of curry down, taking her own seat at the head of the table. "Veer! Is this true? You've found yourself a wife?"

"Oh, shut up, Arjun." Veer had a bite of the chicken curry and rotis and sighed in appreciation at Mom's finger-licking-good cooking. "I paid your college fees today and got the email confirmation. I'm happy about that."

Somehow, the admissions department had accepted the first deposit for now, the exact amount Harsha paid him, and confirmed Arjun's admission to BII. They made Veer sign an undertaking, though, that if he couldn't make all the payments on time, if he missed even one, his brother's admission would be revoked immediately. No refunds.

Veer wouldn't let that happen, obviously.

"Fantastic!" Arjun jumped in his seat as though he were a ten-year-old getting ice cream after dinner. "So the loan application went through? It's all final?"

"Yep," he lied smoothly. "They'd have sent you your class schedule and housing details by now. Why don't you take a look after dinner?

"I will." Arjun grinned. "Oh my god, two more weeks. I can't wait."

Mom wiped a tear from her eye, fiddling with the ring on her finger. "You both make me so proud, every single day. You'll set such great examples for your own children someday, despite your father—"

Veer's jaw clenched. "Let's eat, Mom. Food's getting cold."

Arjun looked down at his plate, while Mom let out a huff. They ate their meal in silence, although Veer's thoughts were a jumbled mess. Dad didn't deserve any space in Veer's life. He'd lost that right when he walked out on them twelve years ago with zero explanations, and yet, here he was, ruining the mood during their family dinner, years after the divorce. Mom still wore her wedding ring to keep up appearances and not be seen as a single mother in society, which broke Veer's heart. She also talked about Dad every now and then, an undercurrent of betrayal and hurt in her words, but Veer refused to engage in those conversations.

He finished dinner and wiped his mouth with a napkin. Arjun looked like he wanted to talk, but Veer shook his head, kissed his mother on the cheek, and headed to his own apartment one floor above. The proximity was at times annoying, especially when he brought a woman back to his place, but it was nice to have his favorite people living so close to him. Family was everything.

Veer had put his phone away for charging on his bedside table. Now he unlocked it to a barrage of notifications, all from Harsha.

Harsha:

> Can we meet at a café tomorrow
> around 9 am to figure out all the
> details? Do you know a good place?

That was an hour ago, after which came a flood of texts spaced a few minutes apart.

> Hello?

> Are you ignoring me?

> You better not ghost me. I've paid
> you!

> And I know where you work!

That last one was from mere seconds ago. Veer laughed and texted back, Oh my god relax. I was having dinner with my family

> Oh okay. Tomorrow then?

Veer:

> Fine, let's meet at Fourth Wave Coffee
> on MG Road

> See you then

As Veer got into bed and pulled the covers over himself, he found himself regretting what he'd done. He was taking five hundred thousand rupees from a woman he barely knew, all the while sacrificing his morals and even risking his job.

But he had no way to pay Arjun's tuition without this opportunity, so he couldn't back out now.

Was he even a good actor? What if he didn't live up to Harsha's expectations? She would only pay him the installments if he did a good job. What if he couldn't? Sure, he'd dated women before. But he'd never been in love, not once in twenty-seven years. Would four semesters of acting school make this charade work? Would he be good enough to impress Harsha's uncle and finally make it in Bollywood?

He was about to turn off the lights and go to sleep when his doorbell rang. Veer shuffled out of bed, stifling a yawn, and opened the front door to find Arjun standing in his pajamas with a sheepish smile on his face. "Hey. Just wanted to talk for a bit."

"Sure." Veer led the way to the couch and sat beside his brother. "Did you get the email from your college?"

At Arjun's nod, Veer's shoulders sank with relief. "Yeah," Arjun said. "I've got some great professors. I'll have my own room, and they've assigned a second-year student to show me around campus, some guy named Salman. But . . ." He shuffled his feet, biting his lip.

"Arjun. What is it?"

"I could have taken the loan in my own name. You didn't have to."

Veer exhaled. Because he had been running short on time, he had filed all the loan applications in his own name, not Arjun's. Good thing, too, because otherwise the banks would have contacted Arjun about the status of the loan application sooner or later, and this humongous lie wouldn't have worked out.

So he patted his brother's shoulder and said, "I'm taking care of it. You should focus on studying and getting a well-paying job after you graduate."

Arjun laughed. "You're a great brother. The best, really. But be kind to yourself too. Not just me and Mom."

"What does that mean?"

"Well . . ." Arjun shrugged. "You encouraged me to apply to the best business schools around the country, but you didn't hesitate to quit acting in Mumbai and come back, as though your dreams aren't as important as mine."

Veer's insides squirmed. "No, I quit because I'm a bad actor and a great barista. You've had my coffee, haven't you?" He ruffled Arjun's hair and forced himself to grin. "Now let me sleep. I have to work tomorrow."

Arjun didn't look convinced, but he nodded. "Good night."

"Good night," Veer mumbled as his brother closed the front door, his footsteps receding. With a slow exhale, he went back to bed and ran a hand across his face, hoping this arrangement would work in his favor.

HARSHA SAT AT A CORNER table at Fourth Wave Coffee and gave the hair elastic on her wrist a gentle tug. It was only 9:05, and she'd already finished most of her vanilla latte (which wasn't half as delicious as Sunstag's). She picked up the fifteen-page document she'd created for today's meeting, flipping through it and rereading the contract—a basic non-disclosure agreement template she found online—and the questionnaire that ranged from "How many siblings do you have?" to "What's your biggest regret in life?" Harsha only hoped Veer would be willing to open up to her.

Speaking of Veer, where was he? She was typing out a text to him when he walked through the café doors, dressed in a printed cartoon T-shirt and jeans, tucking his car keys into his pocket. Harsha craned her neck to spot a faded blue car parked by the side of the street that had definitely seen better days.

"Hey," he said, no sign of a smile on his face. He sat down across from her, interlacing his fingers, and raised a brow. "So? How do we do this?"

Harsha's mouth was dry. She took a hasty gulp of her latte. "Do you want to order something, or . . . ?"

"I'll have a coffee at Sunstag during my shift later. Let's get down to it."

"Right." She slowly slid the document and a pen over to him, exhaling. "The contract is on the first page."

Veer looked from the document to her, his forehead wrinkled, then carefully perused the one-page agreement. His eyes homed in on one line, and Harsha knew which one it was before he opened his mouth. "'Weekly get-to-know-each-other dates'? Is that really necessary?"

"How can we pretend to be madly in love without knowing everything about each other?" she countered.

"Madly in love?" He scoffed. "We've only been 'together' for three months."

She pursed her lips. "Love has no timeline, you cynic."

"I'll have to take your word for it. And what's this?" He jabbed a finger at the next point, his eyes steely. "Intimacy practice?"

"I don't mean sex," she clarified. "I mean being comfortable holding hands, hugging, and . . . other public displays of affection." When he scoffed, she added, an edge to her voice, "The payments are contingent on your acting skills. Don't forget that."

"And yours," he fired back, gripping the edges of the table. "This isn't a one-man show."

She glared at him. "That's exactly why we need to date each other, so we can *both* be convincing."

His eyes narrowed, his knuckles white against the wooden table, and it was only when a barista walked over to clear Harsha's empty cup that their stare-off ended. Veer's fingers loosened, and he nodded, returning to the document to peruse the rules Harsha had carefully laid down:

Kisses allowed only on the cheek or forehead
Posting on social media about each other, weekly
Liking/commenting on everything the other person shares
No telling ANYONE that this is fake, ever
Separate beds when we travel

As Veer read the rules, his jaw tightened, and Harsha let out a soft exhale. For how long was he going to be mad at her? Gone was the cute, funny barista she'd known for the past three months, replaced by a scowling fake boyfriend.

The rest of the terms were clear: the duration of the contract, the mandatory events, and the payment plan—things they'd already discussed. Veer took the pen with shaking fingers and signed the contract. She followed suit, then held her hand out.

He shook it with his own, the movement slow. His large palm was warm and callused against her cool, smooth skin. When their eyes locked, Harsha cursed herself for the trickle of heat that went down to her core. *Focus.*

Next, she showed him the questionnaire they would interview each other with.

Veer frowned at some of the prompts. "These questions are too personal."

"Nothing is off-limits in a real relationship, right?"

He stood up, pushing his chair back with a small, defeated creak. "In that case, I *do* need coffee."

She tried not to laugh.

Once he was back with his filter coffee, they went through the rest of the document, in which Harsha had already printed out some study notes for him. It included not just details of their fake relationship, but also basic information about her: hobbies and interests; favorite movies and songs; names of her friends, exes, and family members . . .

Veer squinted at the page. "You have a lot of cousins. Ah, there's Neha." His body stiffened as his eyes fell on Harsha's uncle's name. MADHUSUDAN GODBOLE. She held her breath, knowing what was to come. Most people went straight into crazed fan mode. Her uncle was the biggest director in Bollywood, and Veer had gone to acting school. But all he said was "I really hate his movies."

Harsha wrinkled her nose. "Well, my *boyfriend* loves them." She took the document from him and turned to the page titled RELATIONSHIP HISTORY. "In fact, our second date was at the movies watching *Dil Se Delhi, Mann Se Mumbai.* You even teared up during the big kiss in the pouring rain."

He chuckled dryly, the sound echoing in the café, empty this early in the morning. "Your boyfriend's a romantic, isn't he?"

"Of course he is. I like to think we all are, deep down."

"Well"—he shrugged, picking up his coffee mug—"I'm not."

Harsha waited for him to elaborate on that. Now would have been a good time for him to share something about his past dating life. Instead, he looked through the detailed bullet points of their "love story," from their first interaction at Sunstag to the development of their relationship over the past three months. "You remember how we met," he said quietly, setting the mug down.

"Of course." She smirked. "That was the beginning of your silly drink joke. It made for an interesting meet-cute, so I put it in there."

Veer's mouth curled into a soft smile beneath his beard. It was the first time he'd smiled at her in days, but why had she only just noticed how cute and warm and *sweet* it was?

Harsha's belly swooped. She licked her lips and turned to the next page. "Let's ask each other the interview questions now."

"Fine." He rolled his eyes, but the smile remained.

She resisted the urge to grin back. "First things first: favorite color?"

"Black," he answered.

"So typical." Harsha made a face. "Mine's—"

"Red?"

Her mouth fell open. "How did you know that?"

Veer's face turned the deepest shade of her favorite color. "You wear red often, your tote bag is red . . ." He paused to gulp his coffee, then set the half-full mug down, giving her mouth a split-second glance. "And, uh, the daily red lipstick."

"Right." Harsha cleared her throat and moved on to the next set of questions: from his go-to comfort film (the 2010s Bollywood hit *Zindagi Na Milegi Dobara*) and his drink of choice (craft beer) to his closest friends (Deepika and Raunak).

"What about your family?" she asked, resting her pen on the page. "What are they like?"

He rubbed the back of his head, leaning away from her in his seat. "They're nice."

Harsha held back a groan. Great. The walls were coming back up. "Nice, and . . . ?"

Veer's eyes closed for a brief moment before he said, "My mom and brother live one floor below me. They're my favorite people in the world."

She held her breath. "And your dad?"

Veer's gaze shifted to his cup of coffee. He picked it up, sighed, and put it down again without taking a sip. "My father walked out on us twelve years ago."

"I'm sorry." Harsha's shoulders slumped. "So your folks are divorced?"

Veer nodded. "Yeah, and we haven't heard from him since then. He must be living with some other woman now. Maybe even has kids he actually gives a shit about."

As messed up as Harsha's relationship with her parents was, it couldn't compare to this. She put a tentative hand on Veer's. "I'm sorry," she repeated.

He gently pushed her hand away and folded his own in his lap. "It's fine. My mom's the best, and so is my brother. We don't need anyone else."

"I always wanted siblings." She smiled softly. "How old is he?"

"Twenty-two."

"Where does he work?"

"He's still a student."

"Nice." Harsha licked her lips, perusing the questionnaire. "So . . . when was your last relationship?"

Veer pushed the coffee aside and rested his arms on the table. "Ended late last year. Dated her for a couple of months."

"Did you love her?" she asked.

His chest rose with a sharp intake of breath. "No."

"Why did you break up?"

"I don't do relationships longer than three months." He looked out of the window, at the dark clouds forming in the sky, his throat bobbing. Harsha was hoping to probe further until he stood up. "It's gonna rain. I should leave early for my shift so I don't get stuck in traffic."

She knew his shift wasn't for another two hours, but she tried not to let her disappointment show and handed him the document. "Go through the rest of my notes a few times and fill out the blank spaces with your answers before our next meeting."

He shook his head and tucked the pages under his arm. "I didn't think I'd be doing homework as a twenty-seven-year-old."

"And I didn't think I'd be giving someone fake dating assignments, but here we are."

A slow smile peeked out from his lips, the smallest of cracks in his defenses. "When do we meet again?" he asked.

She thought about her schedule—not that she had any major commitments to consider, what with her fledgling business and her lack of close friends in the city. "Tomorrow? We should go shopping for your new wardrobe."

Veer looked down at his graphic T-shirt and faded jeans. "Why, what's wrong with my clothes?"

"For the anniversary party," she clarified, although she wouldn't have minded if he never wore that kind of shirt again. "And we can have our first fake date a few days after that."

His lips puckered. "All right," he finally said.

After he left, Harsha sat back in her chair, resting her head against the wall and mulling over their conversation. Veer was so guarded, his body stiffening after the most basic questions every couple in love ought to ask each other. The party was three weeks away. She would have to find a way to peel back Veer's layers and figure out the vulnerabilities of the man beneath the charming, goofy barista exterior.

And the way things were going right now, that would be more challenging than pulling off this ruse altogether.

Chapter

FIVE

"You can't choose who you're attracted to.
You can't engineer a relationship."
—Otis Milburn, *Sex Education*

Harsha might have asked her new fake boyfriend to keep quiet about their arrangement, but that didn't mean *she* couldn't spill the beans to her number one person.

"What the fuck?" Sasha's topknot bobbed up and down as she laughed outrageously on Harsha's laptop screen. "You hired your barista to fake-date you?"

"I didn't have a choice, S. Neha already assumed we were dating." Harsha almost rolled her eyes at Sasha's reflection in the mirror as she applied mascara on her lashes. "Plus, he seemed to really need the cash, so I went ahead with it."

"How much is that in dollars?" Sasha grabbed her phone, hitting a few buttons until her eyes widened. "Six thousand! That's a lot of money for a fake relationship, H."

"Yeah, I know." Harsha returned to the laptop and flattened a crease on the red tank top she was wearing to her shopping trip with Veer. "But it's not just about Neha's snarky comments anymore. It's about my parents finding out I'm single and broke. I just know they'll try to arrange my wedding to a filthy-rich guy who'll expect me to stay home and take care of his entire family. For the rest of my life. And trust me, every guy they have in mind for me is that exact type."

"Which barista is this, by the way?" Sasha asked, then snapped her fingers. "The cute one who's always teasing you about your order?"

"How do you know he's cute?" Harsha narrowed her eyes.

"You just told me." Sasha winked. "Look, be careful," she added, sighing. "You don't want this to go south. This is . . . a big lie; one that involves money."

Harsha dabbed some sunscreen on her face, nodding. "I know. It's only for six weeks, and then things will go back to normal. Once I get some space from my family and have a better idea of what to do with my career, Veer and I can part ways. It won't matter if I'm single again if the rest of my life is figured out. But right now? I *need* this to get my parents off my back."

"Makes sense. Anyway, forget about the fake relationship. How's the business?"

Harsha tried not to groan. She'd barely thought about her freelance photography over the past weekend, thanks to the drama that had taken over her life. She would have to figure something out, and fast, given her depleting bank balance. The secondary account would help her fund all relationship-related expenses, but her pride wouldn't let her spend that money on anything else.

"Slow," she finally answered. "But hopefully I'll find some more leads soon."

"Hope so." Sasha rubbed her eyes and yawned. "I should go to bed. It's almost one A.M. here. Talk later, H."

"Yep, bye." Harsha turned off Zoom and shut her laptop. She and Sasha had bonded on the first day of college, when the racist white professor had whispered a slur under his breath after Harsha answered his question out of turn. Sasha called him out in front of the whole class and eventually wound up getting him suspended. Later that day, they met for drinks and ranted about their experiences of being subjected to racism in America. Sasha, having lived her whole life there as a second-generation Korean American, had a lot more to say than Harsha, who'd been there a week. Best-friendship was inevitable. They had each other's backs through hangovers, finals, or emergencies faked to get out of bad dates.

After graduation, Sasha stayed in Berkeley to get her master's degree while, after a tearful goodbye, Harsha came home to India to find her calling and live life on her own terms. The twelve-and-a-half-hour time difference sucked, but they managed to squeeze in a few minutes of Zoom every week.

Harsha gave her reflection a quick look and decided to apply another swipe of lipstick. Then she paused, her eyes on the maroon shade. The way Veer had blushed and looked at her mouth for that one millisecond while saying he knew her favorite color was red . . .

Sighing, she put her makeup bag aside, deciding not to entertain that train of thought, and hailed an auto rickshaw to the nearest metro station. Veer had offered to pick her up and drive them to the mall, but then he would find out she lived in this run-down neighborhood, and that was obviously not an option. When she was in the auto, she pulled up her social media on a whim and posted a scenic photograph from one of her SoCal trips with her friends, adding a caption that said she had limited spots available for photo shoots this month. Hopefully, it would lead to something. Her love life had been dragged through hell—she couldn't let her career flop too.

VEER FOLLOWED HARSHA RELUCTANTLY AS she scanned the men's clothing section at the mall, looking like a woman on a mission. He didn't mind shopping, but there was really no need for him to change his fashion sense for a short-term relationship, and a fake one at that. Then again, he was Harsha's puppet for the next few weeks, wasn't he?

"This one . . ." Harsha grabbed a burgundy collared shirt from the rack, thrusting it into Veer's chest. "And this one . . ." A blue shirt. "Ooh, these!" A forest-green V-neck shirt and two more collared shirts.

"What's with all the color?" he mumbled, struggling to hold on to the shirts now piling up in his arms. "Am I the lead in a children's show?"

Harsha laughed and guided him to the changing room, one hand on his shoulder. "Trust me, these shirts will look great on you."

The attendant showed Veer to one of the empty rooms. He closed the curtain behind him just as Harsha yelled, "Show me each one!"

Scoffing, Veer took off his Chandler Bing quote T-shirt and tried on the new shirts, which were his dress code for the duration of their relationship. They'd already finished shopping for the anniversary party earlier today: a blue saree for her and a simple black suit for him with a tie that matched.

Veer's fingers fumbled as he buttoned up the burgundy shirt, his mind going to the split-second glimpse he'd gotten of Harsha in the dressing room, her saree wrapped around that snug blouse and her slender hips, before the attendant had asked Veer to turn around to face the front. He couldn't shake off the visual of the soft and creamy skin of her bare waist, couldn't stop wondering how it would feel to touch—

His phone buzzed.

Harsha:

All good in there?

She was such a control freak. Cursing, he put the phone aside and focused on getting dressed, then checked himself out in the mirror, his hands in his pockets. Damn. That color really *did* suit him. He rolled up the sleeves to his elbows and stepped out of the room, doing a slow turn for Harsha, who was standing right outside. "What do you think?"

Her plush red lips parted, her eyes moving from his forearms to the collar, where he'd left the top button undone.

"Harsha?" he prodded.

She cleared her throat, finally looking him in the eye. "Yeah, I like it. Let's take a selfie." Before he could protest, she opened her camera app and sidled up beside him. "Say cheese!" He smiled, and she pressed her cheek to his. Veer stiffened when he caught a whiff of something deliciously fruity—strawberries?—but before he could figure it out, she pulled away, tapping on her phone. "I'm posting this to Instagram. Could you try on the next shirt?"

He rolled his eyes and closed the door behind him.

The green V-neck shirt was actually a great look on him, but the remaining three shirts were the same style as the first collared shirt. Veer wouldn't let Harsha turn him into a Ken doll that she could play with as she pleased. He snapped a quick mirror selfie in the V-neck, then changed back into his T-shirt and headed out.

Harsha was typing on her phone, a grin on her face, and she looked up when he approached. She frowned at the five new shirts draped over his left arm. "What happened?"

"They're all the same size and the same brand. I'm sure they'll fit." He checked the price tag of one—four thousand rupees for a boring collared shirt?—and laughed in her face. "Please tell me you're paying."

She took the shirts from his grasp, sighing. "I am." They headed to the checkout. Harsha handed a card to the cashier, then gasped and gestured wildly for him to stop before he could enter it into the machine. "Wait, sorry, please use this instead."

Veer raised a brow when she held up a different card. Of course, she must have had a billion credit cards at her disposal. Weirdly, though, she kept her gaze on the card machine until it approved the transaction, and only then did she exhale, as if she were scared something would go wrong. She took the card back with shaking fingers and handed the large shopping bag to Veer. Her chest was still rising and falling.

He opened his mouth to ask her what was up, then shut it. It wasn't his business. She'd paid. That was all that mattered.

They went down to the basement parking lot. Veer shoved the large shopping bag into the back seat of his secondhand car and sat behind the wheel. "Can I drop you home?" he asked.

Harsha shook her head. "Just the metro station. I'll take the train."

He jutted his head to the front window, where dark clouds thundered over them. "It's going to rain."

"I'll be fine," she replied testily.

"All right, then," Veer said. As he drove, a message from the Barista Bitches group chat popped up on the car screen, linked to his phone.

Raunak:

Brooo that cute girl who smiled at you last month is back! Get here asap

Veer hit the X button and apologized weakly. "Sorry, you didn't need to see that."

Harsha hesitated, then said, "You should tell them we're dating."

His fingers tightened on the wheel as he turned left. "Excuse me?"

"They'll see our Instagram posts eventually. Besides, I'm always around Sunstag. It'll be good practice for the real thing. Why don't you make something up using the relationship history document and tell them we got together after we met at that bar?"

Veer nodded slowly, knowing she had a point. "All right. I'll tell them today before my shift ends. Will you be at Sunstag?"

"I should be there until evening," she confirmed as the metro station loomed before them. "I guess I'll see you then . . . babe."

The strangled sound that escaped his mouth was a half-laugh, half-groan. "See you, babygirl," he answered, slowing the car, then he bit his lip. Where had *that* come from?

Harsha wrinkled her nose and got out of the car. "Veer, do not call me—or anyone—'babygirl' ever again."

"Noted." He gave her a small salute, then pulled back onto the road after she entered the metro station. As he drove home, he tried to plan a speech in his head that could convince his best friends—who knew him better than anyone else—that he had miraculously caught feelings for Harsha only days after their fallout.

When nothing came to mind, he slammed his palm against the wheel. *Ugh.* This fake relationship was definitely going to be the death of him.

THAT EVENING, HARSHA CLICKED THROUGH some photos she had taken outside the coffee shop a few hours ago. Cold-emailing potential clients hadn't worked so far, but perhaps she'd have better luck selling stock photos of misty pictures of traffic lights and cars whizzing by during a light drizzle? The Pinterest girlies would eat up the blurry and hazy aesthetic. Plus, posting a handful of them on Instagram might get her more followers.

Harsha transferred the photos to her laptop and gave them a closer look. There were a few shots in particular she loved, including one of a foggy, raindrop-soaked car window with a barely-there silhouette of the passenger inside. The driver had scowled when he noticed her, but it was totally worth it.

She'd just gotten down to editing when her phone buzzed with a video call notification. She smiled at the name on her screen: Aunt Pinky. They hadn't talked since before Harsha ran into Neha at the bar.

Still grinning, Harsha adjusted the volume on her AirPods and hit the green icon. "Hi, Auntie," she said, waving with her other hand. "How's the anniversary party prep going?"

Aunt Pinky was lounging on the resplendent four-seater couch in her and Uncle Madhu's million-dollar bungalow that sat atop Pali

Hill, Bandra. She huffed and pinched the bridge of her nose. "Don't ask, Harshu," she said, using her nickname. "Your uncle is hell-bent on Alia and Ranbir attending, but they've both got ad shoots in two different cities that day. He's stomping around the balcony right now, trying to convince them to fly back in time."

Harsha held back a laugh. She'd grown up knowing how far Uncle Madhu's influence went in the film industry, but it was still weird to hear Aunt Pinky refer to Bollywood's biggest celebrities on a first-name basis. "Good luck to him. Is there anything I can do to help?"

Aunt Pinky's forehead wrinkled. "You're a guest at the party, beta, and I know how anxious you must be about it all."

"Why, uh, why would I be anxious?" she stammered out. She'd posted her first-ever selfie with Veer on Instagram after the shopping spree, "hard-launching" their relationship, and most of her friends and family had liked the picture. Sasha had left a comment saying love you both #couplegoals. Had Aunt Pinky gone through Veer's tagged profile and sensed that something was amiss? *Shit*.

"Because you're meeting your parents for the first time since moving back from California," Aunt Pinky said, her eyebrow quirked as if to imply, *Isn't that obvious?*

"Oh, right," Harsha said, relieved.

"I know it feels scary having to see them after so long, but I promise I'll try to ease the tension."

"Thank you, Auntie." Harsha's shoulders sank as she smiled. Aunt Pinky was as kindhearted as Neha was evil, which was saying something. Maybe it was because her aunt had grown up poor, then married rich after a chance encounter with Uncle Madhu during the torrential Mumbai rains decades ago. Her humility and compassion had stayed intact, unlike Maa, whose marriage to Harsha's father had basically been a joint venture between both of their industrialist families.

"And I can't wait to meet Veer." Aunt Pinky beamed, pressing her hand to her chest. "You look so good together. He seems like a nice guy."

Swallowing back her guilt at lying to one of her favorite people, Harsha said, "He is."

"He's cute too." Aunt Pinky winked. "Not as cute as you, of course, but who is?"

Harsha giggled, thinking back to Veer's reluctant and rare smiles. Her aunt was right. Veer *was* cute. Not just based on looks, but also when he apologized for Raunak's text despite his clear disdain for the fake relationship—and her, probably. And the way his jaw clenched when they posed for the selfie, as though he felt the crackling tension in the air too—

"Harshu, are you still here with me?" Aunt Pinky was laughing as she snapped her fingers. "Someone's smitten."

"Please, Auntie. We've been together just a few months."

"I fell for your uncle hours after I met him," she reminded her.

Harsha rolled her eyes, grateful for the blush snaking up her chest and face. It would only make the façade a lot more believable.

The façade.

"I'm going to get back to work, Auntie, but talk to you soon." She blew her aunt an air kiss and hit End Call, then rested her forehead on the cool wood of the table. There couldn't be sexual tension between her and Veer. Nope. It was just nerves and anxiety, both of which were warranted given the stakes of their fake relationship.

Veer walked past her with an empty tray in hand, shooting her a nervous smile. "Hey," she said, but he was already gone. Veer would be done with his shift soon. Had he told his friends yet? She ought to go downstairs and play up the act . . . right?

Her eyes fell on her empty mug. "If nothing else, I need coffee," she mumbled to herself, and went downstairs.

THE MERE THOUGHT OF LYING to his friends about dating Harsha made Veer uneasy, but what terrified him was that they wouldn't buy it. He waited until his shift was almost over and he was ready to dip out, then pulled his friends away from the counter. "So, I have something to admit."

"Everything okay?" Deepika's eyebrows furrowed. "You look a little nauseous."

"I'm fine." He scratched the back of his neck, swallowing the bile rising in his throat. "Uh, better than fine, actually. I've been . . . seeing Harsha. Romantically."

"Wait, what?" Raunak said, as Deepika's eyes widened. "You and Harsha?!"

Veer bit his lip. "Yeah. We, uh, couldn't deny the chemistry between us after we met at the bar. I guess all that anger was just . . . tension."

Deepika's mouth split into a wide grin, then she turned to Raunak and held out a hand. "I win."

Raunak hung his head and rummaged in his wallet until he found a two-hundred–rupee note. "I don't believe this," he grumbled, placing the note in her palm.

"Wait, did you bet on my chances with Harsha?" Veer exclaimed. "I don't even— I mean, I never admitted I liked her."

"It was obvious to both of us." Deepika leaned against the wall, smirking. "Raunak just didn't think you'd ever make a move."

Veer glared at Raunak, who only threw his hands up as if to say, *Can you blame me?* Veer's watch beeped, signaling the end of his shift. "I'll see you guys tomorrow," he said, starting for the exit.

"Not so fast, mister." Deepika yanked him back by the collar, her lips still wide. "Aren't you going to say goodbye to your *girlfriend*?"

He fiddled with the sleeves of his shirt. "Right, um—" Movement from the counter caught his attention. Veer stifled a groan. It was Harsha.

"Speak of the devil," Raunak said.

Okay. Showtime, Veer told himself and turned to Harsha. She was in her usual getup—jeans and a tank top with her curly hair falling down her shoulders—but when she smiled nervously at him, biting that plush red lip, Veer lost his train of thought. Goddamn, that shade of red made her gray eyes pop even more.

"Hi," Harsha said slowly, raising her eyebrow as if to nudge him back to earth.

He tore his gaze away from her mouth and cleared his throat. "Hey, *babe*. Are you leaving . . . babe?"

Harsha gave a split-second wrinkle of the nose. Maybe he shouldn't have said "babe" twice?

"Nope, just getting a refill."

He snuck a peek at his friends, who were giggling. "Can you take my . . . girlfriend's order?" Veer said to Raunak.

"Sure," he replied as he went behind the counter. "Harsha, you want the usual?"

Harsha nodded, handing him her Sunstag card. Veer quickly pecked Harsha on the cheek, ignoring that fruity scent, and said, "I'll see you on Saturday, for our date?"

"Can't wait," she replied, grinning.

Veer rushed out the door and went straight to his car before his face got any hotter. He leaned against the car door, a sigh of relief escaping his lips.

They bought it. No, crazier still, they had been expecting it. He snorted, wondering when his friends had become so delusional. As though he—a broke barista—and Harsha—daughter of a millionaire—could ever really be together.

The mere idea was preposterous.

Chapter

SIX

"If all else fails, you can marry rich."
—Rory Gilmore, *Gilmore Girls*

Veer had to laugh when he pulled up inside the gate of the fancy-schmancy Japanese restaurant Harsha had suggested for their first weekly date. *This* was her idea of a good place for date night? Predictable.

The doorman rushed ahead to open the door of the blue car, the valet close on his heels, but Veer did it himself, flashing the doorman a weak smile. At least the car looked more impressive today—the evening rain had washed away all the grime and dust from Veer's weekly commutes.

He resisted the urge to rake his hand through his gelled hair as the attendant took down his info. Veer didn't like using valet service. Nayanthara, his secondhand beauty named after his mom's favorite Tamil actress, needed gentlemanly love, and who knew if this valet would handle her with care?

Harsha's Uber was less than a minute away according to her text, so he shook off his hesitation, took the ticket stub, and stood by the entrance, tapping his tight, brand-new loafers that he hadn't broken in yet against the ground. He wore the burgundy collared shirt and a pair of sleek black trousers from their shopping spree, hopefully fitting the role of Harsha's perfect, rich, absolutely-not-fake boyfriend.

A car stopped just outside the open restaurant gate in the distance, and Harsha got out from the back seat, her mane of curly hair flowing down her back. She wore a short, tight black dress and high heels that dug into the muddy earth. She looked . . . breathtaking. More so than usual. Veer only saw her in cute tops, jeans, and sneakers at Sunstag, so he hadn't known until now that her long legs went on for days, or that her sharp collarbone perfectly complemented her slender neck. And her usual ruby-red lips that were begging to be kissed—

Cut it out, Veer. "Hey!" he yelled, waving to her, noting how she tugged on the hair elastic on her wrist as she wobbled on those sky-high heels that were not made for Indian roads, especially after a thunderstorm.

Veer didn't think he'd seen her in heels before. He jogged ahead. "Don't want you tripping on our first date." When he reached her, he extended his hand, surprised when she wrapped her arms around his shoulders instead.

"Hi, nice place, right?" she said into the crook of his neck, bringing the scent of strawberries with her.

Oh, fuck, Veer thought as he reluctantly hugged her back, catching a proper whiff of her perfume. Yep, strawberries: his favorite fruit and his go-to choice of jam to slather on buttered toast every morning before work. Not surprisingly, the combination of her heady scent and the softness of her skin made him hungry in more ways than one—

She's paying you, he reminded himself. He pulled away with a tight smile, keeping her at a distance.

Harsha tutted. "That hug is going to need some work, if we're going to convince anyone we're together." Then she gave him a weird look. "Why are you ruining a perfectly good head of hair with that gel?"

He bit his lip self-consciously. "I thought I'd try something different for your boyfriend character."

"Trust me, you don't need it." Harsha wrapped her hand around his arm and grinned. She had the kind of wide smile that was so radiant it overwhelmed everything else, the world fading into a blur around her—the kind of smile Veer didn't want to look away from.

As they walked into the building toward the lift lobby, hand-in-hand so Harsha wouldn't trip, Veer thought back to the first time, three months ago, that Harsha had walked through the Sunstag doors. She'd worn an ankle-length sundress with some kind of bird pattern on it. He remembered because his mom had a saree with birds embroidered on it, too. She walked inside, slid an American Sunstag loyalty card in front of him, and smiled that super-wide smile, her gray eyes sparkling. "I'll have a—"

"That's not an Indian card," Veer said, sliding the card back to her. "You'll have to get a new one made."

Her smile faded, but she nodded. "All right." She waited while he set up her card, then told him her name. "Harsha."

He raised a brow. "That's usually a boy's name here in Bangalore."

"And yet, somehow, it's my name," she tutted, giving her phone screen a wayward glance. "Will you take my order, please?"

As she listed out her customizations, Veer nearly ran out of writing space on the cup. "What if I screw it up?" he joked as she took the wooden table number and started for the stairs.

"Then you buy me another drink," she called out, smiling wide as she disappeared to the upper floor.

She smiled at him a few more times that week, then constantly during his teasing, enough times for Veer to start expecting it every day—and then she roped him into this fake relationship scheme. There hadn't been a lot of smiles since.

Until now.

When they got off the lift at the twenty-first floor and stepped into the sprawling rooftop restaurant, the maître d' led them to a table that overlooked the city.

Veer's jaw dropped. The view was something else. He could see what must have been half of Bangalore, the twinkling lights of moving traffic and city life brighter than the few stars in the cloudy sky. A band played live music across from them, loud enough for Veer to hear the lyrics to the romantic ballad, but soft enough that they could make pleasant conversation if they sat close together.

Speaking of which . . .

There was one loveseat and one table in front of it. He'd have to sit next to Harsha. She'd noticed, evidently, because as soon as the maître d' walked away, she pulled on his arm and sat them down side by side on the cushiony loveseat. "Perfect," she said. "We'll be comfortable touching each other in no time."

Veer shifted in place and nodded in lieu of speaking. The view, the music, the stunning woman interlocking her fingers with his . . . this was the most beautiful first date of his life, and they were only five minutes in.

Correction: It was a *fake* first date. Obviously. So none of those things mattered.

Harsha eased her hand out of his—*thank god*—and flipped through the menu resting on the table, pointing out some dishes as Veer politely listened. So she'd been here before, and quite a few times, too. That ex of hers was definitely loaded. It made complete sense. Veer might not have known any rich people personally, but he understood the way their minds worked. He was sure Harsha would only ever date millionaires. How else would she match up to that cousin of hers?

Harsha smiled at him and scooted closer. "Can we get the lobster curry and jasmine rice? And maybe some duck spring rolls—those are delicious."

Goddamn strawberries. Veer looked at the items on the menu. Combined, they cost more than the sarees he gifted Mom every Diwali. "Sure. Order whatever you'd like. You're paying, after all."

"Technically," she mumbled.

"What?"

"Nothing." She picked up the bar menu. "Something to drink?"

"I'm good." He was driving, plus, he didn't need his inhibitions lowered any further around her.

The server greeted Harsha, a tablet in hand. "Ma'am, nice to see you again!" His eyes went to Veer, his eyebrows rising. "Where is Shashank sir?"

Harsha's smile faltered. "He won't be joining us. But we're ready to order."

"Of course." The server typed into the tablet, then repeated the order. "Duck spring rolls, lobster curry, jasmine rice. And a vodka soda for you?" He tapped a few buttons. "What would Sir like to drink?"

It took Veer a few seconds to realize he was the "Sir" in question. "Oh, I'm good with water, thanks."

"Actually," Harsha put a hand on Veer's wrist and said to the server, "he'll have a Ballantine's Finest scotch, neat. Thanks."

Once the server left, Veer gritted his teeth. "I didn't say I wanted scotch."

Harsha tucked a lock of curly hair behind her ear. "That's what my ex drinks. It would make sense to order that, for the photos."

"Right, yeah." His stomach twisted at the image of a rich, swanky man in a suit sitting with his arm around Harsha in that very loveseat. "So . . . what was Shashank like?"

"Why does it matter?" she asked, eyes narrowing. "Since I've been dating *you* for the past three months."

"I want to know who I'm standing in for," he said.

"Fair enough." Harsha leaned back into the loveseat, arms crossed. "He was attractive, smart, and successful—perfect on paper—but also a mama's boy who was meeting potential wives while dating me."

Veer sighed. "I'm sorry you had to deal with that."

She shrugged, then clapped her hands together, evidently hoping for a change in topic. "Anyway, I've been wondering . . . what do you need the money for? Why would you do this for me?"

Veer averted his gaze to their feet, his unfamiliar loafers and her fashionable high heels side by side. How the hell had he gotten here? "I, uh . . ."

She nudged his shoulder with hers. "Let me guess, you used it to hire a hitman?"

He paused, then nodded, biting the inside of his cheek to keep from laughing. "Yes. I hired a hitman to find and kill my father."

Harsha's head jerked back. She clearly hadn't expected him to play along. She placed her napkin on her lap, wiped her hands on it, and laughed shakily.

"I'm joking." He shrugged. "I wouldn't pay a cent to see my father, dead or alive."

Her red lips pouted, somehow adorable and attractive at the same time. "It sucks that you had to go through something like that. How old were you?"

"Ma'am, sir." The server came back with their drinks, then filled both their water glasses.

"Thank you," Veer said to the waiter. Once they were alone, he cleared his throat. "I was fifteen."

"Fifteen?" She gasped. "The only things a fifteen-year-old should have to experience are new crushes and first kisses, not—"

"A father leaving his wife and sons without warning?" Veer tapped his finger on the table, sighing through his clenched teeth. "Yeah. That whole year really sucked."

"I'm sorry," Harsha said, putting her hand on Veer's and stroking his wrist with her thumb.

The gesture sent tingles to places he didn't want to feel tingles right now. He pushed her hand away and folded his on the table instead. "It's fine," he said, forcing out a joke. "I did have my fair share of crushes."

"Oh? Tell me your first kiss story," she said, her eyes brightening. "Mine was so sloppy."

Veer didn't want to think about any kind of kissing—past, present, or future—while this gorgeous woman sat beside him with her annoying red lipstick, that perfect dress, and the torturous scent of strawberry in the air. He coughed. "You could just read my extremely personal, bordering-on-invasive questionnaire. In fact, I'm surprised you haven't memorized it yet."

Harsha chuckled. "I did. You wrote one sentence: 'First kiss was with a girl from high school when I was 16.' So? How was it?"

He licked his lips. He knew she was just trying to make conversation; nobody whose opinion mattered in this charade would ask her about his first kiss. And why hadn't she whipped out her phone to take a picture of the drinks? Was she waiting for the food?

"Veer?"

"Sorry." He cracked an apologetic grin. "It was a good kiss."

"Was she your girlfriend?"

"No, just a fling." He had no interest in romance after his dad left. His relationships had all lasted only a couple of months—because he could never reciprocate their strong feelings. The hole in his heart had only grown since then, the pain numbing out any possibility of ever wanting to fall in love.

"Okay." Harsha fell silent, pulling on the hair elastic on her left wrist with nails that were painted black. She must have done them specifically to match her dress. Then she picked up her drink, handed Veer the god-awful scotch, and said, "Pretend like we're toasting."

There we go, he thought. Harsha clicked a few pictures, instructing him on how to pose, then smiled as she looked them over. "You're quite photogenic, you know that?"

He chuckled, setting the scotch down. "Coming from a photographer, that's great to hear. How did you get into that, anyway?"

She grinned. "After high school, I traveled around Europe with my aunt and uncle on his shoots. Bought my first camera on a whim and . . ." Her eyes sparkled. "Nothing had ever lit me up like that before."

"Wow." Veer's throat tightened. That was how he'd felt in the third grade during his first school play where he played a tree. One line of dialogue and a few dance moves were enough to cement in his heart the dream of making it as an actor. He opened his mouth, wondering if he should share this with her, when his phone buzzed.

It was a message from Raunak on their Barista Bitches chat, asking how the date was going, and if the cutlery at the restaurant was made of gold, considering the inflated prices on their menu. He exhaled. This morning, during their shift, he'd told them more about his "relationship" with Harsha, as well as where they were going for dinner. They'd had a million questions, of course. It actually made Veer grateful for the stupid relationship history document he now knew by heart.

"My friends are shocked that this is your favorite date place," he said, setting his phone aside. He'd reply to them when he got back home.

Harsha laughed as she sipped her drink. "Who said it's my favorite?"

Veer snorted. "Please. You clearly feel at home here, while I take my first dates to places like CTR."

She frowned. "What's CTR?"

He shouldn't have been surprised, but his brows shot up anyway. "You haven't heard of CTR? Central Tiffin Room! It's only the best South Indian restaurant in all of Bangalore. Their benne dosas are to die for!"

Harsha's mouth twitched, as though she were trying not to laugh. "Okay," she finally said as the server brought over their spring rolls, the pungent smell of soy contrasting the sweet scent of strawberries. "Take me there sometime."

Veer shook his head. "CTR is crowded and noisy, and there's hardly ever seating available. You'd drop sambar on your overpriced shoes and blame me."

"I don't care," she said. "Now I've got to know if these dosas are as good as you're making them out to be."

Veer grinned, though part of him wondered if this was all just a vivid and confusing hallucination. "All right," he said. "Then it's a date."

Chapter

SEVEN

"The show must go . . . all over the place, or something."
—Finn Hudson, *Glee*

Veer sat on his couch on his day off from Sunstag, his laptop open as he read articles and interviews about Madhusudan Godbole's past and future projects so he could figure out exactly what the director might want in a lead actor—and how Veer could become that man.

Harsha's talk about her photography had sparked a small fire in Veer's heart after what felt like months. Though he hoped this fake relationship would turn into a Bollywood career, he needed to explore other options, as difficult as that may be. Sure, being Harsha's "boyfriend" would get him into Madhusudan Godbole's inner circle, but that didn't mean a role was guaranteed, especially given Veer's bare-bones acting résumé.

He sighed, closing most of the Google tabs, and focused instead on the other thing he'd been obsessing over the past week since their first date: the walk-in casting call for a deodorant advertisement happening in Bangalore in about an hour. There was no need to sign up or contact them. He just had to show up, and if he was a good fit, he would be on TV promoting the best deodorant spray in the country. It would be a start to beefing up his résumé for Madhusu-dan Godbole.

As he put away his laptop and got ready, he considered gelling his hair, but remembered Harsha didn't like it. And Harsha had good taste, so maybe gel didn't suit him at all. He wore one of the V-neck shirts she'd bought him, plus blue jeans and a semi-casual blazer. He looked nothing like himself, and hopefully that would land him this role.

He raced out of the apartment, and as he locked his front door, Mom called. "Isn't it your day off? Join us for lunch!" she said eagerly over the phone. "I'm making Arjun's favorite, tomato rice."

He paused at the door, pacing restlessly. "I have plans, but thanks, Mom. I'll order a pizza later."

"All right, love you," she said before hanging up.

Veer was so restless he ran down the stairs instead of taking the lift. He stopped at a photocopy place on the way to the audition to print out his acting headshot and résumé that he hadn't updated in well over a year, since there had been nothing new to add. Better to have something to give them than go empty-handed, he told himself.

He parked in a neighboring lane and jogged to the audition venue, where a line of aspiring actors already stood waiting for their turn. An organizer took his details as he joined them and stuck a numbered piece of paper on his back.

Veer tapped his shoe anxiously against the ground and surveyed the crowd of hopefuls: well-dressed, tall, beefy men who were everything he wasn't. Harsha could have had her pick of the litter if she'd gate-crashed an audition like this in her search for a fake boyfriend.

Should he just give up and leave right away? *You have to be sexy to make it in the entertainment industry,* one of his professors at acting school had told him as she reviewed Veer's headshots. *And you may be cute, Veer, but you're not sexy.* He didn't have a chance.

He took off the blazer as a bead of sweat rolled down his neck, thanks to the harsh sunlight, but then he remembered the numbered paper was on the back. So he put it on again and shifted his shoulders uncomfortably. This was going to be a long afternoon.

After about twenty minutes of waiting, during which all Veer did was try to get a look at the other actors' headshots and compare them to his own, the line moved forward. A woman who seemed to be an assistant or intern handed him the one-page audition brief with a basic script. "We'll call you inside in ten minutes," she said before moving on to the person behind Veer.

Veer looked through the brief. Like most ads geared toward men, this one depicted the womanizing powers of the deodorant in the most outrageous of ways. He went through the script, closing his eyes and visualizing himself in the scene. Shit, he'd missed the adrenaline that was now coursing through his veins. He hadn't prepped for a role in months.

As the line got shorter and shorter, Veer forced himself to inhale and exhale five times, calming his racing heart, until his number was called into the studio.

"Hi, I'm Veer," he said, handing his headshot to the two casting directors sitting at the table. "Thank you for this opportunity."

The female director peered at his headshot through her large glasses, then turned it around to look at his barely-there résumé: one moderately successful play at Prithvi Theatre in Mumbai from two years ago, two plays in Bangalore that had flopped colossally, and one voice-over for a Kannada advertisement that only played on the local radio channels. He hadn't included the failed sitcom, since he had nothing to show for it. She bit her lip. Veer tried not to sigh.

"All right," she finally called out, handing the headshot to her co-director. "The props are on the floor. Let's see it."

At least Veer hadn't been rejected on sight. Nodding, he stepped into the center of the room, falling to his knees and pounding on the invisible wall of rocks he was supposed to be buried under. "Help! Help!" he yelled, scrunching his face up in fear. "Get me out of here!"

He banged his fist against the rocks, fake-wincing as though it hurt him, then looked around the room, thinking. "Wait a minute . . ." He grabbed the stick of deodorant from beside him on the floor and pretend-sprayed a generous amount over himself. The stick was probably empty anyway, but he didn't want to risk smelling too strongly of it. In all honesty, he hated this brand of deodorant.

Veer pressed his ear to the invisible wall, then sprang back in alarm as the rocks gave way to the crowd of imaginary women pulling him to safety, desperate to get their hands on a man who smelled *that* good.

The intern played the raunchy jingle of the deodorant brand on the speakers, giving him his next cue. Veer dusted off his hands and knees and stood, holding the deodorant up for everyone to see. "Who needs a rescue team when you have Manhamm's new Macho Musk deodorant?" He wrapped his arms around thin air. "Ladies, am I right?"

"All right, great," the other casting director said. He studied Veer's headshot again, frowning, then looked up at him. "How tall are you?"

"Uh, five foot eight. And a half," Veer said.

The two directors exchanged hushed whispers while Veer held back his groan. This had happened at nearly every audition. The average height of Indian men was probably five foot seven, but apparently anyone below six feet was just not the right "look" for any project. Ever.

"Veer, thank you so much," the male director said, putting the headshot face down on the table. "We'll be in touch if we need you."

Of course, they wouldn't. Their body language said as much. It was likely the height thing, as always. Veer smiled tightly as the intern held the door open for him. "Thank you." He waited until he was out of sight to rip the numbered paper from his blazer and throw it into the nearest trash bin. So much for that. A deodorant commercial wouldn't have impressed Madhusudan Godbole, anyway. He got into his car and slammed his hand against the steering wheel as his stomach grumbled. He leaned his head back and sighed, deciding he would numb his pain with a pepperoni pizza and a chilled glass of cola in the comfort of his home. While he drove, his phone buzzed with another Instagram notification. They'd been steadily pinging his phone over the past few days since Harsha tagged him in her—their—date night photos.

Veer had had less than a hundred followers on the social media app until the photos went live. Now that number was up by fifty, all thanks to Harsha's friends and family.

He stopped at a traffic signal and checked his notifications. He'd gotten three more follows from distant Godbole aunties and a few comments on the dinner carousel post he was tagged in. There were still fifty seconds to go until the light turned green, so he swiped through the photos again.

In the first, Veer was pretend-hiding his face, as instructed, although there was a visibly wide grin on his lips. The second photo featured them toasting with their drinks in hand. And the final one was a smiling picture of them taken by their server at the end of the night, with Veer's arm around Harsha's shoulder and her soft, small hand grazing his thigh. The smile on his face had never been more fake, because all he'd wanted to do in that moment was take a big, indecent sniff of that strawberry scent and hold on to that breath for as long as possible. Harsha's perfume should be outlawed, he decided furiously, along with whatever moisturizer she used, as well as the designers of that tight, sexy black dress—

Incessant honking from the cars behind Veer jerked him back to reality. He stuck an apologetic hand through the window and drove home, almost on autopilot. If touching her so casually had thrown him off track like this, how would he deal with the real thing? She was coming over next week for . . . intimacy practice: something he was supposed to be totally and completely fine with, because *real* actors touched and kissed each other all the time without making things awkward with their co-stars. Besides, Harsha—with all her world travels and family money—needed a man like Shashank who could fit into that lifestyle. She was only with Veer because she didn't have a choice in the matter.

So that settled it: Veer would be a professional about it, no matter how enticing that strawberry perfume was, and he'd make sure his attraction to Harsha remained a performance he was being paid for—nothing else.

Chapter
EIGHT

"I take all of your recommendations seriously.
I want to know why you like stuff."
—Gregory Eddie, *Abbott Elementary*

Harsha got out of her auto rickshaw with trembling legs and faced Veer's building. It was an old five-story apartment building painted a dull yellow, nestled among a row of independent bungalows and surrounded by tall trees blooming with pink flowers. She craned her neck up at the blue sky and bright sunshine filtering in through the canopy of green. Beautiful. She took a quick photo with her phone, since she hadn't thought to bring her camera.

This was her first time visiting Veer's side of town, but Jayanagar seemed like a homely neighborhood. More homely than where she lived, at least. In the three months since she'd moved to Bangalore, she hadn't invited a single person over. Not even Shashank, who rented a three-bedroom apartment in a gated community and probably would have dumped her much sooner if he knew just how *humble* her living situation was. Home décor could only take an apartment so far. Harsha wasn't quite ready to burst Veer's bubble, either, especially not with the money she was paying him, so meeting at his place made the most sense.

She greeted the security guard with a smile and took the lift to the fourth floor, fidgeting with the hair elastic on her wrist the whole time, and she closed her eyes, breathing deeply, until the lift doors opened.

Time for their first intimacy practice.

God, what had she gotten herself into?

Veer was already waiting for her, his head poking out of his front door at the far end of the hallway. "Hey," he said.

Harsha had seen him every day at Sunstag since their date night, engaging in fake flirting and their usual banter, but now, as she joined him at the door and placed her sneakers in the small shoe rack, she couldn't bring herself to meet his eyes. She stood, taking in the living room instead. The bright green walls clashed with the teal three-seater couch and the purple curtains along the walls. Harsha's apartment might have been small and ratty, but at least her decorating skills were better than Veer's. She turned to him and chuckled. "Did a four-year-old pick out your furniture?"

He rolled his eyes. "I'm renting, and the place was already furnished. Everything else is all me, though. Want a tour?"

"Yeah." She left her bag on the couch and followed him around the one-bedroom apartment, pausing occasionally to catch a glimpse of who her fake boyfriend was outside of Sunstag. In the kitchen, a row of black and white mugs sat beside a coffee machine. One shelf was littered with dusty spice bottles with labels in block letters, ranging from HALDI and JEERA POWDER to PAV BHAJI MASALA—probably given to him by his mother. The balcony was small and airy with Veer's laundry on the drying rack, and it overlooked a children's park. She smiled at the sounds of shrieks and giggles of toddlers playing in the sandbox.

"This is my room," he said, gesturing for her to go inside. Harsha walked in, her mouth nearly dropping open. The paint was a bright, unflattering red; his bed had a rickety old frame with a thin mattress; but the stars of the show were the pictures gracing the walls. From posters of Bollywood movies like *Sholay* and *Yeh Jawaani Hai Deewani* to Western sitcoms like *Schitt's Creek* and *Ted Lasso*, Veer's passion for acting was clearly deeper than Harsha had presumed.

There was also a large framed photograph of Veer next to a blue car with an elderly lady and a young man—his family, she guessed. The car was decorated with garlands, and his mother held a picture of a stylish woman in her hands as she beamed at the camera.

"Who's that?" Harsha asked, pointing at the unknown woman.

Veer snorted. "That's Nayanthara, my mother's favorite South Indian actress. Mom insisted I name my car after her."

Harsha smiled. "How cute." She paused at the cupboard opposite his bed and held back a laugh. Taped on the door, beside the mirror, was Veer's acting headshot. His hair was short and neat, his mouth pulling up to one side in a soft and thoroughly cute smile, his face clean-shaven unlike his usual sparse beard. The photo was black-and-white, but his dark eyes sparkled with hope. Harsha looked at him standing beside her, and her stomach turned. That glimmer of hope was no longer there—especially not when he saw what she was looking at.

"After I moved back to Bangalore, when I still thought I had a shot at being an actor, I put this headshot up so it would be the first thing I saw in the morning." He scoffed, the lean muscles in his arms tensing as he rested his back against the mirror. "Manifestation is bullshit, but I can't bring myself to take it down."

"When was the last time you auditioned?" Harsha asked.

Veer looked away. "Not that long ago. I didn't get it, obviously."

She bit her lip. "Well, maybe if you—"

He straightened and moved away from the mirror, raking his hand through his hair. "Let's get started with this practice session, shall we?"

"Sure," Harsha said, her shoulders sinking as they returned to the living room. So his walls were still up. She couldn't blame him—they barely knew each other outside of their barista-customer dynamic—but if their fake dating ploy was to work, they had to be comfortable with each other.

Since it was Veer's house, she decided to let him take the lead, though this had been her idea. He sat down on the far end of the teal couch, one foot crossed over the other, then gave Harsha a sideways glance and patted the couch. "Uh, join me?"

"Sure." She bit down on her nervousness—and perhaps anticipation—and sat beside him, near enough that their thighs touched. "Let's do this."

"I'm going to put my arm around you," he said, his Adam's apple bobbing.

"Okay."

Veer exhaled through his mouth and wrapped one arm around her shoulder. His hand was calloused, his fingers warm against her bare skin, just like she remembered from their date night. Harsha cleared her throat and scooted closer to him. "See, this isn't so hard."

Veer's gaze was steadily on the floor as he swallowed. "Mm-hmm. Not hard at all."

She tucked her head under his chin, one hand on his thigh, and said, if only to distract herself from the gentle graze of his stubble on her forehead, "I hope you remember the ground rules from the contract?"

"Uh . . . could you remind me?" Veer turned his face toward her, and when she stared up at him, his parted lips were one head-tilt away, hidden beneath that dark beard.

"Ground rules, like . . ." Where was she supposed to look? At his intense gaze? At that full mouth? At the slow rise and fall of his chest beneath the shirt she'd bought him? Instead, she closed her eyes, begging herself to hold it together. "Like, we won't be kissing on the lips, since my family wouldn't find that appropriate, but other kinds of kiss—"

Before she finished her sentence, Veer's lips were on her forehead. "That's fine by me," he rumbled against her skin. When his hand moved down her shoulder to the side of her waist, his fingers curling around her top, she almost moaned, her eyes still shut.

"Harsha, look at me," he whispered.

She did as he said and met his eyes as her body trembled. "I— This is just—"

"Awkward, I know," he said, taking her palm and resting it on his heart, which was beating fast. "But we have to get past that."

She nodded, although "awkward" was the last word she'd have

associated with this situation that had only been her doing. "Agonizing" might have been a better way to phrase it. She pushed down her hesitation and tugged on his shirt, pulling him in closer. Her lips rested close to his neck, breathing in his scent, and then she kissed his cheek as she exhaled.

Veer let out a noise that was somewhere between a groan and a gasp, those fingers now stroking the skin between her top and jean shorts. "I . . ." he started, his lips an inch away from hers—

Harsha's phone buzzed in her back pocket, and she sprang away from him like lightning had struck between them. Veer stood up, turning away from her, and said, "I'll get us some water."

"Sure!" she squeaked.

That was—that—god, what were words?

She held back a sigh and checked her phone. The text message was from her dormant WhatsApp group chat with her parents, finally come to life now that she'd agreed to attend the anniversary party.

Maa:

> Beta u said Veer was a district
> manager right?

She groaned softly, quite certain she knew where this was going. Sure enough, another text popped up on her screen.

> How much does he make every
> month?

Harsha had no idea how much Sunstag district managers earned, but it was definitely not something her folks would think was "enough" for a Godbole.

Harsha:

> It's rude to ask that question, Maa.

Now her father chimed in.

Papa:

> Not when he could be your life
> partner . . . Beta just think about
> whether he can give you a
> comfortable life like we did . . .

Maa:

> Especially since ur not working right
> now

Harsha's thumbs hovered over the keypad, her throat tightening. Before she could defend herself, another message came up.

> Also beta what's his caste? Google
> search results on his last name were
> confusing, so just make sure before u
> get too serious with him

Harsha seethed. Seriously? Caste might have been a big deal when it came to many marriages and relationships, given the regressive mindset most Indians conformed to, but her parents were supposed to be modern, educated, and smart. The only thing they ought to care about was whether Harsha was with someone who loved and cherished her. Then again, how could she have expected anything different from them?

She stood up and shoved the phone into her tote bag, ignoring the persistent buzzing of new messages. Veer came into view with two tall glasses of water. "Here," he said.

"Thanks." She took a sip of water and sat back down, crossing her arms over her chest.

He finished his glass and joined her on the couch, studying her. "Are you okay?"

"Why wouldn't I be?"

He chuckled weakly. "As your *boyfriend,* I think I'd know when you're upset?"

She bit her lip and stared out of the glass doors of the balcony. She owed it to him to be honest about what was bothering her, but maybe not all of it. "My parents are hounding me about you. They're making assumptions about how much you make, or how *little,* that is."

The breath he let out was audible. "Right. Maybe my character can get a new job somewhere. Like a big corporation or a bank."

She scoffed, massaging her temples, which had started to throb. "That's too big a lie to pull off, especially if your actual manager finds out."

"And this isn't?" Veer put his hand on hers. "We'll figure it out. Your uncle and aunt's wedding anniversary is coming up soon. I'll charm them."

"Yeah." She blinked back the dampness in her eyes and nodded at him. "I hope so."

Veer wiped the one stray tear falling down her cheek, his breath warming her face. "Hey. It'll be fine."

She looked away when he cupped her face with one hand, his touch sparking something fluttery in her stomach. "I promise," he said. "We're going to pull this off, and pull it off well."

"You're an actor. I'm not," she whispered.

"You don't have to act like anyone but yourself, Harsha." His fingers grazed her skin, and she sighed softly, closing her eyes and sinking her face farther into his caress. Why did his touch feel so safe already? So familiar?

"Let's go out," Veer said, helping her up, and the moment passed. "Are you hungry?"

She patted her stomach, thinking. "I am, actually. Why don't you take me to that CTR place you love? I checked it out on Google."

Although it hadn't looked like a place she would have frequented with either Shashank or her family, especially seeing as she didn't quite get the appeal of South Indian breakfast food, she was still intrigued. Veer had insisted it was his favorite place, and she needed to peel back the layers and know who he really was.

Because she had to be a believable fake girlfriend, obviously. No other reason.

His eyes nearly bulged out. "Really? Okay . . ." He led the way outside his building to the dusty blue car—Nayanthara, as he'd called her—and they got in. Harsha tried not to look at the tensing muscles of his forearms as he expertly navigated through traffic. Those fingers had touched her face. Her shoulder. Her waist.

If this charade was to work, Harsha would have to get used to the warmth of his rough stubble against her lips and how good it had felt—and the musky scent of his cologne that still hung in the air between them as he drove.

Shit, shit, shit. She looked out the window, trying to ignore the rapid pace of her heart and thinking about how—if she wasn't more careful—this act could really, really, *really* get out of hand.

AFTER FIFTEEN MINUTES OF WAITING at the restaurant, during which Veer answered Harsha's relationship history pop quiz, they were finally directed to a table that had just emptied. The place was packed, with no music playing, just the cacophony of fellow hungry strangers catching up amid the clinking and clanging of plates and bowls.

This was what Veer loved about CTR. It teemed with life. People didn't have to talk in hushed whispers, wear something that fit a dress code, or yell to be heard over the thrum of electronic music. They could just be.

A couple of servers flitted about, but Veer decided to order at the counter to save them some time. Plus, he needed a moment away from Harsha to process what had happened in his apartment.

He didn't know what hidden confidence had come over him when he made the first move of pressing his lips to her forehead, but once he'd done it, it had felt next to impossible to stop. If her phone hadn't buzzed, interrupting the moment, he would have swept her up onto his lap and kissed her—which she'd already specified was off the table—until her lips were bruised and swollen. Because god, she was irresistible. Had she, too, felt that crackle between them, like magnets pulling each other in?

Or was this all just in Veer's head?

He snuck a backward glance at Harsha sitting alone at their table while the cashier rang up his order. She'd put her hair up while they were waiting in the heat, but now she had let her curls out of the bun, and they fell down to her waist like an endless black river.

"Sir, how are you paying?"

He tore his eyes away from Harsha and handed the man some cash. The delectable aromas of butter and spice wafted into his nostrils as a server passed by with a tray of food. Veer grinned; he couldn't wait to make Harsha try everything. When he returned to their table, he debated sitting across from her, but finally decided to pull his chair up adjacent to hers. That was how couples sat, right? So they could be close? He owed it to her to stay in character.

"What did you order?" she asked.

He smiled. "Do you trust me?"

"Yes," she said, biting her lip, "but I don't eat a lot of South Indian food."

"Have a little bit of faith in my favorite restaurant." He shifted his chair closer to her, bumping their knees together, and when she didn't pull away, he added, "Have a little bit of faith in *me*."

"Okay," she let out, looking away. One arm was by her side and the other on the table, so close to his hand that their little fingers nearly touched. If he just moved his pinky finger half an inch to the right—

Harsha snapped the hair elastic on her wrist, and it brought him back to reality, back to this conversation. "Are you nervous?" he asked.

She gulped. "Why—why would I be nervous?"

"This." Veer tugged on her hair elastic and let go. "You always do this when you're anxious or thinking too much." He pulled his lips up into a smile. "Are you so afraid that I have bad taste?"

"No," Harsha said. "I'm just not used to this."

Veer wondered if she meant the intimacy practice or the restaurant, but he only chuckled. "Sometimes, it's nice to pig out on good food and not have it empty your wallet. Not that you'd ever have to worry about that."

Harsha's eyes shifted back and forth as she nodded. "Right."

They looked up at the sound of footsteps. The waiter set two small brass tumblers in the center of their table, brimming with frothy bubbles and the rich aroma of coffee.

Veer handed her one and picked his own tumbler up as a toast. "To filter coffee, which will forever be superior to Sunstag's overpriced lattes. But don't tell my manager I said that."

She giggled. "Cheers to that."

The hot coffee was delicious and milky as always, leaving a subtly sweet aftertaste in Veer's mouth without the sugar rush Sunstag's flavored coffees often delivered. The star of the show, though, was the benne masala dosa, brown and crispy on the outside and packed with yellow potato on the inside, served with coconut and red chutneys. As Veer watched Harsha lick every bit of butter, spice, and chutney off her fingers, his heart swelled three times larger in his chest. She burped, then covered her mouth, her eyes widening, but he only chuckled.

"I loved it," Harsha admitted. "A lot of places in Mumbai sell dosas, but none as good as this."

He rested his head on his hand and studied her. "Do you miss Mumbai?"

"Sometimes. I miss the beach and the nightlife, of course, but I like Bangalore too."

"Why wouldn't you?" He gestured to the restaurant at large with his hands. "It's the best city in the world."

"Now, that's a reach—"

A waiter came by to shoo them away and make room for the people still waiting for a table. Since Veer had already paid at the counter, they returned to his car.

He regretfully put on his seat belt. The day had gone by way too fast, and he had a shift to get to. He started the engine and asked, "Can I drop you home?"

"The metro station is fine," Harsha answered promptly.

He shot her a confused look. Why was she so hell-bent on taking the train?

As they were on their way to the metro station, Harsha perused her phone and gasped.

"What?" Veer asked, looking toward her as he drove.

Squealing, Harsha read the email out loud. It was from a potential client who needed to hire a last-minute photographer. He planned to propose to his girlfriend tomorrow at Nandi Hills, but his original photographer quit on him.

Veer might have been cynical about marriage for himself, but he smiled anyway. "That's cute. I wonder if the girlfriend is expecting it."

"I hope she wears waterproof mascara tomorrow," Harsha said as she eagerly tapped the keypad on her phone, presumably replying to the client. "If not, I'll fix it during editing."

"Nandi Hills is quite the trek, though," Veer pointed out, knowing Harsha probably hadn't been there yet. "No wonder that photographer canceled."

But Harsha only squealed. "Even better. Now I can prove myself. Engagement photo shoots always go viral. This could lead to more bookings!"

Chuckling, Veer pulled up in front of the metro station. "You sure I can't drop you home? Are you worried the security guards will find out your boyfriend drives an old, beat-up car and snitch to your family?"

"Don't say that out loud," Harsha said, patting the dashboard. "You're going to upset poor Nayanthara."

Veer snorted. "Seriously, though, I don't mind driving—"

"I'll be fine." Harsha got out of the car, her tote bag slung over one shoulder. "Thank you for a fantastic fake date," she called out as she shut the car door. "Drive safe."

"Text me when you get home, and good luck tomorrow!" Veer said before pulling back onto the main road and driving home to get dressed for his shift at Sunstag. It was only when he unlocked the door to his apartment, which still smelled faintly like strawberries, that his thoughts returned to the intimacy practice . . . and the upcoming anniversary party. Five days until his acting skills would be put to the test in front of Harsha's entire family, and some Bollywood celebrities, probably. Unlike every moment up until now, though, it wasn't panic or fear bubbling in the pit of his stomach—it was anticipation.

Chapter

NINE

"Look, you didn't ask me for my opinion,
but I'm old, so I'm giving it anyway."
—Sophie Petrillo, *Golden Girls*

In all her years clicking photos of her friends and family for fun, Harsha hadn't expected she would get the chance to document a moment as big as this one . . . for a complete stranger. It wasn't just an opportunity, it was a *responsibility*. One she would do her best to uphold.

Nandi Hills was a good hour and a half from her neighborhood, so she booked a cab for the afternoon journey. The client, Daman, was driving up there with his girlfriend, and had told Harsha not to text him her whereabouts until he could reach out to her on his own. He didn't want to risk Harsha's message popping up on his phone and spoiling the surprise.

In the back seat of the cab, Harsha fiddled with her camera, her fingers shaking, as pop music blasted through her AirPods. Daman had explained that it wasn't really a grueling trek, but still a two-hour walk up a steep flight of a thousand steps, so she'd worn her Nikes. No way did she want to trip and damage her camera before he proposed. Besides, Daman said a few photographers had turned him down, citing the logistics and the long walk, and that had made her eager to show him she wasn't one to back down from a challenge.

The driver dropped her off at the entrance, and she took a quick selfie to send to Veer with the caption I'm here, wish me luck!

He replied minutes later while she waited in line at the ticket counter. Good luck to you and the guy lol! Text me after and tell me how it went 😊

Harsha:

I will!!!

Harsha spotted Daman and his girlfriend up ahead in the queue, chatting excitedly. They were both fit and muscley, dressed in athleisure clothing, looking more than prepared for the two-hour hike. Even with a bare face, the woman was stunningly beautiful. Harsha tried not to snap a picture then and there of how happy they looked as the woman tossed her head back and laughed. They got their tickets and walked up ahead. Daman turned once to nod discreetly at Harsha, who nodded back.

At the counter, the attendant's eyebrows furrowed when Harsha asked for just one ticket. "It's just you?" he said. "No one's joining you?"

Harsha frowned back. "Yes, why?"

The attendant nudged his head, gesturing behind her. "You see the rest of the line? All couples. We never get solo travelers here."

"Right. Well, I'm just here to take photos." She held up her camera. "One ticket, please?" After she paid for her ticket, she looked around, bemused. No wonder Daman had decided to bring his girlfriend here to propose. True to the attendant's words, Harsha was the only person here who didn't have a date or friend with them.

Her phone buzzed.

Daman:

Don't lose sight of us, but just in case: I'll be doing you-know-what right outside the Yoga Nandeeshwara Temple

Harsha sent a quick thumbs-up emoji in response and retied her laces, preparing herself for the trek.

For a Tuesday evening, the place was crowded, which was good, because that meant Daman's girlfriend was busy taking in the picturesque view all around them instead of noticing Harsha. The place was beautiful, and the steep steps leading up to the top of the hill were flanked by lush greenery on either side. The trees swayed lazily in the brisk evening wind, while stray dogs ran around the visitors' legs, hoping for pieces of biscuits. Daman seemed to be in a rush to catch the sunset—only about an hour to go—so he urged his girlfriend onward while others stopped to feed the dogs. Harsha was starting to get out of breath, but she would persist. This was her chance to prove herself.

She climbed the steps through the forts and ruins, the structures made of redbrick walls coated with moss and dust. There really was something incredible about ancient Indian architecture, she decided as she touched her hand to the wall, and the history that went along with it. This place had once been an impenetrable military fortress for a king, and it was now where people bared their souls and confessed their love for each other.

She clicked pictures every now and then of Daman helping his girlfriend up the steps, his fingers interlocked with hers. Harsha stopped to give her lungs a quick break and regarded the photos. They looked so good together against the backdrop of the dense foliage. She smiled at the lump in her throat. God, she couldn't wait for the big moment.

As they continued their hike, she captured the scenic beauty of the eagles soaring overhead in the coloring sky, squirrels scurrying up trees, and a couple of quick selfies to etch this evening into her memory.

Finally, when they reached the top, most of the crowd dispersed to the local restaurant or the footbridge to catch the scenic view from the hills, but Daman led his girlfriend to the Yoga Nandeeshwara Temple, looking back once to make sure Harsha was following close behind.

"This is so beautiful," his girlfriend said, staring up in awe at the tall granite sculptures along the walls of the temple. "Thanks for bringing me here."

"No, thank *you* for bringing me so much joy." Daman pulled her closer, kissing the side of her cheek. Harsha snapped another quick photo. As the sun started to dip into the horizon, painting streaks of orange, purple, and pink all around them, he got down on one knee.

Harsha hid behind a rock and focused her lens on the sight before her. Daman held up the velvet ring box as his girlfriend let out a loud gasp. Onlookers paused, their eyes on the couple, some whispering, others cheering.

"Gauri, will you marry me?"

"Yes!" she screamed, falling to her knees and enveloping him in a hug. They didn't kiss, presumably since they were at a temple and other visitors wouldn't take the public display of affection too well.

Once Daman had placed the ring on her finger, he beckoned Harsha over. "Did you get any good photos?"

She beamed, showing them her camera roll. "So many. You make a beautiful match, congratulations!"

"Babe!" Gauri clapped her hands to her mouth. "You hired a photographer?"

"You deserve nothing less," Daman said, adoration in his eyes.

"Can I take some more pictures with the ring?" Harsha offered.

Gauri wiped a tear from her eye. "Of course. How do we pose?"

She gave them some instructions, using as reference the engagement photo shoots she'd looked up before coming here: Gauri holding up her left hand, showing off the ring, while Daman kissed her on the cheek; her hand on his chest while they looked deeply into each other's eyes; and him kissing the engagement ring while she grinned uncontrollably.

As they made their way back, Harsha chuckled when Daman had to keep reminding Gauri to look down at the steps and not at the rock on her finger. "Can you blame me?" Gauri said, holding her hand out in front of her. "This is the world's most beautiful ring. Where did you get it?"

"It was my grandmother's," Daman admitted, cracking a small smile.

"Babe, I love that!" Gauri exclaimed, stopping to envelop him in another hug. Harsha clicked one more quick photo. When they resumed walking, Gauri told Harsha, "We love the outdoors, and we're always in nature, so I really wasn't expecting this today."

"How did you both meet?" Harsha asked.

Daman laughed. "I was on a hike in Goa, and she was doing a magazine shoot there. I initially assumed she was one of those high-maintenance fashion models who preferred air-conditioning to mountain air, but we got to talking, and . . ." He pressed Gauri's hand to his smiling lips. "She had hiked to all my favorite spots in the country and had a longer bucket list than mine. So, of course, we went hiking on our first date."

"And three years later, this fool finally decided to pop the question. Took you long enough," Gauri teased, smacking Daman on the shoulder.

"That's such a beautiful meet-cute," Harsha said, holding back the lump in her throat. "I want a story like that someday."

Daman quirked a brow. "I thought I saw a picture of your boyfriend on your Instagram."

Harsha's heart pounded. "Oh, our story isn't as movie-worthy as yours," she said quickly. "We met at a café."

"Every meet-cute is movie-worthy." Gauri swung her and Daman's arms as they walked. "A lot of things had to line up perfectly for you and him to be in that café at the same time. That's special."

Harsha only offered a small smile. They reached the exit, and Gauri hugged her tight as a thank-you, while Daman said he would pay her invoice once they got home.

"I'll send the photos your way next week," Harsha told them, then flagged down the cab she had pre-booked.

As she sat in the back seat while old romantic songs played on the radio, she scrolled through the photos she'd taken. The laughter they shared during the walk. The dampness of Gauri's eyes when Daman asked her to marry him. The love in his gaze after she said yes.

When will it be my turn? Harsha wondered, wiping away a tear of her own. Her eyes flitted shut, her head falling back against the headrest. Images swam in her mind of a man getting down on one knee before her, asking her to marry him because he couldn't picture his life without her. When she said yes, he would kiss her, chuckling at his own nervousness. She would hug him and press her forehead into his bearded cheek, smell that musky fragrance she'd loved since the very first time. His lips would melt into that cute, cinema-worthy smile, and then—

Harsha jarred back into the present moment. *No.* Her heart thudded, and she returned to looking at the photos of Daman and Gauri. Nope. It didn't mean anything that she had pictured a certain someone in that dream sequence. He was the closest thing she had to a boyfriend right now, the last person whose arms had held her. That was the only reason her subconscious was playing tricks on her. Right? Right.

She grabbed her phone and sent Veer a text, if only to remind herself that things were as normal as they could be between them.

Harsha:

> It was perfect. She said yes and I got it all on camera!!! How's your day been? ☺

Veer is typing . . .

Veer is typing . . .

He went offline.

She bit her lip. What was that about?

"VEER, PUT YOUR PHONE AWAY," Mom chided from the back seat. Cars honked behind them in line to pull into the departure terminal at the airport.

"Sorry," Veer said, deciding he'd text Harsha back after he and

Mom returned home. He parked by the side of the terminal and got out of the car, his family following his cue. He tugged his brother's heavy suitcase out of the trunk, checked to make sure Arjun's name tag was still in place, and turned to him.

"I can't believe you're getting your master's degree," Veer said, shaking his head at his brother.

"All thanks to you." Arjun fist-bumped him. "I'll pay you back, I promise."

Veer's eyes watered. "You don't have to."

Arjun hugged him tight and whispered in his ear, "Try to think about yourself for once. Please."

Before Veer could reply, Mom exclaimed, "Oh, give your old mother a hug too!" She wound her arms around both of them, her body shaking with emotion. "My son, getting his MBA. It's a dream come true!"

Arjun pulled away, grinning weakly. "I'll miss you both."

"Bet you won't say that in a week," Veer teased. "You'll make new friends and forget all about us."

"Oh, imagine if you met a girl there!" Mom clasped her hands together, gushing. "You'll both graduate and get well-paying jobs, and your kids will grow up rich and happy!"

Arjun's smile twitched for a second. "Uh, yeah. Maybe."

Veer didn't know much about Arjun's love life. Veer had often told him about the girls he'd dated throughout high school, college, and adulthood, but it was always radio silence on Arjun's end.

"Well, I should get going," Arjun said, but he didn't budge. "I'll call once I'm in Delhi."

"Text us after security, when you board, before you take off, and after you land," Mom said, counting down on her fingers. "And video call us to show us your dorm room!"

"Mom." Veer laughed, wrapping an arm around her. "Let's just put a wire on him and call it a day, how about that?"

Mom smacked him on the shoulder, then turned to her other son. "One last hug?"

All three of them hugged for a minute before a security guard came by and asked them to move. With a sigh and a lot more tears, Veer and Mom said goodbye to Arjun and got inside the car so Veer could drive them back home.

On the way, Mom said, "Now that Arjun's getting his degree, don't you think you should plan on settling down? Find a better job, get married, have children?"

"Mom." He tightened his grip on the steering wheel and slowed down at a traffic signal. "I don't want to discuss this right now."

"But why?" Mom sighed, poking her head up from the back seat. Sitting in the front had always terrified her, especially given the sad and sorry state of Veer's secondhand car. Nayanthara might have been Mom's favorite actress, but she had grown to hate the car anyway. "You must be lonely. Surely, you want to do something more purposeful than serve people coffee all day—like acting. What ever happened to that?"

"I like working at Sunstag, Mom, and I need to support you and Arjun for the next two years." He resumed driving and added, "I can't afford to try my hand at acting or go to college for a better job."

Mom sighed. "So maybe if you found yourself a wife with a good job, you could pool your income—"

"That's a great reason to get married," Veer said, laughing aloud, though the irony of the situation wasn't lost on him. "Let me go around stalking rich women and convincing them to fall in love with me."

"Marriage is not about love." Mom sat back in her seat, huffing. "Marriage is about stability and support for both families. It's selfish to say marriage is about love." She paused, then added, "Love doesn't make a difference. It's commitment that does."

Veer almost said, *Tell that to Dad,* but stopped himself in time. Instead, he decided to keep quiet so Mom would have no choice but to focus on something else. He slowed the car at a red light and pretended to tinker with the AC.

Mom cleared her throat. "Did you know your friend Archana has moved back to Bangalore?" she said eagerly.

At that, he turned to look at her, raising an eyebrow. "Archana from high school?"

"She just graduated from college and started her own business," Mom went on. "You should meet her. She's single. I met her mom for coffee last week."

Veer had no interest in dragging a childhood friend into his fake relationship mess. He continued driving as the signal turned green. "I'm sure she's focusing on her start-up right now."

"It's 2025, you know," Mom replied snarkily. "Women can be wives and entrepreneurs at the same time."

"I never said—"

"Besides, her parents are looking at prospective grooms for her, and she's in high demand. I say, you should meet her once, and see if there's—what do you kids call it—a spark?"

Veer tried cranking the radio up in response, but it wasn't working. *Ugh.* The perils of having a secondhand car.

"And if there is a spark, don't you worry," Mom went on, "her parents and I will arrange everything. You won't have to lift a finger."

"Mom—" he started.

"We'll plan the engagement, send out the invitation cards, arrange the wedding. You can focus on your career, and she on her business. It'll work out so perfectly—"

"Mom!" Veer exclaimed. "I *can't* marry her."

"Why not?" Mom smacked the back of his seat. "It's not like you have a girlfriend—"

"But I do!" Veer blurted out before he could stop himself. He bit his lip, but the damage was done.

Mom put a hand to her chest. "You *what*?"

Well, fuck. "Yeah, I'm seeing someone," he said, hating how far the airport was from the city. Another forty minutes of this torture. He braced himself for his mother's long list of questions.

"Who is she?" Mom asked. "How did you meet her?"

"Her name is Harsha," he said, stopping at a toll booth behind the line of cars, deciding to be honest. The beans had been spilled, and he would have to make peace with the mess. "We met at Sunstag. She's a regular."

"Harsha? That's a boy's name." She wrinkled her nose. "Is she pretty, at least?"

"Yes." Veer smiled almost without realizing it and passed his phone over to Mom, open to Harsha's Instagram page, while they waited in the queue of cars.

"She's beautiful," Mom gushed. "You'd make lovely children."

"Mom—"

"Sorry, sorry," she replied, laughing as she returned the phone. Her mood seemed to have done a one-eighty. "What do her parents do?"

The queue cleared up, and Veer bought himself some time by rummaging in his wallet to pay the toll booth attendant. No way would he tell Mom the truth about Harsha's family. She would freak out; as much as she loved Madhusudan Godbole's films, she would never feel secure enough in their own finances to wholeheartedly accept Harsha as a suitable match for her son.

"Her parents have some sort of business in Mumbai," Veer said. Well, it *was* the truth. He just didn't mention the millions in revenue said business generated every quarter.

Mom nodded eagerly. "And when can I meet her?"

He resumed driving and honked repeatedly at an auto rickshaw driver who cut past Nayanthara like he was an F1 racer. "I don't know," he finally said. "Let's talk about this later."

"Fine." Mom tutted, but Veer spotted an upward tilt to her lips in the rearview mirror and heard her quietly hum to herself while he tried not to worry about how furious Harsha was going to be when she found out he'd involved his own family in this mess too.

Chapter

TEN

"Do boyfriends and girlfriends always act so stupid?"
—Michelle Tanner, *Full House*

The night before the anniversary party, Harsha found herself at Veer's place again, this time sitting on the floor, their legs and feet touching as they quizzed each other about their relationship.

"Our first date was at the Japanese place three months ago, the second date was watching your uncle's cringey movie, ow"—Veer fake-winced midsentence when Harsha kicked him—"and the third date was at your place where we Netflix-and-chilled."

"Veer!" She resisted the urge to hit him again. "The relationship history document clearly says 'we stayed up all night talking and bingeing our favorite sitcoms.'"

"Nobody's going to buy that, but point duly noted." He laughed, his finger tracing her shoulder lazily. Harsha had mentally gotten used to the touching by now, but couldn't suppress the shiver that ran down her spine. *How is this not affecting him the same way?* she wondered.

"Okay, next question: What's my mother's name?" Veer asked.

"Manisha," she replied. "How's she doing since your brother left?"

He sighed, his chest deflating. "I don't think being an empty nester suits her. Every time I've visited her since, she's been deep-cleaning Arjun's room. How dusty can a room get in three days?"

Harsha turned her face toward him, catching a stronger whiff of his cologne. "She must be so lonely," she said quietly. "Thank god you live close to each other."

His fingers now moved down her hair, ruffling her curls. "Family is all you have in the end," he said.

She stiffened. That certainly wasn't the case for her—family was the last thing she had, if she even had them at all. Veer must have noticed the movement, because he squeezed her shoulder affectionately. God, he was good at this. "That reminds me," he said, his throat bobbing, "I, uh, told my mom about this."

Harsha's jaw dropped, and she jerked upright to face him. "Wait. About *this* or about *us*?"

"About us," he clarified. "The fake 'us.' She was hounding me about an arranged marriage match, so I told her I'm in a relationship with you so she'd get off my case."

She put a hand to her heart, which was still racing. "What did she say?"

Veer's muscled arm flexed as he scratched his ear. "She wants to meet you, but I told her it was too soon for that."

Thank goodness. Harsha knew what Indian moms were like—hers included. They started to hear wedding bells at the mention of a first date, forget the word "relationship." If she met Manisha Auntie, the fallout of Harsha's breakup with Veer after the contract ended would be messy.

She forced herself to smile. "I'm sure we'll be done with this before she badgers you about it again. Anyway, back to the quiz—" Her phone buzzed with an incoming call. She squinted at the unknown number, then picked up. "Hello?"

"Is this Harsha Godbole?" the man on the other end barked. "From apartment 303?"

Harsha frowned. "Yes . . . ?"

"You weren't answering your door, so I got your number from the building manager. You need to fix the flooding in your bathroom, immediately. It's seeping into my unit downstairs."

Her forehead wrinkled. She whispered a soft apology to Veer and stood, heading to the small balcony. "What flooding?"

"How would I know?" her neighbor said testily. "You need to get over here, *now*." He hung up, cursing under his breath.

Harsha shut her eyes. *Fuck*. She must have accidentally left the water running after her shower, or maybe the semi-functioning plumbing had finally given up on her. Her rent didn't cover maintenance, so she would have to fix it herself.

She let out a long, shaky breath, resting a hand against the cool glass of the balcony door, allowing the sounds of the few giggling children in the park downstairs to soothe her nerves. At least this had happened tonight and not while she was away. But would a plumber be available this late in the evening?

"Is everything all right?" Veer asked, appearing beside her. He put one hand on her shoulder, giving it a light squeeze. "You said something on the phone about flooding?"

Harsha cringed and raked a hand through her hair, stalling for time. She opened her mouth as it dried, her chest pounding. What excuse could she give him? In his eyes, she was rich and presumably living in a gated community with plumbers that worked around the clock. That wouldn't explain why she was freaking out like this.

"Harsha?" he probed. "Can I do anything to help?"

"Just a little problem in my apartment," she squeaked, racing past him to grab her bag. "But it'll be fine—I should run anyway!"

He tugged her away from the door just as she reached for her sneakers in the shoe rack, pulling her by the hand so they were face-to-face. "Like I said before, as your fake boyfriend, I can tell when something's bothering you." His gaze softened. "All that talk about being vulnerable and you're not even accepting my help? Let me in."

She blew air through her teeth. He was right; she was acting like a hypocrite. Why was he such a natural at this role? "Fine," she said, swallowing back her dread—he would have found out sooner or later, one way or another, especially once he met her family. "You can drive me, but please don't freak out when you see where I live."

Veer took out their shoes from the rack and picked up his keys. "Don't worry, I'll mentally prepare myself for a palace or a mansion in the sky," he joked.

Harsha resisted the urge to slap her forehead and followed him down to where his car was parked. Anxiety churned in her belly all the way through the twenty-minute drive, her knees jiggling. How was she going to admit her real financial situation to him?

When Veer pulled onto her dark street, packed with old matchbox-sized apartment buildings and one blinking streetlight, his eyebrows knitted together. "I think I took a wrong turn," he said, giving Google Maps another glance. "Did you put in the right address?"

Harsha sighed. *Moment of truth, here we go.* "No, we're here," she said, unbuckling her seat belt and getting out.

"What?" He froze in the front seat, one hand still clutching the phone propped up on his dashboard. "I don't understand—"

She stomped her foot and glared at him through the open car door. "Veer, please. We have to hurry."

He exited the car, locking it with a beep, and gave her building a confused glance, taking in the faded yellow paint, the rusted gate, and the tiny balcony-less units.

"Come on," Harsha urged, creaking the gate open and leading the way up the cramped staircase to her place on the third floor. She gave Veer a tight, nervous smile, then unlocked the door with shaking fingers and flipped on the light switch. *Here we go.*

WHAT THE FUCK? VEER STEPPED inside the strange, musty living room that was so small it seemed to end before it began, noting the sound of gushing water from somewhere inside. He wrinkled his nose at the heavy smell of mold in the air while Harsha kicked off her sneakers, threw her tote bag on the small two-seater couch, and rushed into the bathroom. "Come on!" she yelled as she ran.

He followed her with slow steps, more questions on his mind than answers. A slow but steady pool of water crept out of the bathroom, and when Harsha opened the door, more poured out. The bathroom was smaller than his balcony and lit by only one dim yellow bulb.

Harsha rolled her jean cuffs up and gingerly walked over to the tap, her feet splashing in the water. While she crouched to inspect the tap at eye level, Veer caught a glimpse of himself in the tiny circular mirror and shut his gaping mouth. "Where am I?" he said.

Harsha sighed loudly from the shower area. "Don't poor-shame me, okay?"

He scoffed. "You're paying me half a million. You are not—"

"Priorities," she said testily. "Help me with the loose tap."

He walked closer and inspected the corroded metal tap, then looked around until he found the knob that controlled the water supply, turning it until the leaking stopped. Then he returned to the loose tap, thinking. "Do you have a toolbox?" he asked.

Harsha's lip wobbled. "No . . . ?"

He wiped his forehead with the back of his hand. "I can't fix this without a toolbox."

She nodded slowly. "Then we'll just have to clean up for now and call the plumber when we're back from Mumbai." She handed him a mop that had been propped up behind the door, and they got to work wringing the excess water into a bucket and draining it in the toilet.

Almost an hour later, they were done. Veer finished washing his hands as Harsha pressed her palms to her eyes. "Thank you so much. I was freaking out."

"Probably not as much as *I'm* freaking out," he said. He used the small, clean towel hanging beside the mirror and walked into her room, trying to make sense of all this. The single bed had a precarious frame, and the closet was too small for a woman he had presumed would have hundreds of designer clothes. The half-empty maroon suitcase on the floor and the multiple scenic pictures on the wall—probably all taken by her—were the only things in the room that proved he and Harsha hadn't broken into someone else's apartment.

He walked out and sat down on her two-seater couch with a thump. It groaned under his weight. "Why do you live . . . *here*?"

She joined him on the couch and took his hands, staring intently at him. "I didn't know how to tell you."

His chest rose and fell as he looked right back at her, nausea in the base of his throat. "Harsha, did you steal the money you're paying me?"

"No." She leaned her head against the wall behind the couch, then explained. Veer could hardly keep up with the dramatic revelation about her current financial situation, and when she was done, she threw her hands into the air. "So yeah. That's my story."

Veer couldn't hold himself back. He burst out laughing.

She narrowed her gaze. "I'm sorry, is my pathetic living situation funny to you?"

He started to explain, but another fit of laughter consumed him, and he rocked back and forth on the couch, nearly kicking his legs up against the small coffee table.

"Fine, laugh at me." Harsha stood up and turned to leave. "I have to finish packing."

"Sorry." Still laughing, he tugged on her arm and pulled her back onto the couch. She nearly fell into his lap, and Veer was grateful she caught herself in time. Holding her for "practice" without getting a raging hard-on had been enough of a challenge for one day.

Right now, though, the warmth slowly unfurling in his chest took precedence over the sparks shooting down his core at their split-second moment of contact. "I like you so much more now," he said, grinning.

Her eyes widened. "You what?"

Veer smiled. It blew his mind that Harsha wasn't living off of her dad's money except to fund the fake relationship, but part of him wondered if he had just been missing the signs, like when she had been anxious and worried at the checkout counters at the mall. Everything made sense now. She wasn't the spoiled, rich, bratty daddy's girl he thought she was. Mr. and Mrs. Godbole were snobby Indian parents who needed her to look successful for the sake of keeping up appearances in front of society. She was trying to make it on her own.

But he still didn't think she was poor; she had a safety net she could rely on whenever she wanted to. If Harsha was ever in *real* financial trouble and couldn't use that secondary account, millions of rupees would be one bank transaction away. She would never have to fake date someone to safeguard the future of her loved ones.

Unlike Veer.

Regardless, he shouldn't have judged her, not when she was in the same place as him, living a humble life and working toward a brighter future, like every middle-class person in Bangalore.

"Come on." He finally got up with a smile, his hand still wound around her elbow. "Let's make some coffee and finish packing your suitcase."

Harsha nodded and followed him into the kitchen.

He looked around the cramped kitchen, from her tiny fridge in one corner to the basic microwave and crumb-riddled toaster on the other side. "Where's your coffee machine?"

"There's some decaf instant coffee powder in the cabinet up there."

Veer whirled around to glare at her; she might as well have slapped him in the face. "Instant coffee powder?" he exclaimed. "How could you, Harsha?"

She giggled and sat up on the kitchen counter, swinging her legs. "Now you know why I come to Sunstag every day."

He rolled his eyes at her. "Okay, coffee's ruled out. Do you have anything else that'll calm you down but won't feel like a knife in the back to me?"

"Ice cream?" she suggested, opening the fridge door.

"Sure."

Veer pursed his lips and took a deep breath as he looked at their options in the freezer: one large tub of vanilla ice cream, or three smaller pints of vanilla ice cream. This woman would never cease to amaze him. "Seriously? You only have one flavor of ice cream in your freezer, and it's the worst one?"

"Shut your mouth." She pointed a spoon at him accusatorially. "Vanilla is the best flavor. It doesn't pretend to be anything it isn't. It's simple. It's authentic. It's—"

"Boring?" Veer suggested, and she scowled at him. "At least tell me you have chocolate sauce, or caramel syrup, or *something*."

Harsha grinned and took something out of the fridge, her body brushing against his. "Ta-da!" She slammed the bottle of Hershey's strawberry syrup down and folded her arms.

"You love strawberries more than I thought," he said, chuckling as he looked around for bowls.

"What do you mean?"

Before he could stop himself, he said, "You smell like strawberries, all the damn time." Then he turned around to grab two bowls from the cabinet, hoping it would hide the blush on his face.

"You noticed," Harsha said. She scooped ice cream into their bowls, generously drizzling it with strawberry syrup. A drop of syrup fell on her index finger, and she absentmindedly licked it off. Veer swallowed back a groan. He did *not* need that visual in his head.

She led the way to the couch, tapping her spoon to his. "Cheers," she said with that trademark Harsha Godbole smile. "You deserve all the strawberry syrup in the world for helping me tonight."

"Of course," he said, grinning back. "What are fake boyfriends for?"

Harsha frowned, and Veer couldn't tell what she was thinking. "Let's eat," she said simply, and dug into her ice cream. They finished their bowls and got to work packing Harsha's suitcase, chatting about the Mumbai trip and the big family lunch with the Godboles tomorrow before the anniversary party.

"Make sure to bring all your new shirts," Harsha reminded him, making room for her shoe bags in between her clothes, "and the suit you picked up from the tailor last week."

"Roger that." He saluted as he handed her another pair of heels from the closet.

Harsha packed the heels and let out a shaky breath. "Veer, I'm honestly so anxious. What if we mess this up? What if my family sees through me?"

Veer hesitated, then pivoted the topic. "Do you think your cousin Neha would know how to fix a leaky tap?"

Harsha giggled. "She stays in the kind of gated community you thought I lived in, with around-the-clock maintenance. She doesn't need to *know* what a tap is, forget having to fix one."

He studied her, wondering what the real backstory was between the cousins' rivalry. "How do you feel about seeing her tomorrow?"

Harsha let out a shaky breath and tightened her fist around the sock she was holding. "Terrified. She's always been able to get under my skin and bring out my worst side. If she ever found out the truth about us, she'd destroy me."

"I won't let that happen." He uncurled her fingers from the sock and interlaced them with his own. She smiled, squeezing his hand in return, and his gaze dropped to her mouth. Usually painted red, the color had faded after the long events of the night, revealing her natural pink lips that he now knew were softer on his cheek than he'd first imagined. What if he just reached out and pressed his—

Harsha dropped his hand and fidgeted with her hair tie. "It's late. You should go home. See you at the airport in the morning?"

"Right, yeah," he said, his stomach squirming. He said good night at the front door and returned Harsha's hug, pulling away at the faintest whiff of her strawberry scent.

"Night." The door shut behind him.

He walked down the flight of stairs, his footsteps heavy, and got into his car wondering what went wrong. Maybe nothing—to Harsha, this was a business relationship, and he needed to respect that.

Cursing under his breath, he started the engine, pulling back onto the main road. Tomorrow was the first test of their contract, but as much as he had to convince Harsha's family that he was madly in love with her, there was another thing on the to-do list: remind himself that this relationship was fake and only for show, and nothing—not even the fluttering in his chest—could change the reality of this situation.

Chapter

ELEVEN

"Old people are arseholes."
—Michelle Mallon, *Derry Girls*

It had been years since Veer visited the Indian equivalent of the city that never sleeps. The damp, salty smell that always lingered around the city greeted them as they stepped out of Mumbai airport after their ninety-minute-long plane ride, searching for their Uber driver. "I haven't been here in forever," Veer said, fanning his collar, as memories of failed auditions washed over him. "It's so hot."

"It's humid, not hot," Harsha said plainly.

"Same thing," he grumbled. "It's still just as terrible as I remembered it."

Harsha laughed, giving him her suitcase to hold while she flagged down their approaching driver in the distance. "Considering the fact that my entire family lives here . . . yep, 'terrible' about sums it up."

Veer shoved their suitcases into the trunk, and they got into the Uber, en route to the hotel Harsha had booked for them near the venue of tonight's party in Bandra, which was also where her uncle and aunt lived.

They hadn't touched at all during the plane ride, but now that

they were in Mumbai, the city hosting their first real test, maybe
that should change? Veer cleared his throat, and when Harsha looked
away from the window, he asked, "Should we revisit the intimacy
practice?"

Harsha's face flushed, but she nodded. "Good idea. Lunch is only
a few hours away."

He slung an arm around her shoulder, and she sidled closer to
him and rested a hand on his thigh as though it were instinctive.
Then she went and tugged on her hair elastic, her forehead wrinkling. *Old habits die hard,* Veer mused. "Do you want to talk about
it?" he prodded.

She shook her head. "I don't know how to explain what I'm feeling."

He smiled softly and nudged her sneaker with his shoe. "Try."

Harsha leaned her head back into the seat, her gray eyes flitting
shut. "All these weeks, I was nervous about whether we'd pull this
off, but it was just a what-if in my head. Now? It's real, and there's
no escaping it."

"The only way out of this situation is through it," he reminded
her, although his own heart hammered. "I promise it'll go great."

"Okay," she said, swallowing. "Can you turn up the radio?" she
asked the Uber driver, who happily obliged. She returned her gaze
to the window as contemporary Bollywood music boomed from
the speakers, and Veer rubbed a hand along his jaw. He might have
been putting on a brave face in front of Harsha, but that was his duty
as the more experienced actor between the two of them. In reality,
though, he was also shitting his pants thinking about how he was
going to make Harsha's parents, and especially her uncle, like him.

No—it didn't matter if they liked him. It mattered if they *believed*
him. Veer didn't want any doubt in their heads to risk this deal, because that would risk Arjun's education.

He could *not* afford to let that happen.

Harsha hadn't spoken a lot about her parents since she admitted
they considered him to be poor (which was true, in their defense),

but it was all he'd thought about since. And now, when he was mere hours away from meeting the people who would determine the fate of his family's future, he almost started to consider Mom's suggestion: Marry someone nice, pool your income, live a good life.

It was a tempting offer.

They sat in silence the rest of the ride as the Uber driver sang along to the radio, and it was only when they wheeled their suitcases into the hotel that Veer's chest relaxed, and he could breathe again.

The hotel room, thankfully, had twin beds, as stated in the contract. They would be spared the awkwardness of sharing a bed and putting a pillow between them. It was a cozy space with cream-colored walls, a narrow closet with some hangers and a safe, and a mini-fridge that didn't work underneath the desk and chair.

They were meeting the Godboles in an hour for lunch at a gourmet restaurant that Harsha had picked, knowing it was her mother's favorite. "At least there's no risk of a bad meal ruining her mood," Harsha said as she took out a yellow sundress from her suitcase and held it up against her body in front of the mirror.

"Pretty dress." Veer tilted his head and smiled. "We've got this, okay?"

"Right." She shut her eyes and nodded, though she didn't look like she believed him.

While she changed, Veer went to the bathroom and put on a baby blue collared shirt over his jeans, hoping he wouldn't sweat too much in the heat of not just the city, but Harsha's family's expectations. He used a generous amount of cologne and ran shaky fingers through his hair. Harsha knocked, then came inside.

"Love the shirt," she said, leaning against the bathroom door in her yellow dress that was tight along her chest and flowy below her waist, the spaghetti straps accentuating her sexy, toned shoulders. "I bet your girlfriend picked it out for you."

Veer tossed his head back and laughed at the teasing tone of her voice. She was adorable. "My girlfriend has good taste," he agreed. "You look beautiful, by the way."

Harsha smiled, slowly but surely. "Thank you." She reached for his hand, and he took it without a moment's hesitation. "Let's go."

As THEY WAITED OUTSIDE THE hotel for their Uber, Harsha adjusted her tote bag on her shoulder. Veer had brought some sweets from a Bangalore shop to give to her family, and Harsha fought the urge to snack on them out of anxiety. She wiped sweat off her face and suggested they discuss sections from the relationship history document in case anyone decided to walk down memory lane.

Somehow, Veer remembered every detail, even ones that she didn't. "You were wearing a dress with birds on it," he said of their meet-cute at Sunstag. "And you were so confident, handing me your American Sunstag loyalty card."

She frowned as the car pulled up in front of them. "You remember that?"

He held the door open and got in after her. A beat passed, then he said, shifting in place, "Of course. You were so close to arguing with me, but I suppose my cute smile charmed you."

"Right." Harsha cracked out a grin at his attempt to joke, deciding to let it slide. She turned to the window instead, pretending to marvel at the city she had lived in for eighteen years, while Veer texted his friends. She took out her phone to capture the sights.

The beautiful outfits hanging in the window of a clothing store. The cawing of a crow sitting in a tree. *Beautiful,* she thought as she snapped a pic.

You were wearing a dress with—

She would just have to focus her phone on something else. Ah, there was a chaat stall where a young teenaged couple were downing pani puri after pani puri. She clicked a photo. Perfect, that had absolutely no relation to—

You were wearing a dress with birds on it.

Stop it, Harsha scolded herself, setting her phone back down. So what if Veer remembered what she wore all those months ago? It didn't mean anything. Maybe he just liked fashion. Cartoon T-shirts counted as fashion! In Veer's head, at least. It was more important to focus on the lunch, anyway.

Fifteen minutes later, as she clung to Veer's arm in a death grip, the maître d' led them to a large, empty table in the middle of Maa's favorite French restaurant. Nobody else was here yet, to her relief. She sat down in the center chairs, Veer beside her, when her phone chimed.

Aunt Pinky:
Almost there! See u soon Harshu ☺

"They'll be here any minute now," she told Veer. When he didn't respond, she looked up to find him in a tug-of-war with his collar, though the top button was open. "There's no possible way the shirt is choking you." She quirked a brow. "Are you more anxious than you let on?"

"Yeah, there's just so much at stake, and . . ." His voice trailed off, and he straightened as part of her family approached. Neha, Uncle Madhu, and Aunt Pinky walked over to the table. Harsha got up and gave Aunt Pinky a tight hug, then reluctantly air-kissed Neha on either cheek while Veer shook Uncle Madhu's hand and said hello.

The server filled up their water glasses, and they all took their seats, waiting for Maa and Papa to arrive before ordering lunch. Veer handed two boxes of Dharwad peda to Aunt Pinky and Neha, and while Aunt Pinky thanked him excitedly, Neha simply smiled, her lips tight. "Oh yeah, I've been to this shop before. They've got decent pedas."

Harsha gritted her teeth. Why couldn't Neha just say thank you for the gesture like a normal person?

"So, Veer, are you liking Mumbai?" Neha added, her fingers interlaced on the table.

"Oh yeah," he said, taking Harsha's hand in his. "It's good to be back."

"Back?" Aunt Pinky smiled. "Have you been here before?"

Harsha's shoulders tensed. The relationship history document didn't have a lot of information about Veer's time in Mumbai, mostly due to his walls being up all the time. "Oh, he . . ." She coughed. "Veer, why don't you tell them?" He was an actor. He would hopefully be good with improv.

Veer ran a hand through his hair and chuckled, his eyes going to Uncle Madhu. "This is embarrassing, but I was here a couple of years ago, trying to make it as an actor."

"Oh?" Neha gave him a once-over, her eyes lingering on his broad shoulders and his short beard. "I'm surprised that didn't work out."

"Same here," Aunt Pinky said, sipping her water. She nudged her husband. "Madhu, don't you think he's got the face for Bollywood?"

Uncle Madhu studied Veer, then gave a sharp jerk of the head. "He sure does. Veer, what kind of acting are you into?"

Harsha wanted to redirect the conversation to something else, perhaps his career at Sunstag, her photography, or where the hell her own parents were, but Veer spoke up first. "Advertisements. Drama. Television."

Neha raised a thin brow. "Would we have seen you in anything?"

"A few years ago, I did a few stage plays and one radio commercial." Veer shrugged casually and drank his water. "But now I think I'm ready for something bigger."

"Hmm." Uncle Madhu's lips thinned, and he looked Veer up and down, as though sizing him up. He had just opened his mouth when Harsha's parents arrived. *Finally!*

Harsha stood, wondering if they would want a hug, but Maa and Papa only eyed her, tight smiles on their faces. "Nice to see you," Maa said, and Papa nodded politely. *Typical,* Harsha thought. They were meeting in person after so long, and yet, why had she expected anything different? She swallowed the lump in her throat, hating that she craved affection from the two people who thought she didn't deserve any.

Her parents took the last two empty chairs and called the server over. "I'm parched," Maa said, without so much as a glance at Veer, who had also gotten up to greet them. "Shall we order my favorite wine?"

"And food, please," Papa barked, signaling to a server. "Get us today's special appetizers and roast chicken for the main course. And two bottles of Chenin Blanc."

Once the server had noted the order, and they had the table to themselves, Harsha forced herself to smile. "Maa, Papa," she said, "this is Veer."

Veer handed them the box of pedas. Papa took it, staring at the picture of the sweets on the lid, then said, "Thank you, Mr. Veer Kannan. We've heard so much about you."

Harsha didn't miss the twitch in Veer's eye as he asked, "You have?"

"Of course, you two are the talk of the town. Harsha is trying to make it on her own, *and* she's fallen for a coffee shop manager? It's unlike anything any Godbole has done before!" Papa held a hand out, chuckling.

Ouch. If Neha's words during that first night at the bar had upset Veer, he would probably be extremely offended by what Papa just said. But all Veer did was briskly shake hands with him, then address Maa. "It's lovely to meet you both."

Maa's face morphed into a barely-there smile, thanks to her Botox, no doubt. "So you're a district manager at Sunstag?"

"Yes," he said. "And I'm so grateful I have a girlfriend who shares my love for coffee." He put an arm around Harsha and kissed the top of her head. She beamed, her cheeks flushing without having to force it.

Maa didn't look impressed, but Aunt Pinky's smile widened. At least they had *one* person on their side.

The server reappeared with the wine and a complimentary mini charcuterie platter. Uncle Madhu cleared his throat, readying himself for a toast, but Papa beat him to it. "To family," he said, a gleam in his eye. "It's all anyone has in the end."

Harsha's stomach nearly turned as she clinked her glasses with the others, all of whom cheered.

Veer pressed his fingers to her wrist, giving her hair elastic a light tug, as if to say, *Relax, we're in this together.* She met his gaze and smiled. Aunt Pinky must have noticed the tension in the air too, because she said, "The smoked gouda is delicious! Has everyone tried it yet?"

"Speaking of gouda"—Neha swirled her wine around in her glass—"we're going to have one of those cheese towers at the wedding. Rohan's friend from med school recommended this artisanal cheese place in Bangalore, and I was mind-blown by their ideas."

"Oh, where in Bangalo—" Veer started, but Papa spoke over him. "So how is your career going, Harsha?" He smirked as he dipped a cracker in hummus. "Or is your manager boyfriend footing all your bills?"

Holy shit. "I, um . . ." Her mouth opened and closed, bile rising in the base of her throat. Maa simply sipped her wine, while Uncle Madhu almost choked on a piece of cured meat, and Aunt Pinky had to hand him a glass of water.

Veer raised his chin, squeezing her knee once to reassure her. "She did an engagement photo shoot just this week, and it went really well. Her career is taking off."

"Faster than yours, Mr. Manager?" Papa raised his glass of wine like he was saying cheers and drained the last of it. Across from him, Aunt Pinky paled as though insulted herself.

"Exactly," Veer said, giving her a fond smile that made her heart clench with gratitude. "I couldn't be prouder."

Harsha had never been more relieved to have picked Veer as her fake boyfriend. But she had to return the favor and be his hype woman too. "He's being modest. Veer might get a promotion soon," she said and popped a grape into her mouth. "We're just waiting for the formal announcement from the company." She elbowed him discreetly, and he nodded.

"Yeah, of course." Then Veer cleared his throat. "I might not take it, though."

Harsha whipped her head around to subtly glare at him—why was he going off-book? But he went on, addressing Uncle Madhu, "I'm hoping to resume my career in acting now that I have some savings."

"Really?" Uncle Madhu quirked a brow.

"How much can you have in savings as a twenty-seven-year-old district manager?" Papa countered, shaking his head. "God, I need a smoke break. Madhu, join me?"

Once they had both moved to the outdoor smoking area and out of earshot, Aunt Pinky said, "Harshu, did you have time to pick up those personalized party cupcakes from the bakery near your hotel?" She wiped her hands on the napkin, almost as though she were deciding what to say next. "They close early on the weekends, so I'd leave now, before they lock up."

Harsha exchanged confused glances with Veer. What cupcakes? Was Aunt Pinky trying to give them an out? *We need one,* Harsha thought. "We were going to pick them up later, so we wouldn't have to cut lunch short," she said, "but if they're closing soon . . ."

"Go," Neha said, rolling her eyes. "This lunch is giving me secondhand anxiety, anyway."

Harsha looked back at Papa and Uncle Madhu in the outdoor lounge, still chatting over their cigarettes. She turned to Maa. "I'll see you at the party tonight, then?"

"Sure," Maa said, blank-faced as ever as she sipped her wine.

As Harsha stood up hesitantly, wondering if this was even the right move, her phone chimed with a text from Aunt Pinky. Go have fun with ur man!! I'll handle ur father 😊

She gave her aunt a final grateful smile, mumbled a "bye" to Neha and Maa—who had already started talking about something else—and headed out of the restaurant, hand in hand with Veer. Her eyes were burning with tears as she opened the Uber app. "I'm sorry about that. Back to the hotel?" She figured the lunch was enough excitement for one day.

"Actually, I spent a lot of time in South Bombay when I lived in

Mumbai." He made a "hmm" sound. "I haven't been there in ages. Maybe we could make a stop?"

She blinked slowly, her face scrunching up in confusion as his words sank in. "I thought you hated Mumbai."

He paused to wipe a tear from her cheek with his thumb, his other fingers cupping her face. "Maybe I like giving second chances."

Harsha smiled up at him. "All right. But we're going to commute there like the Mumbaikars do. Ready to brave the local train?"

Chapter

TWELVE

"If you don't believe in love, what's the point of living?"
—Ron Swanson, *Parks and Recreation*

Veer tried not to drag his feet as he followed Harsha into the train station. While she bought them two tickets, he looked around at the hubbub of people bumping into one another, then rushing off with no time to apologize. That was the hustle culture Mumbaikars had been born into and raised on, and it was also one of the reasons Veer preferred Bangalore. The city was growing at an alarming rate thanks to the tech boom, but it was still quieter and softer than Mumbai. That was home for him.

"All right, let's go." Harsha wound her arm around his—he told himself it was because of the crowd—and they walked to the nearest platform. The next train to Churchgate was two minutes away.

Harsha yawned and adjusted her Gucci tote bag over her shoulder, which she seemed to carry everywhere, the straps digging into her skin. "Hey," Veer said, stretching out his hand, "can I carry that for you?"

She blinked in surprise. "Thank you."

He took the tote bag and slung it over his shoulder. Some passersby stared, probably because they couldn't deal with a man holding a woman's bag, but all Veer thought about was how this bag was probably the most expensive thing he'd ever put on his body. Harsha had likely bought it before the falling-out with her parents.

The train arrived at the platform and they got into the general compartment and found two empty seats by the window. It was a little after three P.M. on a Saturday, so the train was mercifully not as packed as Veer had experienced during his acting days. The commute from his studio apartment in Worli to Goregaon, where his sitcom was filmed, had been brutal in the early hours of the morning. Veer would never forget the sight of men holding on to the edge of the train door for dear life because there wasn't enough breathing room for all passengers to sit or stand comfortably.

"It'll take us around half an hour," Harsha said, yawning again as she settled into the seat. "I'm going to take a quick nap. Today's been such a long day already."

Veer nodded and carefully put the tote bag between his legs for safekeeping. "I'll wake you when we're close to Churchgate."

She tied her hair up into a messy bun and rested her head against the window, closing her eyes. Veer watched stray strands of her hair flying around in the hot, sticky breeze, and how she swatted them away from her mouth every few seconds, her forehead wrinkling. He hesitated before saying, "Do you want to use my shoulder as a pillow?"

Harsha opened her eyes and stared at him, thinking, then rested her head on his shoulder. "Thank you. I'm just so tired . . ." Seconds later, she was asleep, her face safe from the oncoming breeze. Veer smiled as he looked at her, doing his best to ignore the strong scent of whatever spicy floral shampoo she used and the desperate urge to kiss her forehead. He wanted to take a picture of this moment, one that would likely never come again. She was so pretty; he'd known and thought it since day one—but never before had he truly felt it in his bones.

Anyone would agree that Harsha was conventionally attractive with her perfect black curls, those gray eyes, and a wide smile that made people stop right in their tracks—but there were nuances to her beauty that gave her personality, ones he had only noticed up close. The small acne scars dotting her cheeks. The slight upturn of her long nose. And the way her plump red lips parted slightly as she breathed in and out—

Fuck it. Veer pulled his phone out from his pocket, careful not to wake her, and took a selfie: her head on his shoulder, his lips buried in her sweet-smelling hair . . . and the smallest of smiles on her face as she snuggled closer to him in her sleep.

He woke her up with regret when the train reached the station, from where they took an auto rickshaw and got off in front of Chowpatty beach, bustling with life and laughter.

Veer looked at the crowded beach in the distance, the people giddily playing in the sea and lounging on their towels as the sky grew cloudy. Harsha took off her heels, handed them to Veer, and pulled her phone out of her purse.

"What are you doing?" he asked as she turned on airplane mode.

"I don't want my family bothering us," she answered. She put the phone back inside and swung their arms together. "So, how long has it been since you last visited the beach?"

"Hmm . . ." Veer's eyes slid away as he reminisced. "Over a year ago. Juhu Beach. We shot the final scene of my pilot episode there and—" *Shit.* He hadn't told her about that yet.

Harsha yanked on his hand, forcing him to stop in his tracks. "Pilot episode? Like, for a television show? Veer, how could you not tell me? Where can I watch it?"

"It didn't get picked up," he said, hanging his head. "The producers pitched it to all the TV networks and streaming platforms, but nobody wanted it. My agent dumped me after that."

"I'm sorry." Her eyes shone. "Do you miss acting?"

He didn't dare admit the truth to himself, so why would he admit it to her? Instead, he held up their interlocked hands. "Isn't that what we're doing now? Acting?"

Harsha's lips thinned, and she pulled her hand away. "Sorry."

"I'm kidding." Veer took her hand again, pressing his fingers into the gaps between hers, relishing the cool touch of her palm. "Yeah, I miss acting, more than I'll admit to anyone else. It lights me up. Or at least," he chuckled sadly, "it used to."

She was silent for a moment as they walked. Then she said, "When you talked about acting with Uncle Madhu, you were trying to get his attention, weren't you?"

His eyes widened.

She shrugged. "I'm not mad. You were shooting your shot. But my uncle isn't your only way back to your dream career, Veer. There's a thriving cinema industry in Bangalore too. And there are new advertisements and webseries being filmed every day."

"I went for an audition two weeks ago, and I didn't get it." Veer looked up at the blue sky, avoiding her gaze. "It's not that easy to make it—"

"Nothing is, but you know you have to keep trying."

He sighed as his heart clenched. "I do."

"When we get back," she said, "you're going to try harder to get back to acting, not to prove a point to anyone, not even yourself or me, but to finally let your soul be happy."

Veer kicked at the sand ahead of them, watching as it settled. "Working at Sunstag isn't soul-sucking."

"Then don't quit your job there until you have your foot in the acting door."

He nodded slowly, squeezing her hand. "All right."

"So," she asked, looking out toward the sea, "what scene were you filming at the beach for the pilot?"

Veer didn't need to even think about it; he still had the script memorized. "My character had a bad first week at law school, so his friends took him to the beach, and they made sandcastles."

"Really?" Harsha's eyes glinted as she stopped in place. "Let's do it, then."

"Do . . . what, exactly?"

"Make sandcastles!" she exclaimed, now pulling him into the crowd.

Veer raised an eyebrow at that preposterous idea. "No way. We don't have a bucket or shovel, and—"

She dragged him along to a corner where three kids between seven and ten years of age wrestled in the sand, their colorful buckets and shovels lying ignored next to them. "Hi," she said to the kids, bending down. "Can we borrow your sandcastle toys for a little while?"

"Sure," the oldest girl said as she pinned a screaming younger boy to the ground.

"See?" Harsha smiled smugly at Veer. She took her heels from his hand and gave him two buckets in shades of neon pink and green. "Fill these up with water. I'll get some sand."

"But—"

"Go!"

He walked to the water, racking his brain. He'd never imagined that this woman—with her Gucci bag and expensive manicures— would want to make sandcastles with him, all for nostalgia's sake. But there she was, glowing in that yellow dress, two-inch heels in hand as she shoveled sand into another bucket.

Twenty minutes later, they had built the ugliest sandcastle to ever exist. Harsha took some pictures, but no amount of Photoshop could fix . . . this. The levels were uneven, the foundation shaky, and globs of wet sand dripped from the edges. When the kids came back for their toys, the youngest said, "Eww, that's ugly!"

Even Harsha laughed in relief as the waves took the sandcastle away. They washed their muddy fingers in the sea, giggling and splashing water on each other. Then she took his hand in hers once more, and they walked along the shoreline. Minutes went by, and though their palms were getting slick with sweat in the humid, salty weather, neither of them let go.

It was nearly five P.M. now, and the beach was jam-packed with couples and friends alike. Hawkers and vendors walked here and there, enticing the visitors with everything from pani puri, masala chai, and cotton candy to plastic pinwheels and bubble blowers.

Veer was enjoying this a lot more than lunch, although there was a thought in the back of his mind that they shouldn't have left early. Hopefully, Mr. Godbole would buy Aunt Pinky's excuse instead of getting offended. Veer didn't want any more bad blood between Harsha and her family.

But walking along the beach felt . . . cathartic. He didn't know how he could miss Bangalore and his memories of Mumbai at the same time, but he did. Maybe he missed who he was when he had lived here—bright-eyed, hopeful, excited for a future where his sitcom would be an instant classic that propelled him into a lifelong career in cinema and television.

But it made no sense to miss a future that never had a shot at existing.

Harsha was laughing as she told him about her friendship with Sasha, and although he was listening, his thoughts went to his friends back home. Deepika and Raunak. He would have to come clean to them soon enough, no matter the risks. Not just because this was a huge secret to keep, but because he was on the brink of . . . feeling things. And he really, really, really didn't know what to do about it.

Harsha let go of his hand, and his heart dropped, wondering if she'd somehow overheard his thoughts. But all she did was smile apologetically at him, wipe her sweaty hand on her dress, and take his palm in hers again.

"Sasha's like the sister I always wanted," Harsha told him, her hair blowing away from her face in the seaside breeze. "I don't have a lot of friends, honestly. I've never been good at making them. But I just know she and I are forever."

"That's how I feel about Deepika and Raunak," Veer admitted. "We met at Sunstag, and they're like family to me, especially Deepika. She's the straight-headed one among us."

Harsha nodded. "She always seems so into her work at the café."

"She is," he told her. "She has big dreams of starting her own coffee shop once she has enough savings, and she's hoping to get promoted next year to store manager and build a network of contacts. Maybe after that, she'll be an actual district manager." He chuckled. "I know she'll make it."

"How would you feel about that?" Harsha studied him. "I mean, she's your friend, but she'd become your boss."

"She deserves it the most out of all of us." Veer stopped. They were nearly at the edge of the beach, and the crowd had dwindled at this point. The rushing of the waves, the cool air punctuated with some sort of heat that emanated from their bodies, and the gentle twanging of someone's guitar in the distance . . . it was almost romantic.

No, scratch that. It *was* romantic.

Veer pulled his hand out of her grasp and feigned checking his wristwatch. "You should turn your phone back on, in case your dad texted you about us leaving."

She switched her phone back on, waited for it to load, then smirked, holding her phone out for him to see. No messages. No calls. No WhatsApp texts.

"They don't care about me," Harsha said, sounding the slightest bit disappointed even as she laughed. "Maa must be catching up on the latest gossip with Neha, and Papa probably doesn't even care that we're gone."

"Then they're assholes." Veer bit his lip. "I'm sorry. I shouldn't have said that."

"They mean well," Harsha said. "But we don't have that sort of bond. Papa thinks love equals money, so he's pretty much just tried to buy my love all my life. Maa . . . I'm sure she cares about me, but doesn't know how to show it."

"What about your uncle, aunt, and Neha?"

Harsha hesitated. "Aunt Pinky and I are quite close. She bought me my first bicycle and my first lipstick, and we still talk on the phone every few weeks. Uncle Madhu's always been busy traveling for his job, so she and I kept each other company when I lived here. We even traveled to Europe together. And Neha"—she exhaled— "we've always butted heads about the most random things, and that's led to a lot of tension between us over the years."

Veer cringed. "I'm sorry."

"If it weren't for Aunt Pinky trying to pacify the situation at lunch, I probably would have gotten into an argument with Papa." She blinked back tears, tilting her neck to the other side, and Veer knew she was trying to hide her face from him. "I can't remember the last conversation I had with my parents that didn't end in some sort of fight."

"That really sucks. Do you know why they're like that?" he asked.

Harsha looked up at the afternoon sun bathing the beach in warm light. "I think it's because they were raised by parents who didn't know better. And they passed that experience on to me. I hope I can change that pattern for my future kids."

"Of course you will," he said, as something softened in his chest. "You're gonna make a great mother someday. I mean, well, if you want that for yourself."

She faced him, her cheeks reddening almost as much as her cherry lips. "I do want it—if I ever meet someone who'll want to have kids with me."

"It'll happen," Veer said, and he meant it. "Only a fool would say no to you."

Harsha rolled her eyes. "You're the best fake boyfriend, you know that?"

"Thank you." He felt the slightest hint of color peek through his own face. He pressed her hand to his lips before he knew what he was doing. "You're pretty good too."

She didn't seem to mind—in fact, she curtsied. "Why, thank you."

Her hand was still near his lips, so he slowly let go and turned the other way. "Shall we walk back?"

"Yep," she agreed. She took his arm now, resting some of her body weight along his side, and Veer noted something that felt both light and heavy: He wasn't on the brink anymore. He'd caught feelings. Oh, he'd caught feelings *real* bad.

BACK AT THE HOTEL, HARSHA peered at the YouTube tutorial on her phone, which was propped up against the desk, then looked down at the long cloth she'd wrapped around herself like a cocoon. "Ugh!" she yelled. She started the video over and unraveled the fabric, trying to figure out where she was going wrong.

"What happened?" Veer asked as he ambled out of the bathroom, looking handsome in a black suit and baby blue tie. He paused in place when he saw her standing in the corner of the room, dressed in just a thin petticoat and sleeveless blouse. "Oh, um—" He whirled around. "Sorry, I can come back—"

She groaned loudly. "This isn't the time for your gentlemanly nonsense. We're already late, and I can't figure out how to drape this stupid saree. If Maa was here—" She huffed at the long-gone memory of her mother helping her get dressed for her high school graduation, where all the girls had to wear sarees. "Forget it."

Veer walked to the desk and put the video on 0.5x speed. "Let's see if this helps."

Together, they got to work, pleating and folding the midnight blue fabric and tucking it into the petticoat. Harsha was thankful she could chalk up the tensing of her body and the hitching of her breaths to her anxious nerves, not to the gentle grip of Veer's fingers on her bare waist as he helped her pin the saree in place. He placed the pallu over her shoulder, his hand grazing along that sensitive spot on her neck, and she shut her eyes and nearly hissed through her teeth. *Fuck.* He was not supposed to have this effect on her.

This is fake. This is fake. This is fake, she repeated on a loop in her head.

When the video ended, Veer took a step back to admire Harsha, who put her hands on her hips, still feeling the ghost of Veer's touch. "What do you think?" she said, posing.

He beamed. "Gorgeous. And the saree doesn't look half bad, either."

She rolled her eyes at him. "Let me check my makeup before we leave," she said, walking past him into the bathroom. Veer's phone was still on the counter, and it buzzed with a text from a WhatsApp group titled Barista Bitches while she was swiping some more mascara along her lashes. She couldn't help but look at the screen.

Raunak:

Wait, there are gonna be celebrities there???? Broooo, you've hit the dating jackpot with Harsha lol

Harsha averted her gaze to the mirror and ignored the subsequent buzzing from whoever else was on that group chat. Veer must have told them about Uncle Madhu's anniversary party. They were no doubt starstruck; she was surprised how coolly Veer had taken all of this, considering he went to acting school. She pushed down the shame quelling in her belly. From what she knew of Veer, he'd grown up poor, and his friends likely had the same kind of lifestyle as him—and no matter how much Harsha tried to pretend she wasn't like the rest of the Godboles, she would never be able to relate to Veer or his barista friends, either.

No wonder Harsha's parents were disapproving of their relationship. It wouldn't have made sense to anyone.

She exited the bathroom, Veer's phone in hand. "You left your phone in there."

He took it from her, smirking as he swiped through his notifications. "My friends are freaking out about this party. Raunak thinks you're a total catch"—he winked at Harsha, who couldn't bring herself to smile—"and Deepika wants me to send her pictures of all the celebrities who'll be there."

Harsha put on her favorite Jimmy Choo stiletto heels from two years ago. Thank god her shoe size didn't change. "What is your mom saying?" she asked as she fastened the strap over her ankle. "She knows we're here together, doesn't she?"

Veer ran a hand across his beard, wincing. "I told her I'm here to meet some friends from acting school. If I mentioned you were bringing me here to see your family, she'd want to meet you sometime too, and I know you're not okay with that."

Harsha nodded. This charade was ending in a handful of weeks, and then they'd have no reason to continue their relationship beyond barista and customer. Why should he get his mother's hopes up about a relationship that made no sense and had no future?

Because it didn't, she reminded herself as they headed downstairs. It had no chance at lasting outside of the contract. It was surprising, though, how three weeks of this fake relationship felt so much more fun than anything with Shashank.

She rubbed along the goosebumps sprouting up her arms at the thought, even in this sweltering nighttime heat. Veer must have noticed, because when they got into their Uber, he pressed his fingertips into the spaces between her knuckles. "The worst is over," he reminded her. "Just try to breathe. You look amazing."

"Thank you." Harsha looked away, pretending to scroll Instagram on her phone. All that ran through her mind was: If Veer was this caring as a fake boyfriend, how much love would he have shown her as a *real* one?

Chapter

THIRTEEN

"If I wanted to avoid doing things with people I hate,
I would literally never leave my house."
—Dina Fox, *Superstore*

Veer let out a whoosh of breath. Here he was, at the venue of his first-ever Bollywood party. Or rich-person party, for that matter. He scratched his collar—boy, his suit was starchy—and got out of the Uber. He looked up at the fancy building before him: Taj Lands End, one of Mumbai's biggest and best five-star hotels situated by the sea. Against the dark night sky, the hotel was lit up in a multitude of golden hues, and sweet, romantic Bollywood music already boomed from one of the lower floors. That was probably where the party was being hosted.

After the quick security check, he followed Harsha to one of the smaller, more intimate ballrooms in the hotel. He now recognized the Bollywood song playing as a classic romantic song from a '90s Aamir Khan movie.

"There are so many people here, I can't seem to spot my family," Harsha said, turning her neck left and right in her search.

Meanwhile, Veer took in the wood-paneled room. Bright white pillars jutted out around the corners, sparkling from the light of the yellow chandeliers. Regal artwork, possibly from renowned painters, decked the walls, matching the carpeted floor perfectly. Metallic gold balloons and silver streamers hung from the ceiling, swaying with the breeze of the air-conditioning. A stage was set up at the front with a large framed photograph that looked to be from Uncle Madhu and Aunt Pinky's wedding day, twenty-five years ago. Flowers and gifts were stacked on the table in front of the photo frame.

Was Veer supposed to bring a gift? He sighed internally.

There were perhaps seventy to eighty guests here already, some flocking about the buffet, others in small groups, all of them with a drink in their hands. Waiters holding trays moved in and out of the crowd swiftly, refilling those drinks before they were even done.

Then his eyes landed on some of the guests, and he did a double take. Was that the King of Bollywood, Shah Rukh Khan, taking a selfie with his wife? And a few other Bollywood actors who Veer could only have dreamed of being in a room with? *Holy fuck.*

He tugged on his collar, then pulled his tie back up. He had to look the part of a successful boyfriend and future movie star. He had to impress Uncle Madhu and bring up his acting skills in conversation again, so he wouldn't ever need to wonder what could have been.

"You okay?" Harsha touched his side gently with her purse.

"Yeah," he lied, nodding. "Just overwhelmed by all the people here, I guess."

"Really?" Harsha raised her eyebrow. "And here I thought you were unfazed by my family being so, um . . ."

"I get it." He laughed, then spotted Uncle Madhu and Aunt Pinky at the bar chatting with a Hollywood actor. "Want to grab a drink?"

She nodded.

They greeted her uncle and aunt, wishing them a happy anniversary, and Harsha called the bartender over to order their drinks. "Vodka soda for me," she said, "and what beer would you recommend for my boyf—"

"Actually," Veer said, shooting a furtive glance at the drink in Uncle Madhu's hand, "I'll have a scotch on the rocks with a twist?"

Harsha's brows furrowed, but Uncle Madhu must have over-heard, because he raised his own glass of scotch at Veer. "The boy has good taste."

"Thanks." Veer cracked a grin.

Aunt Pinky smiled in return, rubbing her palm along Uncle Madhu's arm. "Enjoy the party. We'll be a little busy, but thank you for being here. For us and for Harshu." Then they turned away, back to their conversation with the actor.

Harsha handed him the glass of scotch, and he took a sip, nearly pulling a face. He hated scotch, especially whatever overpriced brand they'd served him. Beer was the only right choice of poison, in his opinion.

"Did you only order scotch to impress my uncle?" Harsha laughed into her vodka soda.

"How did you guess?" he asked dryly, swirling the glass around.

She gave him a teasing look. "As your *girlfriend,* I'd know when something's bothering you, wouldn't I?"

Veer blinked. "Are you quoting me? I'm flattered." How could anyone be *this* adorable? And sexy. And smart.

Harsha smirked as she sipped her drink. "Don't get used to it."

"I'll try not to." He set his drink aside and pulled her closer, pressing his cold fingers into her bare waist below that sleeveless blouse, eliciting a gasp from her. Harsha blinked, confusion on her face, then looked around at the crowd. A few people were looking their way, probably surprised by the PDA.

"Veer—"

"Shush." Chuckling, he grabbed a tissue from the bar and dabbed at the spot next to her lower lip, ignoring the way her throat bobbed. "You had some smudged lipstick. There. All done."

"Thanks. Now . . ." She put her drink next to Veer's and took his other, warmer hand. "Let's dance."

They walked to the center of the ballroom where people were already slow dancing to another retro Bollywood song. "Put your hands back on me," Harsha whispered as her arms wound around his shoulders. "And look at me like you can't believe you get to dance with me."

I already am, he thought. He wrapped his fingers around her waist again, pulling her even closer in, flush against him. The small noise she made in the back of her throat at the proximity sent blood rushing down to his groin. *This isn't the time or place, Veer,* he told himself. *Keep it PG-13.*

Veer had never found one good thing about being a five-foot-eight actor. The industry had changed since the '90s and the early 2000s, when talent trumped nepotism and looks. Now, a male actor needed a tall frame and muscles for days whether he was filming an action thriller or a sappy rom-com. But Harsha was nearly his height with her stiletto heels, and as they danced, their bodies pressed together more than they'd ever been, her lips were hardly a couple of inches away from his. Okay, that cinched it: five foot eight was the perfect height for Veer.

"You're doing a great job," Veer murmured, dropping his mouth to her ear. "Nobody's going to doubt that we're in love." He spun her around in time with the music and pulled her back in again.

She looked away, biting that red lip. "Yeah," she said after a pause. "Nobody."

He wished he could get a pulse check on what she was thinking. He dipped her low, and when she came back up, she said, "I never thought the cute barista from Sunstag would be such a good dancer."

Cute barista? Veer tried not to blush. "Dancing lessons were part of the curriculum at acting school," he said as he swayed with her to the slow beat. "You're not so bad yourself."

"Please," she laughed as he twirled her around and pulled her closer again, "I can barely focus. I'm trying so hard not to fall flat on my face in this saree and heels."

He lowered his chin, so their lips were less than a hair's distance away. "There's no way that'll happen, because I won't let go of you until you ask me to."

She exhaled; he felt it on his face, hot and slow. He took one hand off her waist and cupped her cheek. God, those lips, so close and yet so far away . . . Veer knew the contract had said "no kissing," but this dance they were doing, between the lines of real and fake—it was impossibly hard not to break that rule then and there. He had to try. "Harsha," he started, "can I—"

"Veer!" A voice interrupted the tense air between them. Harsha pulled away, clearing her throat, while Veer looked behind him at the grinning man who'd called out his name.

His eyebrows shot up. "Ibrahim?"

"Man, how have you been?" Ibrahim gave him a hug, thumping him heavily on the back. "I haven't seen you since you left Mumbai!"

Veer returned the hug, dazed. "I've been well," he said, then gestured to Harsha. "Uh, this is Harsha, my . . . girlfriend. Harsha, Ibrahim is a friend from acting school."

Harsha smiled politely at Ibrahim. "Nice to meet you. Didn't you play a minor role in Kunal Jowar's latest movie? I remember seeing you on-screen."

Ibrahim nodded, looking pleased that he'd been recognized. "Yeah. One of my co-stars invited me to this party as their plus-one, so here I am. How about you, Veer?"

Veer took Harsha's hand. "Harsha is Madhusudan Godbole's niece."

"Wow." Ibrahim let out a whistle. "Are you still acting?"

"Just here and there, when I get the chance," Veer said, then added, "If you know of any opportunities in Bangalore . . ."

"Of course, man! I'll hit you up. It was great seeing you." Ibrahim gave them a smile and headed to the bar.

Veer held his hand out, and Harsha took it again, although he made note of the distance she kept between them this time. They swayed to the music, not talking, not even meeting each other's eyes, until Neha and her fiancé, Rohan, appeared beside them, half-dancing and half-giggling. Neha might have been mean, but they were a cute couple.

"Hey," Neha said as Rohan spun her around. "Enjoying the party?"

"Mm-hmm." Harsha scooted closer to Veer, and he squeezed her waist in reassurance. "Uncle Madhu sure knows how to throw them."

"As we both know," Neha agreed. After a moment of silence, save for the music, she added, "My friends and I are going wedding shopping at Renuka Mishra's boutique next weekend for their outfits. That's where I got mine too."

"How nice," Harsha replied tightly.

"Have you been there?" Neha asked, smiling against Rohan's chest. "Nobody makes designer lehengas like her."

Veer felt Harsha go rigid against his body. "I don't think so," she said, and as the song ended, she mumbled a "see you soon" to Neha and pulled Veer away from the dance floor. "Let's have dinner and get out of here," she said, her voice lowered. "My parents are still mingling, and maybe it's for the best if we leave before they come up to us. I don't really want to see them after the way they treated us at lunch."

"Okay." Veer led her by the hand to the buffet, sighing to himself. He wanted to dance with her more; he wanted to hold her in his arms for longer. The moment they'd had—if he could call it that—had passed, and who knew if there would be another one?

WHY COULD HARSHA STILL FEEL the warmth of Veer's breath tickling her lips? As they took the elevator to their hotel room, she was keenly aware of the hot, stifling air between them that urged her to step closer to him and finish what he'd initiated in the ballroom.

Thankfully, Harsha was a woman with self-control. At least, she hoped she was.

Veer used the key card and the door opened with a beep. Should she bring up the moment in the ballroom, just to see what would happen? Just to gauge his reaction, prove her theory that he hadn't been acting in that moment? Before Harsha could so much as open her mouth, Veer said, his voice stiff, "I'm gonna take a shower. Be right back." He rummaged in his suitcase for a fresh pair of pajamas and disappeared into the bathroom.

She tilted her head back and groaned. So much for that. She changed into a silk night suit and lay back against the fluffy white pillows of her bed, pulling the comforter over herself and checking her phone. Her parents hadn't texted her at all, but they'd uploaded a selfie to Instagram. Uncle Madhu (or perhaps his assistant) had already posted videos of all his celebrity friends dancing to Bollywood music. Neha's story showed her flanked by Uncle Madhu and Aunt Pinky, their lips pressed to her cheeks. The caption read: I am nothing without them 🖤

Harsha's stomach squirmed. The mutton biryani and veg kebabs she and Veer had eaten at the party threatened to make themselves known. She took a sip of water, staving off the nausea, and decided to post something too, if only to stop feeling left out and unwanted. Earlier today at the beach, she'd clicked a video of Veer working on that mess of a sandcastle, his hands muddy, while she laughed out loud in the background. She posted it to her Instagram stories.

She knew her parents and Neha wouldn't care for it, but Aunt Pinky DMed her within minutes. Beta u both seem so happy! Sorry we couldn't talk much at the party 😊

It's okay, Auntie, Harsha texted back despite the hollow sadness in her gut. I hope you enjoyed your big day! And I wish I could have stayed longer at lunch. It was just hard 😖

Aunt Pinky:
Love u beta

Harsha put her phone away and wiped the side of her nose. She curled her knees up into her chest, wishing she could be independent enough to stop caring what her family thought of her. Maybe that was the curse and blessing of being brought up Indian. After all, she'd been raised to believe that family was the only solid foundation a child could rely on, that their parents knew what was best for them and would give their kids the life they deserved, as long as they complied.

It had taken her a lot of growing up to realize that her parents wanted what was best for her only as long as it made *them* look good—and she didn't want any part in that.

Her phone buzzed: a video call notification from Sasha. Harsha got up eagerly, adjusted the straps of her silk camisole top, and answered the call. "Hi! Oh my god, S, today was such a disaster."

Sasha was standing at her kitchen counter beside her coffee machine, her face bare of any makeup, but her eyes widened. "Fuck. Tell me everything."

The water in the shower turned off, so Harsha put on her Air-Pods and went outside the room. She leaned against a pillar in the hallway and summarized everything to her best friend.

"Your dad sounds like the worst." Sasha set her coffee down and slapped a hand to her forehead. "But forget about him—how's it going with Veer?"

"Good," Harsha said, nodding slowly. "Yeah. Pretty good. He's, um," she tucked a strand of hair behind her ear and cleared her throat, "he's quite convincing."

Sasha shot her a funny look. "Convincing to your family, or convincing to you?"

Damn Sasha for being such a mind reader. Harsha didn't know how to answer that. She fumbled for words, but her best friend got it. "Are you falling for him?" she asked.

Harsha looked to the closed door, then said softly, "What? No way." She scoffed unconvincingly. "I'm just so attracted to him. And it doesn't hurt that our banter is fantastic. Why couldn't he have been one of those good-looking men with nothing in their brains?"

Sasha chuckled. "If he wasn't smart, you wouldn't have picked him."

"What do I do, S?" Harsha said. She heard the sound of footsteps inside the room and lowered her voice another octave. "I almost leaned in for a kiss when we were dancing—"

"For starters, don't you dare do that again," Sasha said sternly. She rubbed her temples. "This situation is too precarious to give in to your attraction. I hope you've got separate beds?"

Harsha nodded. "If I had to share a bed with him, I wouldn't make it through the night. Have you seen his smile? No, forget his smile, S—have you seen his forearms?"

Sasha's mouth twitched. "I will never understand your forearm kink. Maybe next time, you could buy him shirts with sleeves he can't roll up?"

"Screw you," Harsha fired back, then sighed. "I should go back inside. I'll call you when I'm home?"

"Be careful, H," Sasha said. "Love you."

Harsha nodded and hung up. Then she shook out her shoulders and returned to the room. Veer stood by the bed, dressed in a cartoon T-shirt and gray sweatpants. He smelled like the hotel's lemony shampoo. "Cute video," he said as he held his phone up. "I wish we had footage of that kid calling the sandcastle ugly, though. That had 'viral' written all over it."

She forced herself to laugh, trying not to think about how bad they had both been at sandcastle-making, yet how fun it had been spending time with Veer. Not just at the beach, but at the party, too, with the dancing and the banter and the sizzle of their almost-kiss—

Nope. Don't think about that. She exhaled and crawled under the covers, as he did the same on his bed.

"Good night, fake girlfriend," Veer said, switching off the lights.

"Good night, fake boyfriend," Harsha said, then hesitated as something Veer once said popped into her mind: *I don't do relationships longer than three months.* Why, though? He had the looks and the charm needed to get a woman's phone number, and the kindness to be a good partner. He'd already been a fantastic fake boyfriend to her in the span of a few weeks. So . . . what did he have against a serious relationship?

She had to know. With a tentative voice, she asked, "Veer, you still awake?"

"Yeah," he rumbled out. "What's up?"

Harsha shifted on the bed, facing him, but he was still looking up at the ceiling, one muscular arm under his head. "You told me once you don't do relationships longer than three months. Can I . . . ask why?"

He didn't speak for what felt like the longest second of Harsha's life. Finally, he said, "It's not like I enforce a rule, but it's just never happened. I'm not . . . that kind of guy."

She peered at him in the dark. "What kind of guy are you, then?"

"The kind for whom love doesn't make any sense." He sighed. "I've never been in love. I'm twenty-seven years old, and I've never said those words to someone."

Harsha frowned. "Why not?"

He sighed again, loudly. "You know," he said, "some of my high school classmates' parents were divorced too. But those kids still had both their parents coming to PTA meetings and school events. I didn't even get a card in the mail from my dad on my birthday."

"I'm so sorry," she whispered.

"After that, I didn't want to let people in. Or rather . . . I couldn't. The only people I've trusted in a long time are my mom and brother, Deepika and Raunak, and now—" Veer cleared his throat. "It's getting late. We should sleep."

Was he about to say her name? Harsha didn't have the courage to ask. So all she said was "Thank you for telling me that. I know it's not easy to talk about this stuff with new people."

Veer let out a noise that was somewhere between a scoff and a laugh. "You're not 'new people' anymore."

She couldn't stop the wide grin from splitting across her lips. "Sleep tight," she said, rolling onto her back.

Veer's light snoring filled the room within minutes, while Harsha stayed awake, watching the spinning ceiling fan and replaying the past week over and over in her mind. It had been the longest couple of days, full of chaotic upheavals, from the leak situation last night to the snide comments of her family during lunch.

And Veer had been the balm to Harsha's pain through it all. When was the last time someone had made her feel this safe? No way could he be pretending to care about her. And she cared about him, too. More than she wanted to let on.

Go to sleep, she commanded herself. Feeding these thoughts was dangerous. The longer they consumed her, the harder she would fall—and falling for her fake boyfriend was the one thing she couldn't afford to do.

Chapter
FOURTEEN

"Listen, buddy. It's not who brings you into the world.
It's what you do when you're there."
—Jay Pritchett, *Modern Family*

The queue to get away from the stuffy heat and inside the air-conditioned respite of the airport was moving at a snail's pace, so they stood in line patiently. At least, Veer did. Harsha kept throwing anxious glances at her phone, cringing as the minutes went by.

"We'll make it," Veer assured her when she pulled her hair out of its ponytail and started tugging on the hair elastic. He gestured to the large screen ahead of them. "See, our flight's delayed by thirty minutes."

"Oh, thank god." Harsha sank against his body, her curly hair tickling his nostrils. He tried not to take a great big whiff of her spicy-floral shampoo. This woman was a melting pot of intoxicating scents. First the strawberries, now this?

The line moved forward by a few people. Harsha busied herself with swiping through some photos she'd taken this weekend while Veer looked around at the airport. Next to the crowded queues was the arrival hall, equally as packed with loved ones eager to see the people who'd just landed in the city. Cab drivers stood holding name placards, waiting for their assigned passengers to spot them. The drivers were from different hotels, companies, banks, and—

Veer froze.

One of the drivers was holding up a placard with the logo of a midsized corporate bank headquartered in Mumbai. It said: WELCOME BACK, MR. KANNAN!

It couldn't be. No way was that referring to Narayan Kannan, father of Veer and Arjun Kannan, breaker of Manisha Kannan's heart. It couldn't be. When Dad had left, he'd been a teller at a government bank with big dreams of making it in corporate someday— not that he ever put any effort into those ambitions. Kannan was a common Tamilian last name. There was no way the placard was—

The driver waved to someone walking out of the arrival hall. Veer craned his neck, hoping to see who this banker was, if only to give himself closure.

A middle-aged, balding, portly man in a suit came into view, wheeling a small overnight bag. He turned sideways, greeting the driver with a familiar smile—

It was him.

Veer blinked back tears as he pulled on his collar and tried to take in a big gulp of air, but his throat had closed up. Time came to a standstill; his heart nearly stopped, but Dad kept walking, out of sight, out of Veer's life yet again.

Just like when he was a kid. And now, here he was, presumably rich and successful, while the people he once called family were struggling to pay their bills—

"Veer? Veer, are you okay?"

Harsha's frantic voice pulled him out of his stupor. Veer looked around, gasping for breath, and stumbled into Harsha's outstretched arms. They were closer to the check-in counter now, but everyone was staring at him in concern. He didn't need a mirror to know his face must have looked pale and sickly.

"I'm here," Harsha said soothingly, patting his back. "Do you want some water?"

"Y-yeah," he stammered out.

A man standing behind them in line handed Veer a bottle of water that he downed in three quick gulps. "Thanks."

"Sir, do you need medical help?" a security guard asked from up ahead.

Harsha opened her mouth, nodding, but he spoke first. "No. I'm—I'm fine. Thank you."

Veer let Harsha take the lead with check-in, quietly following behind her and mumbling "We're late" every time she tried to ask him what happened.

Once they were through with security check and sitting in front of their gate, Harsha held his hand. When she spoke, her voice was thick with emotion. "Veer, please talk to me," she said. "You almost collapsed, and I didn't know what to do. I just froze. I—I'm so sorry."

He smiled, despite the exhaustion he felt down to his toes, and wiped the first tear that slid down her cheek. "Hey, I'm fine now."

She squeezed his hand three times in reassurance. "Was it a panic attack?"

Veer looked away, thinking. "I don't know. I've never had one before. I, uh, I saw my dad outside."

Harsha gasped. "Your dad?"

He explained what he saw and sat back in his chair, shoulders sinking. "He was wearing a suit. And he had a driver. And—and he looked happy."

"Veer . . ."

"How can he be happy after everything that happened?" A wave of anguish was threatening to break out of him, but he tried to hold it in. He didn't want to cry in front of Harsha. "Anyway, I'm sorry if I embarrassed you—"

She got up from her chair and crouched in front of him, cupping his face with her soft hands. "Listen to me," she said, her voice fierce. "You could *never* embarrass me. You are smart, and sweet, and so much fun, and you've proved it countless times this weekend.

If your father can't see your worth, then he doesn't deserve your grief. All right?"

Veer nodded. "Thank you. I needed to hear that."

Their flight had commenced boarding, so they joined the queue. Harsha held his hand right up until they slid into their seats, and she only let go to place her tote bag under the seat in front of her. "Do you want the window?" she asked as he fumbled with his seat belt. "I can take the middle, if you want to cry without anyone noticing."

That made Veer laugh. Fuck, she was so cute. "I'm fine, thanks. But I definitely could do with a nap."

Harsha smiled. "Want to use my shoulder as a pillow, this time?"

He suppressed the rush of affection that flooded his senses at those words and scooted closer to her. "Yes, please."

WHILE VEER SLEPT ON HARSHA's shoulder as the plane flew to Bangalore, she looked out the window at the blue sky. The city below them grew smaller with each passing second, but dark clouds ahead threatened turbulence. What a perfect metaphor for this weekend.

The more time Harsha spent with Veer, the more it solidified her belief that she was doing the right thing. Once Neha and Rohan's wedding was over, Harsha would have some breathing room to figure out her shit. Everyone would be focused on Neha's honeymoon, her married life, her plans to start a family—they wouldn't notice if Harsha stopped posting pictures with Veer. Hopefully, by the time they started asking questions again, she would have a head start with her career and love life.

The problem was . . . Harsha couldn't remember the last time she'd connected with a person to this extent. When she'd turned around in the queue and seen Veer's deathly pale face and trembling limbs, her heart had stopped. A multitude of thoughts had raced through her mind—*Is he having a panic attack? Is he going to collapse?*

Why didn't I notice it sooner?—but there was a quiet voice whispering, *I need him to be okay, or I won't be.*

She didn't want to lose Veer after the contract ended. She couldn't afford to. In the past month, he had become more than just her contracted fake boyfriend—he'd become her friend.

But did he feel the same way?

Veer roused, lifting his head from her shoulder and rubbing his neck. "What time is it?"

Harsha checked her phone. "We're fifteen minutes from landing. Did you sleep okay?"

He yawned as he nodded. "Kinda." He stretched his arms in front of him as much as he could, given the packed economy class flight, then said, "I had a dream about Dad."

"Wow, your subconscious works fast," Harsha joked.

Veer chuckled; it made Harsha's heart bloom. "In the dream, he showed up to Sunstag in that fancy suit and tie and ordered a nitro cold brew to go. He didn't recognize me, and when I told him who I was, he said his real son would never work at a café." At Harsha's raised eyebrow, he let out an anguished exhale. "Was he judging me for being a barista? Or am I judging myself, since it was my dream and my subconscious?"

Harsha shifted toward him, placing her hand on his knee. "I don't think it's about you being a barista at all. I think you'd have had this dream even if you were an engineer, a banker, or anything else."

He snorted. "Are we jumping right back into the acting conversation?"

"You know I have a point," she said.

A flight attendant stopped by their row to remind them to prepare for landing. Veer slowly pushed his seat back upright. Finally, he spoke. "You and my brother would get along so well."

Those words made her stomach flutter, but she kept a straight face. "Meaning what?"

"Arjun is always on my case about getting back into acting." Veer ran a hand along his hairline. "But he doesn't understand that I *can't.* Some of us have financial responsibilities."

Harsha didn't know the extent of Veer's monetary obligations. He still hadn't told her what he was using the money for. "Following your passion has a cost, but isn't that risk worth it?"

Veer took a sip of water from his bottle, his jaw clenched. "Not everyone can afford to take risks."

She opened her mouth, then shut it. What could she say to that? Instead, she took his left hand in hers, her heart dropping when she noticed how much colder it was than usual.

He pinched the bridge of his nose with his other hand. "Should I . . . tell my mom I saw Dad at the airport?"

Harsha thought for a minute, wondering what she would do if she were in Veer's shoes. "It depends on what you want to do about it. When was the last time you made contact with him?" she asked.

Veer's eyes went back and forth. "Maybe a couple of months after he left, when I didn't know for sure that he was really gone. Mom gifted me my first cellphone for my sixteenth birthday, and I called his number to ask where he was, why he wasn't home." He sighed. "But he had switched his number, and that was that."

"So you haven't looked him up? Ever?"

"No. I told myself I didn't need to know." He put his empty water bottle in the seat pocket ahead of him, swallowing. "But maybe that's changed now."

"Then that's another thing you need to do. And I'm here for you, Veer. Always."

"Thanks," he said, pulling his hand away from her grasp and turning to the front as the captain announced landing. Harsha didn't miss the distant look in his eyes or the way his shoulders had tightened.

After they got out of the airport and headed to the Uber pickup line, Harsha said, "Do you want to hang out a little longer? We could get some lunch, or watch a movie—"

He walked on, dragging his suitcase behind him. "I'm fine. I think I need to be alone."

She nodded as she spotted her Uber. It was so hard to understand what went on in this man's head. "That's me," she said, nudging her head toward the car. "Call me later today, okay? I just want to make sure you're all right."

"I will," he said, avoiding her eyes. He helped her put her suitcase into the trunk and opened the car door for her. "Get home safe," he said, turning away before she could wave goodbye to him.

"Sure," she mumbled as her car sped home. So much for thinking they were letting each other in, at long last.

FIFTEEN

"And I know we can't fix every ache inside of us.
But I shouldn't have to pretend it's not there, either."
—Colin Hughes, *Ted Lasso*

Veer unlocked his front door and slammed it closed behind him. He kicked off his shoes, leaving his suitcase by the door, and fell into the couch, clutching his forehead. What a chaotic weekend. He hugged a fluffy cushion to his chest, then jerked away when he caught a whiff of strawberries, probably from the last time Harsha was here.

No. Veer threw the cushion aside. He couldn't let his mind wander in Harsha's direction again, or he'd stay up all night thinking of her kindness, her compassion, her beauty. Of that almost-kiss and the way he was forcing himself to get some space from her, for the sake of what was still at stake. He wouldn't let himself dream of any sort of real connection with her—at least not until the third payment was in his bank account, Arjun's tuition was taken care of, and his future was safeguarded.

He changed out of his airport clothes and decided to take a nice, long nap when his phone chimed with a text from Harsha. I got back a while ago. Hope you did too?

He sent out a quick text. Yep. Could you send over the second payment when you get a chance?

> Harsha is typing . . .

> Harsha is typing . . .

Harsha:

> Okay

He paused, then texted the Barista Bitches **WhatsApp group.** I'm back home. I know it's only noon, but anyone up for drinks?

> Raunak is typing . . .

Raunak:

> Hell yes! It's always 5 p.m.
> somewhere!

Deepika:

> Yep, see you in an hour after my shift!

Guess that nap would have to wait. Veer headed to the shower instead, grateful for the distraction his friends would hopefully give him.

At their favorite bar, his friends caught him up on all the drama that had happened at Sunstag while he was away. Apparently, two customers had been caught hooking up in the bathroom; their grumpy, introverted store manager's boyfriend dropped by for the first time; and Deepika's coconut mocha latte recipe won a barista contest and was added to the menu of every Sunstag store in the country. Then, finally, the topic shifted to Veer.

"You didn't send me a single picture of any celebrities," Deepika whined, "but I'm so glad you're back. We missed you!"

"I missed you both too." Smiling, Veer clinked his mug of beer with theirs. "But I, uh, decided to take another couple of days off from work."

"Why?" Raunak asked, frowning.

"This weekend has been a lot," he admitted. "I just need some R and R."

His friends nodded in understanding. It hadn't been an easy decision to extend his break from work, since he'd used up a chunk of his paid time off for the Mumbai trip, but he needed some time to figure out his next steps with Dad . . . and Harsha. And he couldn't do that if she was at Sunstag every day, right in his inner orbit.

She had texted him when he was on the way to the bar, asking when he wanted to do their next date, but apart from confirming to her that he'd received the second payment installment, he hadn't kept the conversation going or answered her question. Veer hadn't imagined being so vulnerable and baring his soul to anyone ever again, let alone the woman he was fake-dating. He couldn't face her until he knew what to do about his feelings.

Over their next beer, Raunak told them about his most recent Tinder date with a woman from Delhi who had seemingly only come over because she needed a place to crash until her flight the next day. As Deepika told Raunak this was karma for his fuckboy ways, Veer's phone chimed with a selfie of Harsha holding up a morsel of masala dosa and a flask of filter coffee.

Harsha:

Guess who just found out CTR delivers to her apartment?

He chuckled and started to type out, CTR: 1, Gourmet Restaurant: 0. You're welcome 😉, but before he could press Send, Raunak snapped his fingers in Veer's face, making him jump. "Hey! Stop texting your girlfriend when you're with us. Didn't you fly back with her just this morning?

Veer pocketed the phone. "Yeah, sorry."

Deepika smiled. "You've never met a girlfriend's family before. This is fast for you, but it's going well, isn't it?"

Before Veer could reply, Raunak chimed in, "Bet you he'll come back from the cousin's wedding and start shopping for engagement rings."

Veer's face flushed. He opened his mouth to tell them off, then closed it when Deepika spoke, her eyes twinkling. "Should we start looking up baby names? What letter are we thinking? Girl or boy?"

He tightened his grip on his mug. Any high the beer had given him was slowly dissipating, replaced by sheer dread. There was no way they believed that Veer was serious enough about Harsha to want to marry her. They knew most of the details about his father. Dad's abandonment had left him emotionally unavailable. Stunted. Empty.

Then why did his heart feel so full at the thought of Harsha's smile? Why did part of him know he could potentially think, say, and promise those three words to her, and mean them forever? Why didn't that scare him in the slightest?

"I know!" Raunak slammed his hand on the table. "They should combine their own names to create a new one. Maybe Harshveer if it's a boy, and Varsha if it's a girl!"

The emotions swirled around in him—Harsha's softness as he navigated his panic attack, her support of his acting career, and that almost-kiss—god, it was all a bit too much. He didn't know how to function or deal with his feelings for her.

Especially because the longer this went on, the harder it got for him to imagine a life without her in it.

"Would Harsha let you get a stripper for your bachelor party?" Raunak asked. He swirled the last of his beer around in the mug. "I know this woman who does—"

"Just stop it!" Veer roared, loud enough for other people to hear over the pounding EDM beats. He lowered his voice an octave. "There's not going to be a bachelor party, or a wedding. Or—or babies!"

Deepika and Raunak exchanged confused glances. "Why not?" She tilted her head.

Veer's shoulders sank as he said, "Because it's not real."

Deepika's mouth fell open, her sentence dying on her lips. Beside her, Raunak choked on his beer. "What?" they both said in unison.

Veer finally admitted the truth about the contract, the money, and Harsha's complicated family history. He hung his head when he was done, bracing himself for their outrage. And boy, were they pissed.

"Are you out of your mind?" Raunak said, his jaw tense. "Why would you ever agree to something like this?"

"I had to do it, for Arjun's sake—"

"You could have asked *us* for money," Raunak insisted. "We would have pooled our savings, asked other people in our network for help."

Veer sighed. "I didn't think of that."

"Do you think this is some kind of Bollywood movie?" Deepika shook her head. "Veer, you can't be serious."

He rubbed his temples. "I *am* serious."

"You're practically an escort without the sex part," she said, while Raunak nodded furiously. "There is no universe in which this ends well."

"But it's fake," he murmured in his defense.

"Is it, though?" Deepika raised a brow. "Or are you taking time off from work because you've caught real feelings for her?"

Veer wiped his sweaty hands on his jeans. "I . . . may have."

His friends exchanged glances, some sort of unspoken agreement between them. Then Deepika said, "We've always liked her for you, but this sounds too complicated to ever work."

"So what do I do now?" he said weakly.

"Well, you have to keep it in your pants," Raunak said, "and keep her out of your heart."

"Agreed." Deepika frowned. "Her dad sounds like bad news. If the truth comes out, he'll ruin your life, and that could affect your mom and Arjun too."

He gulped. They were right. Fuck, they were so right.

"Okay, so the wedding is in two weeks." Deepika drummed her fingers on the table, ever the planner of the group. "Hold it together for now, then cut it off with Harsha completely."

Veer nodded dismally.

Slowly, the conversation switched to relationship horror stories, Raunak's upcoming dates, and the new coffee blends Deepika wanted to introduce to Sunstag. Veer chimed in with occasional uh-huhs and mm-hmms, replying half-heartedly to whatever his friends were saying, but his mind was still on their warnings and how right they were.

If he wanted to get over this crush and stop it from turning into full-blown feelings, he needed space. He would keep up the deal to the best of his abilities, but no way would he let himself bare his soul to Harsha again.

It wasn't worth the risk.

VEER CAME BACK HOME EARLY, around four in the afternoon, weary from the conversation with his friends, and spotted a Tupperware container on his doorstep with a note: *Welcome home! Leftover idli chutney for breakfast tomorrow. Keep refrigerated. —Mom*

He laughed and stowed it away in the fridge. As he walked into his room, his thoughts drifted back to Dad and the panic attack.

Both he and Mom deserved to know the full truth about the man who had left them, not just the bits and pieces he had gathered at the airport. He picked up his laptop, his fingers hovering over the keyboard, but he couldn't bring himself to type out his father's name.

What if he saw something he wasn't ready for? Dad's financial success, fame, maybe even a new family? All while leaving Veer, Arjun, and Mom in the dust?

On the other hand, how would Veer pretend that life was back to normal without satiating his burning curiosity, one that had lain dormant for the past twelve years?

Fuck it. He would do it.

The results were instant, turning the blood in Veer's veins ice-cold. A LinkedIn résumé boasted eight years at the corporate bank, climbing the ranks steadily to where he was now senior vice president. Facebook photos of young children and a woman with silver-black hair. And . . . a work cell phone number.

Funny how Veer had gone twelve years without caring about Dad and what he was up to. He'd moved past the grief of losing his father a long time ago. But after today, every single emotion that fifteen-year-old Veer had bottled up crashed over him like a tidal wave. And he didn't know if there was an off switch to the heartbreak he was reliving all over again. Perhaps the only way out was to face it head-on.

Veer deliberated over it, then punched in the numbers and hit Call before he could second-guess himself. His father might not even pick up, this being a Sunday afternoon, but he had to try. Five agonizingly slow rings later, someone answered. "Hello, Narayan Kannan with LPK Banking here, may I know who's speaking?"

That voice had been etched in Veer's mind his whole life, but hearing it after twelve years, knowing everything his father had missed out on in the time since—from Veer's play performances and Arjun's success in academics to all the recipes Mom had perfected—it broke Veer. It broke him to know that Dad was out there sitting in an air-conditioned office or a fancy apartment, answering his phone with no idea his estranged son was calling. And even if he knew, he probably wouldn't care.

"Hello? Is anyone there?"

A strangled gasp escaped Veer's lips as he hung up. His heart thudded, his stomach turned and twisted. He clapped a hand to his mouth to stave off the nausea. *Fuck, fuck, fuck. Not another panic attack. Please, no—*

His phone vibrated with a call. *Shit.* Was his dad calling back?

No. It was Arjun.

Veer's head hurt with guilt. He hadn't spoken to his brother in a while, what with all his focus going toward Harsha, dodging Mom's questions about the relationship, and his friends' incessant teasing.

He accepted the call, then set his phone on his stomach and sat back. "Hey, little brother," he said, trying to keep his voice steady.

"Don't 'little brother' me," Arjun said playfully, and just the sound of his brother's voice relaxed him. "Guess who got the highest grade on all four of the assignments we turned in since the start of the semester?"

"I don't know, some nerd with big glasses and oil in his hair?"

"Ha-ha. Very funny." Arjun laughed. "I can't believe I'm doing so well at one of the best business schools in India. Sure, engineering was a piece of cake, but how am I juggling numbers and strategy so easily too?"

"Maybe you've found your calling," Veer said, smiling, as he thought of Harsha's family and how successful they were. "Maybe you'll start a business of your own someday."

"Fat chance," Arjun scoffed, "because most people who graduate from here inevitably end up at multinational corporations. Or at banks. Can you see me as a banker?"

"Uh . . ." Veer's thoughts drifted back to their dad. Maybe banking ran in the Kannans' blood. "I don't know." Veer paused, wondering if he should mention seeing Dad at the airport. But Arjun's spirits were at a high . . . "Hey, I'm gonna take a nap. Talk soon?" he said instead.

"Love you, big bro. Sleep well!"

Veer hung up and crawled into bed. Arjun's life was going perfectly on track—thanks to his efforts and the fake relationship—and if Veer wanted to ensure a good future for his brother, he had to do as his friends said, and keep his head on straight.

Some risks weren't worth the cost, after all.

HARSHA WALKED INTO SUNSTAG CAFÉ in a better mood than the previous day. The Nandi Hills photo shoot clients had finally posted their engagement pictures on social media and tagged Harsha's account as the photographer—and it turned out that Daman's girlfriend wasn't just a model, but also an influencer with over two hundred thousand followers. Now Harsha had four other inquiries in her email, one of which she'd already agreed to. If all went well, she would have a busy and profitable month.

So it didn't matter that Veer had been ignoring most of her text messages, for whatever reason. She would focus on brighter, happier things and push down the disappointment she felt at his silence. But just out of *curiosity*, Harsha made the trip to Sunstag, knowing it was Veer's regular shift.

"Welcome to Sunstag!" Deepika called out as Harsha made her way to the counter.

Harsha slid her card across the counter, her eyes darting around the café. No sign of Veer. "Can I have the usual?"

Deepika lowered her gaze to the system. "Sure."

Raunak surfaced from behind the coffee machine, his eyes narrowed. "Oh, hey."

Harsha frowned as the cash register chirped. Why were they being weird? "Hey"—she looked around—"where's Veer?"

"Veer?" Deepika and Raunak exchanged glances. Raunak opened his mouth, hesitated, then said, "Uh, he's not here."

Harsha jerked her head back. "But I thought today was his first day back after our Mumbai trip?"

"He's taken a few more days off," Deepika said, scanning Harsha's card against the machine.

"What for?"

Raunak glanced at Deepika. "Uhh . . . his mom's not well."

She shifted her feet, wondering why they were all acting so off. Not just Veer, but the other baristas too. "Okay, then." She took her card back and headed upstairs.

As she sipped her coffee and started on the next of those emails, she couldn't help but let her mind wander to Veer. The dancing at the party, the way he'd tugged her closer, his lips mere inches from her, how she'd replayed that moment in her head over and over last night in the shower to let go of the tension pent up in her body.

Then her thoughts shifted to the airport incident and how Veer's demeanor had changed since landing in Bangalore. Forget playing it cool—she had to know what was wrong. She sent him a text. Hey, I heard your mom is sick. Anything I can do to help?

His status changed to "online" and blue check marks appeared under the message.

Veer:

All good. Thanks

She tugged on her hair elastic. Something was definitely wrong, but what? Veer had always been honest with Harsha about his feelings, even when they were negative. This stone-cold exterior was completely new territory.

Didn't he find it odd to start his day without their usual inside jokes at Sunstag, or the smiles they exchanged every time he passed by her table? And more than that . . . didn't he miss her the way she missed him?

Harsha needed advice, and fast. Sasha was probably still up, since it was just past ten P.M. there, so she video called her and filled her in on everything.

Sasha pursed her lips, her nightly mug of chamomile tea in her hands. "He's being weird, yes. But maybe his mom is really sick and he's just too busy taking care of her?"

"Maybe . . ." Harsha let out an *ugh* at the phone screen. "Something feels off, though. Just in general. He's acting distant."

"I say give him another day and then just have a conversation with him about it. Call him, instead of texting."

Harsha nodded, sinking into her chair as her eyes dampened. "Okay. I'll try that. Thanks, S. I wish you were here." God, she missed her best friend; she missed their weekly cocktail girls' nights and daily coffee hangouts spent talking about boyfriends, girlfriends, and—of course—college gossip.

"Actually," Sasha bit the inside of her cheek, "I may know how to fix that."

Harsha's brows wrinkled. "What do you mean?"

Sasha's camera went out of focus for a second, and then she said, "Check your messages."

Confused, Harsha opened their chat and loaded the screenshot Sasha had just sent her.

Of a plane ticket.

To Bangalore.

With Sasha's name on it.

Harsha put a hand to her mouth as a tear fell down her cheek. Was this a dream? She hadn't seen her best friend in four months, the longest they'd been apart in four years. This couldn't be real.

Sasha came back into focus, grinning. "Two of my friends from grad school are getting married in Jaipur, so I thought I'd make a quick pit stop in Bangalore and see you."

Harsha shook her head, wiping her cheek. "I don't believe this. You're just—you're the best!"

Laughing, Sasha said, "I know. And hey, if you need someone to be your backup while you beat Veer up, I'm all for it."

"Hopefully, it doesn't come to that," Harsha said with a genuine smile. "I have to get back to work, but I'll text you soon."

Sasha blew her an air kiss and hung up.

Harsha put her phone aside and pressed her hand to her chest, soaking in this perfect moment. It was the best timing—Sasha was visiting a few days before Neha's wedding. At least Harsha would be in a good mood before the wedding from hell.

Grinning, Harsha opened up her laptop to pull up an Excel sheet, deciding to create the greatest itinerary of all time for her best friend.

Chapter

SIXTEEN

"I'm really tough. And when I do stumble, I have the most
amazing mom who is always right there to pick me up."
—Elena Alvarez, *One Day at a Time*

It was day three of being ignored by Veer, and in an attempt to distract herself, Harsha sat at her usual warm and cozy desk at Sunstag. She uploaded Daman and Gauri's engagement pictures to her website along with their official testimonial and sat back, grinning at her slowly growing online portfolio. The next project she had lined up was a teen influencer's sweet sixteen birthday party.

She was slowly starting to fall in love with this career path. She'd initially thought freelance photography would be a side hustle until she figured out her shit, but what if this was Harsha's real purpose? To celebrate people's big moments with them and help them document it forevermore?

Her parents might never approve, but Harsha had a feeling she'd finally found her calling.

When her phone chirped with an incoming video call notification, she blinked and shifted her focus from work. It was nearly three P.M.; Sasha would be fast asleep now. Who else could it be? Veer? *Oh, please let it be Veer,* she thought as she turned her phone over.

It wasn't Veer. It was Neha.

"Why is she calling me?" Harsha mumbled under her breath, then took the call. "Neha, hi," she said, her voice shaking as Neha's makeup-free, sweaty face came into view. Was she . . . at the gym?

"Hey," Neha said in a totally casual, energetic voice, as though she weren't running at breakneck speed on the treadmill. She had her AirPods in and wore a neon green sports bra under a white tank top. Her hair was up in a tight bun, not a single strand out of place as she moved her body vigorously. "How are you, Harsha?"

"I'm fine," Harsha said, wondering what this was about. "Busy work day at Sunstag."

"Lovely." Neha exhaled softly through her lips and continued running. "Just wanted to tell you the wedding venue has changed."

"Oh, I thought I saw on your stories that it was supposed to be at The Leela Palace?"

"Yeah, we had our eyes set on it," she said, now starting to briskly walk on the treadmill, "but there wasn't availability for the ceremony on the one day the panditji said was auspicious. And Mom's not willing to change the date. So instead, it's going to be at a really fancy wedding venue in Nandi Hills. Daddy pulled a few strings and booked it for four days, last-minute. It's absolutely gorgeous; just wait until you see." She slowed her pace and squealed.

"I bet," Harsha said, forcing out a grin, although her stomach lurched. Harsha had a hundred excuses ready to leave the wedding early, since it was scheduled to be in Bangalore. But Nandi Hills was a two-hour drive away. Now they would be expected to spend at least a night or two. She held back a sigh and said, "Congrats. Veer and I will be there."

"Yay!" Neha said, pumping her fists in the air. The treadmill stopped, and she wiped sweat off her forehead with all the grace of a ballerina. "I'll have someone book one of their on-site hotel rooms for you two. The mehendi's on the afternoon of the fifteenth, so make sure to leave early that morning—"

Harsha almost laughed. Four days of Neha? No thank you. "I

don't think Veer can miss that much work, with his promotion coming up, but we'll attend the wedding ceremony at the very least."

"Oh." Neha cringed. "That might be a problem."

"Why, exactly?"

Neha hopped off the treadmill and walked over to the cycling machine, taking the phone with her. "See, the reason I called is because my photographer can't make it on all four days due to the venue change, so he's going to duck out right after the sangeet ceremony on Tuesday."

"That sucks," Harsha said.

"Which means I have to hire another photographer for the wedding and reception," Neha said, moving her body vigorously as she cycled, "and I thought that could be you."

Harsha rubbed the back of her neck. "Are you asking me to be your wedding photographer?" She hadn't heard anything *this* preposterous coming out of Neha's mouth before.

"Only for the final two days." Neha slowed her pace and blew air through her mouth. "And I'll pay you whatever your usual rate is, of course."

There was no universe in which Harsha wanted to spend more time with Neha or her family, least of all as an employee. "Doesn't Uncle Madhu know someone who can step in?" she asked.

Neha slowed her cycling to a halt. "He can, but I *wanted* to ask you because—ugh, never mind, I shouldn't have bothered—"

"Wait." Harsha sighed, thinking. She wouldn't have liked to be in most of the wedding photos as a guest anyway, so maybe she should just say yes. At least it was a good opportunity to pay her bills for the next few months, make Aunt Pinky happy, *and* keep Neha from going full-on bridezilla at the wedding. "All right, I'll do it. Veer and I will drive down to the venue the evening of the sangeet."

"Thank you! Thank you!" Neha squealed. She turned her face away and wiped her cheek, then said, "Gosh, it's so hot in this gym. Send me an invoice, okay? See ya!"

"Okay . . ." Harsha frowned as the call dropped. She sat back, mulling over this turn of events. On one hand, Neha could intentionally be trying to make Harsha feel like an outsider at the wedding. On the other hand, Harsha was already an outsider and had made her peace with it a long time ago.

She returned to her phone, adjusting her AirPods. She'd better make sure Veer was okay with this change in schedule. Her teeth gritted when he didn't pick up after ten rings. He hadn't even responded to her texts from two days ago. Either his mom was really, *really* sick, or he was ghosting her. She finished the last dregs of her latte, grabbed her tote bag, and raced to the metro station, desperate for answers.

VEER STOOD IN HIS KITCHEN, making an omelet for a late breakfast and humming an old Bollywood song he'd heard . . . somewhere? Right. The anniversary party. The dance. The almost-kiss.

He sighed as he poured the masala egg mixture into the skillet. Every thought in his head inevitably led him down the path of wondering how Harsha must be doing.

It had been, what, three days since they had talked? And already, he missed her. He missed coming up with weird drink names as he brought her that sugary latte. He missed their practice dates that somehow felt like the opposite of fake, and he missed . . . her.

Looking at her.

Talking to her.

Touching her.

Veer jerked himself out of his thoughts before he did something stupid like burn the omelet. He flipped it over, then grabbed a plate and some cheese while the other side cooked.

The doorbell rang as Veer was ladling the omelet onto his plate. He frowned. Mom wasn't coming over until later with some leftover carrot halwa. He set the plate on the coffee table and checked the peephole.

Shit. It was Harsha.

Honestly, Veer should have seen this coming. Harsha was stubborn and didn't take no for an answer. Did he really think he could avoid her forever? He opened the door, wincing.

Harsha stared at him, her arms folded. Her curly hair fell to her waist, one lock pinned up and away from her face. Her striking gray eyes were narrowed, and her lips were painted a fiery shade of scarlet. She looked the way she always did, and yet somehow, she was a hundred times more attractive than he could recall in his mind's eye.

"Hi," he said.

She let out a scoff. "Really, Veer?" She pushed past him into the house, kicking off her sneakers, and looked around, an eyebrow quirked.

"Are you hungry?" He gestured to the cheesy masala omelet on the coffee table behind them.

Harsha put her tote bag aside and studied the omelet, hands on her hips. "I wouldn't mind one, along with a serving of the truth, thank you very much."

"Great. Why don't you wait here?" Veer headed to the kitchen to make another cheesy masala omelet—and figure out what the hell he would say to her.

He returned to the couch with the omelet and two mugs of coffee, and sat beside her.

"So, I'm assuming your mother isn't actually sick," Harsha said, accepting the coffee and plate from him.

He shook his head, sipping his own coffee. "Raunak made that up when you asked about me. I'm sorry, Harsha, I was too overwhelmed with it all. The Mumbai trip, seeing my dad, and us"—he gestured to the air between them with his mug, blushing—"I just needed some space. I know I should have asked you for some time—"

"Exactly," she said, sitting upright, avoiding eye contact. "You should have communicated like a real adult, not an avoidant fake boyfriend." She paused to take a bite. "This omelet is delicious, but it's not a good enough apology."

He took a bite of his own omelet, now cold. "What can I do to make it up to you, then?"

"First, I need to fill you in on everything that's happened recently."

"Oh?" Veer quirked a brow. "I'm listening."

"Well, here's the short version," she said, her eyes finally sparkling as she turned to him. "I booked two new photography clients, Sasha is visiting Bangalore a few days before Neha's wedding—oh, and the second client is Neha herself, who's now getting married at Nandi Hills."

Veer gave himself a few seconds to take in all of the information he'd missed in three long days. "That's fantastic about the clients and Sasha," he said. "But . . . why exactly are *you* the photographer for Neha's wedding?"

Harsha groaned, covering her face with her hands. "I don't know why I said yes. But I did, so now we have to drive down there the evening of the sangeet. Is that okay?"

Veer had done a lot for the sake of this deal and Arjun's future; he could afford to do a little more. "That's fine," he agreed. "I'll talk to my manager about the extra day off. Hopefully he's not too mad at me for asking again."

She gave him an appraising look. "Were you not at Sunstag these past three days because you were avoiding me? Or did you really need a break?"

"I needed a break," he lied swiftly. "So, how can I make it up to you?"

"You could drive me to shop for a lehenga for the ceremony?" Harsha showed him Neha's most recent Instagram post, where she and some friends of hers posed with matching shopping bags from a designer called Renuka Mishra. He vaguely recalled Neha mentioning it at the anniversary party. One look at those shopping bags told him this store was "Designer" with a capital *D*. Or maybe all block letters. Obviously, Neha and her friends wouldn't be caught dead shopping from the countless local small businesses in the city that needed more sales, like Deepika's family boutique. All they cared about was showing off their wealth. He knew Harsha wasn't like that, but maybe she needed to do this to keep up appearances. Her trust fund would definitely cover the expenses. "How about we go next week? Maybe Thursday?"

"That'd be great." Harsha smiled slowly as she finished her omelet. "Can I use your bathroom?"

"It's at the end of the hall," he said, jutting his head in that direction.

While Harsha stood up and went to use his bathroom, Veer picked up the plates and coffee mugs and ran water over them in the sink. So much for his brilliant idea of pushing his feelings down by avoiding Harsha. It was going to be impossible to do either of those things. So be it, he decided. Maybe he'd let himself enjoy her company—and this fake relationship—for as long as she would allow him to. What was the alternative, anyway?

His doorbell rang, and he scoffed. Who was it now?

Mom was smiling up at him through the peephole, a Tupperware container in her hands. The leftover carrot halwa. Of course. Mom had perfect timing. Harsha was still in the bathroom. Hopefully, he could take the halwa from Mom and get her to leave before she came back.

He held back a sigh and opened the door. "Hey, Mom."

She took off her slippers and barged past him into the house, tsk-tsking at the state of the apartment. Veer always thought he did a great job taking care of his place until Mom showed up and told him off for missing a dust bunny under the couch. "Are you hungry?"

"Not really—"

She went into the kitchen and put the container in the fridge. "The halwa will stay fresh for at least a week if it stays refrigerated. Don't you dare leave it out in the open."

"I won't."

She appraised the plates in the sink, and her nose wrinkled at the smell of egg still in the kitchen. "Do you not wash your dishes before going to bed?"

He raked a hand along his stubble. "That's from brunch."

The flush sounded. Mom's eyes widened as the bathroom door creaked open from the other side of the apartment. "Do you have someone over? Is it Harsha?"

Veer suppressed the urge to face-palm himself. "Uh, yeah."

Mom speed-walked into the living room as Harsha said, "Veer, you really should wash your hand towel—"

Both women stopped in their tracks when they saw each other. Veer hung back, scratching the back of his head. His two worlds had finally collided, and he had no idea how to go forward from here. He'd never introduced a girlfriend to his family before. If only the darned relationship history document had covered this.

"Hi, Auntie," Harsha said, lifting her hand up in a hesitant wave. "It's nice to—"

Before she could finish her sentence, Mom had wrapped her arms around her, joy in her voice. "I can't believe I'm *finally* meeting my son's girlfriend!"

Veer caught Harsha's frantic expression and mouthed, *It's okay.* She nodded and hugged his mother back.

Mom pulled away to cup Harsha's face in her hands. "And you're so pretty too. Veer, you never told me the photos don't do justice to how pretty she is!"

"You're right, Mom." He stood beside them, hands in the pockets of his pajamas, and smiled at Harsha. The words fell out before he could stop himself: "She's beautiful."

Harsha's cheeks flushed. "Thank you."

Mom looked back toward the kitchen. "Were you here for breakfast?"

Veer knew she would assume Harsha had stayed over. He was sure Mom wouldn't approve; she was always put off by premarital sex scenes in movies. He was about to do some damage control when Mom clapped her hands. "Doesn't Veer make the best masala omelets?"

"He does," Harsha agreed. "I love the labeled spice containers on his shelves. Did you do that for him?"

Mom's chest puffed out. "I did. This boy wouldn't know garam masala from jeera powder if it weren't for me."

Veer had a feeling Harsha was no master chef herself, but she laughed at his expense anyway. "You've taught him well," she said, then shuffled her feet. "Um, Veer, should I . . . get going?"

His heart sank; it was his final day off, and he wanted to catch up on all the time he'd missed with her, maybe introduce her to one of his favorite sitcoms she hadn't seen yet. "All right," he said finally.

"No." Mom lifted a finger and turned to Harsha. "You must come home for lunch. I made my famous chicken kari kulambu last night, and there's still plenty for everybody. It's one of Veer's favorites."

"Oh, we just had brunch, and I . . ." Harsha hesitated, a question mark on her face as she locked eyes with Veer. "I don't want to overstay my welcome—"

"Nonsense. You must," Mom insisted.

"I think it'll be fun," Veer said. He was afraid of Mom getting her hopes up about a potential future daughter-in-law, only to have them come crashing down after the inevitable fake breakup, but . . . he liked seeing Harsha here, in his home, standing beside his mother—like she was a real part of his life. Like it wasn't all just for show.

"Okay." Harsha smiled and barely grazed the hair tie on her wrist with her thumb. Veer's shoulders loosened. She was nervous, not anxious. The thought comforted him.

Mom went to the bathroom to wash her hands, complaining about the dusty surfaces in the apartment. Once she was out of sight, Veer put his arm around Harsha and whispered in her ear, "This is okay, right?"

She tilted her face up, so close he could feel her warm breath on his lips. "It's okay," she said, pulling away just as Veer was once again considering closing the space between them, the consequences be damned. She tucked a strand of hair behind her ear and cleared her throat. "I can't wait to hear all about your childhood."

He forced himself to laugh. "You're in for a treat, then. Mom loves embarrassing me."

Harsha fastened the laces on her sneakers and grinned at him. "Oh, I'm counting on it."

Mom returned, and they headed out. Veer watched his two favorite women walk down the stairs to the floor below, chatting and laughing like they'd known each other for years, not minutes. Something blossomed in Veer's chest—a gentle flicker of hope that maybe, just maybe, the sight in front of him could all be real someday.

Is this what a mom is supposed to be like? Harsha wondered to herself. Manisha Auntie barely paused to take a breath as she said praise after praise about her son. "I'm so proud of how hard he works to support us," she said, leading Harsha into the Kannans' family apartment. "Did you know he was employee of the month at Sunstag five times in the past year? Five!"

"Mom, please," Veer said, chuckling as he slipped out of his loafers at the front door. "She goes to Sunstag every day. She knows."

"He's the best barista there," Harsha agreed. She gave Veer's hand a squeeze.

"I'll be right back with the leftovers." Manisha Auntie walked into the kitchen, calling out behind her, "Veer, set the table!"

Harsha stood, wanting to help, but Manisha Auntie flat-out refused to let her into the kitchen. "You're our guest," she insisted, pushing her into a chair at the dining table with a cold glass of water. "Sit tight." Then she scurried back to the kitchen.

"I hope this isn't overwhelming," Veer said to Harsha. He placed three plates and some cutlery on the table along with a jug of water. "Mom talks a lot."

She shook her head. "Are you kidding? I love her. She's so supportive of you."

"I don't know about that." He leaned against an empty chair and laughed. "She's always telling me to find a better job, get married, move on with my life . . ." He exhaled. "Moms, am I right?"

Harsha let out a wry smile. Veer didn't know how good he had it. She wished Maa was like Manisha Auntie. "Veer, she's encouraging you to aim higher when it's just the two of you, but raving about what you've already achieved in front of me. Trust me"—her voice broke—"she's a real gem of a mother. My mom has nothing nice to say to me or about me. Ever."

Veer's face fell. He sat in the chair and took her hands in his. "Your mom doesn't know you like I do," he said. His thumbs zig-zagged along her wrist, the gesture equal parts electrifying and soothing. "I can safely say her opinion of you is bullshit."

"Mind your language, kanna," Manisha Auntie said in a faux-stern voice, appearing before them. She placed the steaming hot bowls in front of them and served everyone a portion of rice and curry, smiling when Harsha thanked her.

Veer's mother was an amazing cook. Harsha hadn't had a flavor-ful homecooked meal since moving to Bangalore, since she mostly ordered takeout, and despite not being that hungry, she found her-self asking for seconds. Manisha Auntie regaled her with some highly anticipated embarrassing stories from Veer's childhood. At the age of six, he had tied a towel around his neck and jumped off a second-floor balcony because he wanted to fly like Superman. One broken ankle and a sprained wrist later, he gave up on his superhero dreams.

"I might still be Batman, for all you know," he grumbled under his breath when Harsha burst into peals of laughter.

"And he was an important part of every single Drama Club pro-duction from the sixth grade until he graduated high school," Man-isha Auntie gushed. "One year there were no male roles available, so he auditioned in a wig and a dress to play Amy from *Little Women*."

"Oh my god." Veer bent over and thumped his forehead against the table. "I think we went twelve years without bringing that up. Thanks a lot, Mom."

"Are there pictures?" Harsha asked, her voice teasing. "Please tell me there are pictures."

"We have a whole photo album dedicated to Veer's acting phase," Manisha Auntie said. She paused to serve herself some more rice. "It's an impossible career path, but he's got so much talent. Have you seen him in any of his roles, Harsha? I have some recordings—"

Veer choked on his spoonful of rice, hastening to drink water. "Can we talk about literally anything else?" he said.

Harsha smiled politely as the topic shifted to Manisha Auntie's favorite TV show. She had seen Veer's acting firsthand over the past month, and knew his mother was right. He was phenomenal, from his easy demeanor and charming smile to the depth of his kind words as he fake-dated her. Veer was born to be a romance hero. If her parents didn't like him, that was their flaw, not his.

Wait . . . Harsha blinked. Neha asking her to be the photographer had made it clear that she was a Godbole, but not quite in the right way. Then why did her family's opinion even matter?

Why did she care so much that they approved of Veer, a man she was going to end things with in two weeks?

Because I want them to like him too. The thought hit Harsha like a truck, freezing her insides and then melting them down to her core. Because she wanted him around for way longer than the end date of the contract.

Veer got up before she could ruminate on that dangerous thought any longer, finished with his meal. He gave her a cute smile and headed to the kitchen with his empty plate.

Manisha Auntie put her hand on Harsha's wrist, her eyelids crinkling around the edges. "Harsha, you don't know how happy I am that he's met you."

"Me too." She smiled back. Harsha had always wanted to meet her significant other's parents and find the motherly love she'd lacked most of her life. Aunt Pinky was wonderful, but she would always be her aunt. How bittersweet that she finally got her wish with Manisha Auntie, but with the condition of a looming expiration date.

"You're good for him," Manisha Auntie went on, fiddling with the wedding ring on her finger. Harsha wondered how hard it must be for her to still wear that, over a decade after Veer's father had left. "He's softer around you. Warmer. And . . . happier."

Harsha's eyes misted. "I'm happier around him too," she admitted softly, and Manisha Auntie nodded like she could see it as well.

LATER, VEER DROVE HARSHA HOME. She kept her gaze locked outside the car the whole time, reminding herself that there were only around two weeks to go until Neha's wedding, after which the façade was supposed to come to an end.

But what if their relationship went from fiction to fact? What if they just . . . kissed? What if he wanted this—wanted her—as much as she wanted him?

"You okay?" Veer's voice broke through her conflicting thoughts.

"I'm just sleepy from all the food." She rested her head against the warm window, letting sunlight wash over her closed eyes.

Harsha couldn't forget that she was paying him half a million rupees and had no idea what he had done with the money. As much as she had shared with him about herself, parts of Veer's life remained a mystery to her. Despite things being back to normal between them, there were still so many unanswered questions. Maybe, after this was over, he would do the sensible thing and meet someone he could break his three-month rule for without needing the incentive of money.

The sooner Harsha came to terms with this fact, the better.

SEVENTEEN

"The bottom line is, in life, sometimes good things happen, sometimes bad things happen. But, honey, if you don't take a chance, nothing happens."
—Dorothy Zbornak, *Golden Girls*

Harsha refreshed her bank balance on her phone, certain the number blinking back up at her was a lie. Neha had promptly paid the invoice in full for the wedding photography gig, while the other client had sent over a small deposit, and gosh, that was . . . a lot of money in her own account.

Maybe it wasn't a lot for any of the other Godboles, who would only need one shopping spree to bring that number down to zero, but for Harsha, who'd done her fair share of hustling and struggling this year, it was more than she could have dreamed of.

When Veer's car honked thrice from downstairs, Harsha put on her sneakers and jogged to where Nayanthara was parked. Veer reached forward to open the car door for her before she could, and she smiled at him graciously as she tugged on her seat belt. He wore one of her favorite collared shirts that she'd bought for him—light pink, the sleeves rolled up to his forearms in a sexy way—and his hair was slightly shorter than usual, buzzed on the sides.

"New haircut?" she asked as he pulled onto the main road and braked in traffic.

"My barber cut one side too short," he said, touching the buzz cut as though self-consciously. "So it had to be done. Hope I don't look ugly, though."

Harsha rolled her eyes. "You're fishing for a compliment."

He tutted loudly. "And you didn't take the bait."

The road erupted with the noise of horns as the signal turned green, and Harsha waved her hand forward, smiling at how quickly he could soothe her nerves. "Just drive, you goof." She set her phone on his dashboard, Google Maps displayed front and center. Twelve minutes until they got to the designer wedding clothing store, and maybe she'd luck out and find something she could buy with her own, hard-earned money. Now that her career was going places, there was no way she wanted to rely on the secondary account for anything other than Veer's payments.

"Here we are." Veer parked the car under a shady tree in front of Renuka Mishra's designer boutique, where a guard swiftly opened Harsha's door for her. Impressed, she said a quiet thank-you and reached for Veer's hand, pulling away at the last moment.

When they walked inside, Harsha's heart melted. The store was decked out with yellow chandeliers, artistic Indian wallpaper, and rows upon rows of the most beautiful, high-end, fashionable ethnic wear she had seen in her life. No wonder Neha had proudly shown off this place on her Instagram.

One of the store attendants, dressed in a neatly pleated red-and-gold saree—signature bridal colors, and the colors of Renuka Mishra's logo—folded her hands in namaste. "Welcome to Renuka Mishra's boutique. Would you like something to drink?"

"Filter coffee, if you have some," Veer said.

"We do. Ma'am?" the attendant asked.

"I'm good, thanks," she said, and the attendant headed somewhere inside the store.

Veer bent closer and whispered right into Harsha's ear, ruffling her hair with his breath, "Is my coffee the only kind you like?"

"You mean Sunstag's coffee, not yours," she said, shifting away. Her neck still tingled.

"Po-tay-to, po-tah-to," he said.

"Nobody says po-tah——" she started, but gave up and addressed the other attendant who was waiting patiently for instructions. "I'd like to see some lehengas. My cousin's getting married next week."

"Of course." She gestured for them to follow her to the other side of the store, which opened up into an explosion of colors: green, blue, pink, yellow, silver, everything but red; clearly, it only showcased lehengas for guests of the wedding. "What style or color are you looking for, ma'am?"

Harsha thought for a minute. She'd stayed up all night, googling lehenga designs with Sasha diligently commenting on them via Zoom, and decided sea-green was the way to go. It was a classy color that would set her apart from the other guests *and* bring out the flecks in her gray eyes. Or so Sasha had said.

"Something in sea-green or turquoise," she said, and the store attendant picked out three lehengas from the rack and set them on a table.

Harsha turned her back to the attendant and tried to shield herself as she combed through the first lehenga to find a price tag, curious since the website didn't advertise prices. When her hands came up empty, the attendant cleared her throat. "Ma'am, this range starts from a hundred and seventy thousand rupees. We have another range that's priced a little lower at a hundred and fifty thousand——"

Harsha almost gasped at the cost. She slowly faced the attendant again, forcing out a weak smile. "I was just feeling the fabric."

"Of course." The attendant lowered her gaze.

"Excuse me." Ignoring Veer's concerned look, Harsha walked farther into the store, nearly stumbling into the first attendant who carried Veer's coffee in a dainty, pink-rimmed mug. She apologized and took out her phone, her fingers punching in keys on the touchscreen until her own bank balance flashed before her eyes: a little over one hundred and sixty thousand rupees, more money than the account had seen in months.

Her stomach dropped to her knees. And yet, there was no way she'd be able to afford anything from this store within that price range and still pay all her other bills on time. What had the attendant said? One hundred and fifty thousand? She laughed dryly. Nope. Not happening.

Why had Harsha even wanted to shop at the same store as Neha, anyway? Wasn't she above all that competition and drama now? She exhaled, refusing to let her tears fall. No. She wouldn't let Neha get to her again.

"What's wrong?" Veer's warm hand clasped hers, and she sank into his half-embrace. "Aren't you using the secondary account?"

She licked her lips. "I wanted to get something with my own money."

He spun her around and placed his hands on her shoulders, his gaze soft and smiling. "Let's get out of here."

"But where would we even go?" she said. "These wedding boutiques are always so expensive."

He grinned—no, smirked—as he took out his phone and started to dial a number. "Trust me. I have a place in mind."

Veer's body thrummed with nervous energy—part anxiety, part excitement—as he pushed the door open to Anuja Pillai's wedding boutique and led Harsha inside. Deepika had told her mom they were coming, and she was on the way to the store herself to help them find the right lehenga. So far, Veer's friends hadn't let it slip to Harsha that they knew the truth, but keeping his secret wasn't the focus right now. What mattered more was making Harsha smile and solidifying in her the belief that she could make it on her own.

Her eyes were bright and wide-eyed with all the innocence of a kid in a candy store as she spun around, marveling at the cozy boutique so different from Renuka Mishra's: no attendants at their beck and call, no bright explosions of colors, no chandeliers, but rows upon rows of beautiful Indian ethnic wear in pastel shades, from light blue and yellow to pink and green . . .

Harsha's hands went to the pastel mint-green lehenga on the mannequin on display in the center of the store. "Veer, look!" she said. Her fingers walked along the embroidered blouse. "How did you know about this?"

"Veer, is that you?" Anuja Auntie walked up to them from a small room in the back, beckoning him over. He bent low to hug her short, stout frame, then tried not to laugh as she sized him up through her large glasses like only Indian aunties could. "You've lost weight. Are you not eating all your meals on time?"

He had only met Deepika's mother a handful of times in the past two years, but she was a sweetheart. "I promise I'm eating just fine," he said, then took Harsha's hand in his. "This is Harsha, my girlfriend. Harsha, this is Anuja Pillai—Deepika's mother."

"Namaste, Auntie," Harsha said, folding her hands politely. "What a beautiful collection you have here."

Anuja Auntie grinned, her cheeks heating from the compliment. "Thank you, and it's clear you've already found the one you love." Harsha looked at Veer, confused, but Anuja Auntie pointed to the mint-green lehenga on the mannequin. "Let me bring it out. What's the occasion?"

The door swung open behind them, bringing a rush of cool air as Deepika walked in. Veer gave her a hug. "Thanks for coming over."

After Anuja Auntie headed to the back room, Harsha smiled at Deepika. "I didn't know your mom was a designer. These lehengas are beautiful!"

"Yeah, thanks," Deepika replied curtly.

Veer spoke, if only to break the awkward silence. "Deepika wants no part in the family business. Like I told you, she wants to start her own café someday."

"You'd make an amazing coffee shop owner," Harsha said. "Veer told me the new coconut mocha latte at Sunstag was your original recipe?"

Deepika nodded, shuffling her feet. "Yeah. It is."

Harsha blinked as the silence stretched on. Veer shot his best friend a glare, but she shrugged at him like she didn't know what else to do.

After a second, Deepika headed to the back room, and Harsha sidled up to Veer, her voice low. "I'm pretty sure she hates me."

"No, don't think that." Veer put a hand to his neck, feigning ignorance. "Maybe she had a bad day."

"Veer, I'm telling you—" Before Harsha could finish her sentence, Deepika and her mom brought out the lehenga, draped over Anuja Auntie's arm with the hanger. Deepika was now wearing a tape measure around her neck. "Do you want to try it on?"

Hesitantly, Harsha stepped forward, running her fingers through the shimmery fabric once more. Her forehead was creased, lips set in a line, her back straight. Veer had no idea what she was thinking. Finally, she asked, "How much is it?"

A bead of sweat rolled down Veer's neck. Deepika had said they were cheaper than Renuka Mishra's lehengas when he had texted her, but by how much?

"It's thirty-five grand, and we can also discuss a friends-and-family discount."

Harsha's eyes lit up. "I'll be right back." She headed inside the only dressing room in the store and drew the curtain across the rod.

"Let me know if you need any help," Anuja Auntie yelled, then grabbed both of Veer's hands. Her eyes were shining. "Business has been so slow. Thank you for bringing her here, kanna!"

Veer squeezed back. "Of course, Auntie." She showed him around the store, explaining that they had only one other staff member who came to the store on weekends when it would ideally be a little busier. Sales weren't going as expected, though, because Anuja Auntie had hardly sold any designs in the past week. "I hope your girlfriend likes it," she said, sighing. "This has been the slowest wedding season in years. Everyone just wants to flock to those famous designers so they can show off to their friends. What about the rest of us?"

He fell silent, unsure of how to respond when he and Harsha had also gone to Renuka Mishra's boutique first.

"Okay," Harsha's call echoed around the small store, pulling him back into the present moment, "are you ready to see this?"

"Let's do it," Deepika said. They headed toward the dressing room as, with a flourish and a "ta-da!," Harsha pulled back the curtain and stepped in front of them.

Veer's heart fluttered, his breath whooshing out of him. Harsha looked like a dream. The gold-embroidered blouse, cut high at her neck but dipping low at her back, enhanced her curves like no tight dress ever could. The mint-green lehenga skirt flowed straight from her natural waist and fell to the floor; little silver sequins in the fabric emitted a soft glow that mimicked the beauty of her gray eyes. The pastel green dupatta she'd draped along her arms completed the look. "Well?" she said, almost nervously.

"Hold on." Anuja Auntie helped Harsha tie the strings across the back of the blouse, then beamed. "You're going to look more beautiful than the bride."

"I hope not, or my cousin will start a war," Harsha said, chuckling. She picked up the folds of her skirt and tiptoed closer to the mirror.

Veer nodded along. He couldn't think or speak. What were words? Deepika stood in his peripheral vision, her eyes on him, but there was no chance in hell he could look away from Harsha, not even if he wanted to.

"Do you want to look around some more?" Anuja Auntie said, gesturing to the store at large. "As you can see, pastel is our zone of genius. Pink or yellow would look lovely on—"

"I think this is it." Harsha's cheeks colored as she turned back to the mirror. "I don't need to think about it. This is it."

"Oh!" Anuja Auntie put her hands on her head as though she couldn't believe it. "Let me just take some measurements so it's the perfect fit for you. Deepika, hand me the tape?"

Deepika did as told, her face impassive, then dragged Veer by the arm to the entrance, away from Harsha and her impossible beauty.

He reluctantly tore his eyes off of Harsha and turned to his friend. "What?" he said, pulling his biceps from her grasp and massaging it. Damn, she was strong.

Deepika stared him down, her arms folded across her chest. "You're going to fuck this up for yourself."

Veer glared back. "What are you talking about?"

"You should have seen your face when she came out of that room," Deepika said. "I've never seen a man more whipped. Fake relationship, my ass."

"Lower your voice," Veer mumbled. "And like I told you, I can't help that she's attractive—"

"And I can't help but worry about you," she fired back, though mercifully her voice was softer now. "I've seen you date around a lot over the years, and it's never been like this."

"What is that supposed to mean?"

Deepika shook her head. "You're going to fall in love with her, and then this contract will blow up in your face, and you'll be devastated."

He ran a hand through his hair, gripping the strands for a second before letting go. "I've got this under control, all right? You know me; have I ever fallen in love before? I'm not capable of it—"

Deepika swallowed. "We both know that in this case, you *are* capable of it. Please be careful."

He sighed, knowing she was right, knowing he had no chance of winning this argument. "All right."

Anuja Auntie called them back inside. She had tightened the blouse and skirt in certain places, so the lehenga now fit Harsha like skin. Veer tried not to gawk like an idiot, especially not after his conversation with Deepika.

"Could you please share a picture on social media and tag my account?" Anuja Auntie asked, clasping her hands together, while Harsha smiled at her reflection. "Every post helps a small business."

She's going to say no, obviously, Veer thought. Because Harsha probably wouldn't her parents and Neha finding out she was shopping from a smaller designer. But she said, "Of course. Veer, do you want to take a selfie? Maybe we can just show off the blouse and save the rest of the outfit for the day of."

"Yeah, okay." He took out his phone and sidled closer to Harsha, putting one hand on her back, where golden strings held her blouse together. Her skin was soft and warm, and he realized as he pressed their cheeks together that he had never touched her bare back before.

"Veer?" Harsha said, and there was a slight edge to her voice. "Are you going to click it, or . . . ?"

"Uh, yeah, sorry." He clicked a few pictures as they smiled. In the last one, before she could protest, he turned his face and kissed her cheek, and the blush (and surprise) on her face was so natural he wondered if her family would think something amiss if they saw it.

"You should post this one, since you brought me here," Harsha said as she walked back inside the dressing room and tugged the curtain closed.

"You make a lovely couple," Anuja Auntie said, beaming.

"Thanks." Veer shared the post on his Instagram feed, captioning it: Got to take my girl shopping for her cousin's wedding. Am I the luckiest man or what? He tagged Harsha and the boutique in the picture and pressed Post, all too aware of Deepika's concerned eyes on him.

Chapter

EIGHTEEN

"It's comforting to know that the ones you love are always in your
heart. And if you're very lucky, a plane ride away."
—Carrie Bradshaw, *Sex and the City*

Harsha unzipped her blouse and shimmied out of the lehenga skirt,
breathing hard as she recalled Deepika's words, clearly audible in the
small shop: *I've never seen a man more whipped. Fake relationship, my ass.*

So Veer had told her, and probably Raunak, too. Now it made
sense why they'd been looking at Harsha all funny since she and
Veer got back from Mumbai. They knew the truth.

And then there was the other thing Deepika said: *You're going to
fall in love with her.* Harsha tried to push down the hope that swelled
in her chest. If Veer's best friend, who knew him better than anyone
else, thought he might have feelings for Harsha . . .

Then maybe he did? Maybe this wasn't just in Harsha's head. She
cleared her throat, pressing her lips together to hold back her grin,
then changed into her normal clothes and left the dressing room
with the lehenga over one arm.

Anuja Auntie was waiting at the checkout counter. Harsha
handed her a debit card and didn't take her gaze off the cash machine
until the transaction was approved. Then she let out a slow, soft
breath and handed the shopping bag to Veer, butterflies thrumming

in her stomach at the slight contact of their fingers. "Let's go home. Deepika, thanks for everything."

Deepika gave her a terse smile. After they said goodbye to Anuja Auntie, Veer put his arm around Harsha, guiding her back to his car. "Well, that worked out perfectly," he said, grinning.

Harsha giggled, pressing her body into his shoulder. "It did," she agreed, although all she wanted to do was ask him what he really thought about her. Did he, too, think he could fall for her?

They got into the car, and Veer drove back to her place, seemingly deep in thought. When the car slowed in traffic, he asked, "When's Sasha getting here?"

"Tomorrow," Harsha said as a grin came to her face automatically. "She just boarded her flight. It's like, a twenty-plus-hour journey, and she'll only be here for three days before she has to fly out for her friend's wedding in Jaipur, but gosh, I can't wait."

Veer frowned, shooting her a quick look as the light turned green. "Wait, isn't your sweet sixteenth photo shoot tomorrow too?"

He remembers, she thought, her heart fluttering. "I'll have to rush from the airport to make it on time."

"That sucks," Veer said. He turned down the volume of the music, then added, "Will you have enough time to show her around the places I recommended?"

Veer had sent Harsha a longer itinerary than the one she'd come up with herself. CTR was, of course, on his list.

She laughed. "Yes, but we'll be ordering in CTR instead of going there. No way am I braving that crowd without you around to guide me." Harsha was hoping they would all be able to do something together, but Veer would only have a few hours to spare every day in between his packed shifts. Maybe it was for the best if Sasha didn't spend too much time with Veer. She already wasn't supportive of the fake relationship turning real.

Just like Deepika.

Harsha's smile faded. Veer didn't notice, though, because he said,

"Is it weird that I'm both happy and sad that you get to see Sasha this week?"

"Why is that?"

Veer stared into the distance as he drove. "You'll have some quality time with your best friend after so long, and that's great. But I won't get to hang out with you as much. I'll . . . miss you."

He turned to her, but Harsha averted her gaze to pretend-wipe some dust off her tank top. "I'll miss you too," she said, meaning it. In moments like this, when he showed her how much he valued their connection, it was so difficult not to ask him the question that had been bothering her for weeks now: *What happens to us after Neha's wedding?*

Funnily enough, Harsha didn't know what she wanted his answer to be. Because no matter what, it meant change. They couldn't go back to how things were before, when Veer was just her barista; at the same time, no way could they continue living in the murky gray area of their current dynamic: not friendship, not love, but something dangerously in between.

And as for the possibility of starting something new—something real—what would that look like? Would they hide the origin of their relationship from the rest of the world forever?

What about the money she was paying him? Would that overshadow their future?

Biting her lip, she tugged on her hair elastic. Veer must have noticed, because he took her hand and pressed it to his chest. His heart was beating steadily, slowly. "You're nervous about the wedding, aren't you?"

"Yeah." It was easier to go along with this more obvious truth than the one hidden deep in the recesses of her mind. "We're in the endgame now. What if we fuck it up?"

"We won't." He let go of her hand to continue driving, but he smiled. "Do you trust me?"

Harsha didn't hesitate as she said, "More than anyone else."

Smiling, Veer pulled up a playlist on Spotify, singing along to it loudly. Harsha joined him, belting out the lyrics to The Weeknd, as her heart continued to thud. As much as she knew both Sasha and Deepika had valid points, she couldn't suppress her feelings for him for much longer.

It was all getting too real.

When he pulled up outside her gate, Harsha slid out of her seat belt. "Deepika's mom's designs were beautiful," she said. "Thanks for taking me."

"Of course," he said, his eyes twinkling.

Before she could stop herself, she kissed him lightly on the cheek, took the shopping bag, and ran upstairs without another look back at him, her face burning red.

Sasha:

At baggage claim. See you in a bit!!!!

Harsha:

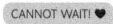

CANNOT WAIT! ❤

Harsha bounced on the balls of her feet, waiting outside the arrival hall at Bangalore's international airport terminal, a bouquet of lilies in hand—Sasha's favorite flowers. They had gone four months without seeing each other in person, and now Sasha would finally be here, even if it was only for three days before her friends' wedding.

Groups of foreigners trickled out from inside the airport, most of whom talked in typical SoCal accents. They were likely from Sasha's LAX flight. Harsha craned her neck and tried to spot her best friend, pursing her lips. Sasha's visit couldn't have come at a better time. Especially since Harsha needed a distraction, not just from the anxiety of the looming wedding, but also from Veer's Instagram post about lehenga shopping—the one she'd sworn she wouldn't keep looking at.

A blond white woman raced out of the crowd toward a dark-skinned Indian man. He scooped her up in his arms and kissed her, seemingly unconcerned about the prying eyes of strangers. Harsha's belly flip-flopped at that public display of love, her thoughts drifting to the way Veer had kissed her cheek at the boutique yesterday for that picture on Instagram. *Okay, fine,* she chided her stupid, traitorous mind. *You win.* She pulled out her phone and looked at the post again.

It really was such a cute photo, she decided, from her cherry-red mouth open in a soft, smiling gasp, to his crinkling brown eyes fixed on her. What wasn't visible in the picture was Veer's warm fingers grazing her bare back through the cut-out on the lehenga. She let out a shudder, going back to that moment. That touch had felt so intimate, so precious, and it wasn't even for the cameras. It was just . . . for them.

Oh, she was in trouble.

Hurried footsteps approached. Harsha had barely looked up from her phone when Sasha tackled her with a hug, making her stumble back a few feet. They held each other, squealing and jumping for a whole minute before pulling apart.

Harsha handed her the flowers, grinning so wide her cheeks hurt. "I was going to bring garlands and a puja thali to welcome you to India, but I thought that was a little too cliché."

Sasha pressed the flowers to her chest. A tear fell down her cheek. "I've missed you so much, H," she whispered, brushing her straight black hair away from her eyes.

"Me too." Harsha's face crumpled. They hugged again, then booked an Uber to Harsha's apartment. She had already crammed a mattress into the small gap between her single bed and her cupboard for Sasha to sleep on. Harsha had suggested Sasha book a hotel room so she would be more comfortable, but Sasha was adamant that she didn't care about moldy walls or sex-crazed upstairs neighbors as much as she cared about spending quality time with Harsha.

In the Uber, as Kannada songs played on the radio, Sasha looked out the window, squealing with excitement at the brightly colored mom-and-pop stores, the cows ambling about on the street, and the different kinds of vehicles in traffic. "This city is so alive!" she exclaimed, her eyes wide. "Like, there must be a hundred people on this street right now! Isn't that cool?"

Harsha laughed, throwing her head back against the leather seat. "Mumbai is even more alive. It literally never sleeps. Bangalore goes dead silent after midnight."

Sasha quirked a brow. "Well, what's home to you now? Mumbai or Bangalo—"

"Bangalore," Harsha affirmed without thinking twice. "It feels like where I belong."

"Because of your photography biz taking off . . . ?" Sasha said, more like a question than a statement.

Because of Veer, Harsha wanted to say. But Sasha was already suspicious of this whole fake relationship and its consequences, so all she did was nod. "Exactly."

Sasha's phone chirped. "My mobile data pack is working, finally!" She exhaled through her teeth as Instagram loaded. "The Wi-Fi on the airplane was so wonky. I need to catch up on—" She fell silent.

Harsha's neck prickled with sweat. She didn't have to look at Sasha's phone to know which picture had made her speechless.

"That's a cute photo of you and Veer," Sasha said, her voice stiff. "Is that from yesterday's lehenga shopping spree?"

"Yeah, isn't the lehenga gorgeous?" Harsha said, hoping it would distract her. "And it was a steal, too, compared to the other store we went to."

Sasha sighed as she set her phone aside. "H, why are you doing this?"

"You know why." Harsha thumped her head against the leather seat. "My family—"

Sasha smacked her on the arm. "Bullshit! You and I both know that this is so much bigger than your family and what they think of you."

"Oh, really?" Harsha rolled her eyes at her best friend and rubbed her biceps. Sasha was petite, but strong.

"You're starting to fall for him, and you don't want this to end. Isn't that right?"

Harsha ran her finger along the car seat, gulping. "Maybe . . . ?" When Sasha didn't speak, she looked up to find her best friend smiling. "Wait, you're happy?" Harsha exclaimed.

Sasha pressed a hand to her face, her eyes shining. "You were so defeated after your parents ghosted you at graduation . . ." She shrugged. "You deserve more joy than anyone I know. And I think Veer gives you that, doesn't he?"

"He does," Harsha said softly. "But S, there's more." At Sasha's confused expression, Harsha explained what she overheard during their shopping trip.

Sasha gasped. "H, this is a green light! He has feelings for you too."

"But Deepika had a point." Harsha sighed as she rested her head against the seat. "Making this relationship real would complicate everything."

"Like what?" Sasha rolled her eyes. "The money thing? He could pay you back!"

Harsha blinked back tears, yanking on her hair elastic. "Like my dad. If he finds out the truth, who knows what he would do? Besides, it's technically his money, not mine—"

"You've been afraid of your family for far too long, H. Don't give them that power again."

"But—"

"I haven't seen you this happy in a long time, and I'm sure his friends would say the same about him." Sasha stared at the Instagram photo. "Promise me you'll think about this."

"Okay," she replied softly, not knowing what else to say.

The rest of the Uber ride was devoid of conversation, but Harsha's thoughts were louder than a torrential downpour. Even the upbeat Kannada music and the Uber driver's constant honking weren't distracting enough.

Sasha's jet lag finally hit her by the time they wheeled her suitcase into the cramped bedroom. Harsha tucked her in, pulling the covers up to her neck and promising to be back from the birthday party as soon as possible. Sasha fell asleep within minutes. Harsha wore her camera around her neck and headed to MG Road.

While she stood in the metro, holding her breath in the sweaty train compartment, she texted Veer to let him know Sasha had arrived safely. Now on my way to the gig, she added. How's work?

She didn't expect him to reply right away. He hadn't been online for hours—Sunstag's anniversary sale was probably keeping him busy. They'd slashed the prices of their drinks to two hundred rupees for one day only, which was bound to draw in more customers than usual.

The train lurched to a stop at the next station. More people came in; the air was stifling despite the air-conditioning. Harsha pushed herself against the wall to keep from being squished by a student's large backpack. Her phone buzzed.

Veer:

Sunstag is packed, I barely have time to breathe. Talk soon ok? Tell Sasha I say hi though

Harsha:

Yep, take care ☺

She put the phone back and smiled. Despite his chaotic workday, he'd responded right away, his distant behavior long gone. Harsha envied the woman he would date after their fake relationship ended. If he was this attentive with her, she couldn't imagine how much love he would shower upon someone he actually wanted to be with.

Guess I'll never know, she thought glumly. Sasha might think it was worth giving a shot, but Harsha knew better. This wasn't just a fake relationship like in all the movies—it was a paid contract. If any of the Godboles found out the truth . . .

No. Harsha wouldn't ever let that happen.

Chapter

NINETEEN

"Maybe you could be my emotional support human."
—Sam Gardner, *Atypical*

For someone who had only met Veer minutes ago, Sasha sure had taken an instant liking to him. The café was packed during Sunstag's anniversary sale, so the only chance Harsha got to introduce them was during Veer's twenty-minute break later that night.

Veer sat across from them, wearing a jacket over his uniform and listening as Sasha gushed about his coffee while Harsha tried to contain her grin. "This is the best pour-over I've had in my life," Sasha said and took a big sniff of her drink. "And that's saying something, because I brew my own coffee. You're good."

"Takes one to know one," Veer shot back with a smile. He dipped his sandwich in ketchup and winked at Harsha, who looked between her two favorite people and tried to hold back her excitement.

"It really is great coffee, isn't it?" Harsha said, holding up her mug.

Veer and Sasha gave her identical dirty looks. "That does not qualify as coffee," Sasha pointed out, while Veer nodded in agreement. "That's barely a latte."

"Exactly what Veer thinks." Harsha sipped her oat milk vanilla latte and relished the sugary, syrupy taste. "I didn't think you both would get along so well."

"Why wouldn't we?" Sasha rested her arms on the table. "We both like *you*."

Harsha nearly choked on her latte. What the hell was Sasha thinking?

Sasha's lip twitched. Before she could play matchmaker any further, Harsha changed the topic to her last gig. It had gone great in terms of the pictures she snapped, but in true high school fashion, there was all kinds of chaos. Three mean girls got into a huge fight, two couples broke up, and one parent cried.

"Teenagers are so brutal these days," Veer mumbled as he ate his sandwich.

"They've always been brutal, like at *my* sweet sixteenth party," Harsha said, chuckling. "It was more drama than a Netflix reality TV show."

"Why?" Veer asked.

Sasha already knew this story and she burst out laughing. Harsha held back a smile, pretending to think about it. "Let's see: Neha wore the same shade of pink as me, so I yelled at her for stealing my thunder. Cut to ten minutes later, there was cake all over both our designer dresses and someone uploaded the video to YouTube. The whole school saw it."

Veer put his sandwich down and opened the YouTube app on his phone. "Is the video still up, or do I have to track down your former classmates to get the link to it?"

"Don't you dare," she said, swatting at his hand. "It was the most embarrassing moment of my life. I looked like a cartoon character with strawberry cake all over my pink dress."

"Strawberry, again?" Veer chuckled. "Cute."

Harsha's blush darkened as Sasha giggled. "Well, you should get back to work," Harsha said to Veer.

"Right." Veer exhaled softly, definitely getting the message. He stood, tray in hand. "It was great meeting you, Sasha. I'll see you both tomorrow, for my big surprise?"

"We'll be there," she replied, waving.

His footsteps thudded down the stairs. Harsha didn't look up at her best friend until Sasha let out a loud, exaggerated sigh. "He's adorable. How could you not pursue this?"

Harsha put her coffee down regretfully. "It's too complicated, S. If only I hadn't come up with this whole arrangement—maybe I'd have gotten to know him better outside of Sunstag, and then we'd have had an actual chance at . . ."

"Love," Sasha finished.

"Yeah."

"Well, you might not have the perfect love life, but at least your career's going in the right direction." Sasha rested her head on her hands, a smile on her face. "Today's birthday party, then Neha's wedding? You're in demand."

Harsha beamed at her. "Hopefully, it only goes up from here."

"It will," she promised. "You deserve only good things. Especially after all the shit you went through before moving here." Sasha rolled her shoulders back and stood up. "I need another coffee to go."

Harsha nodded and closed her eyes as Sasha went downstairs.

Honestly, it almost felt like a lifetime had passed, not just since the day she met her ex on the flight to Bangalore, but since the night the fake relationship was born—thanks to Neha, of all people. She and Veer had come such a long way, from that awkward hug as strangers during their first fake date, to their now unflinching support and affection for each other.

Her eyes dampened, and she wiped them away resolutely. Sasha might have thought Harsha ought to be selfish and give things a real shot, but Harsha wouldn't. There was simmering attraction between them, and the start of romantic feelings—but she wasn't in love, right? And neither was he, not after everything he'd told her.

Love was hard to ignore—but feelings could be kept in check. And that was what Harsha would do.

THE NEXT DAY, HARSHA GRUDGINGLY got dressed, rubbing her bleary eyes, as a yawning Sasha put on mascara. After ordering takeout from CTR, they'd stayed up most of the night talking and watching rom-coms, finally falling asleep around four A.M.

And if it weren't for the fact that Veer had apparently planned something "super fun" for them to do this morning, Harsha wouldn't have gotten out of bed at all.

Veer's car honked thrice from downstairs at nine A.M. on the dot. "Can't we just go back to sleep?" Sasha groaned, wearing her sneakers.

It was a nice, breezy day, with bright rays of light filtering in through a sky of clouds after last night's rains. "It's a great day to be outdoors," Harsha said, if only to convince herself. Veer had told them to wear something comfortable that they wouldn't mind getting dirty.

"Morning!" Veer greeted them, full of energy, when they slid inside his car, Harsha in the front and Sasha in the back seat. "Are we ready?"

"Only barely," Sasha mumbled, stretching her arms as much as she could within poor Nayanthara's cramped interior. "Where are we going, by the way?"

"It's a surprise," he said, grinning from ear to ear. He started the engine, and they drove with the windows down through the city, which was quieter than usual this Saturday morning. Harsha closed her eyes and soaked in the sunshine as the cool wind whipped her curls around. She never could have enjoyed a car ride like this in the stifling Mumbai humidity. Bangalore was home now—she had no doubt about it.

Veer stopped the car in a shady spot outside Cubbon Park and gestured for them to get out. While they complied, he opened the trunk and took out a large shoulder bag.

Sasha eyed the bag, looking doubtful. "If that bag was any bigger, I'd think you brought us here to bury a body."

Harsha snorted, then covered her mouth as her best friend burst into giggles. "I haven't heard that snort in months!" Sasha said, clapping her hands.

"Let's go," Veer said, locking his car with a beep, "before you two get sentimental."

"Too late for that," Harsha said and wound her arm around Sasha's, smiling.

Veer led the way through the lush, green park, which was a welcome refuge from the chaos of city life that Bangalore usually promised. A group of women dressed in workout gear ran past them, their breaths fast and loud. People walked their dogs, stopping to let passersby pet their furry babies, while couples sat on benches and chatted, their time only each other's.

Harsha didn't live too far from Cubbon Park, but she'd only passed by here once on her way to a lunch date with her ex. It looked like the perfect place to click some photographs, get a morning jog in, and gush over cute puppies. "Where are we going?" Sasha asked when Veer got off the jogging track and led them into the grassier lawns of the garden.

Veer smiled as they approached an area filled with people . . . painting.

"What is this?" Sasha asked as she took in the scene alongside Harsha.

Veer stretched his arms wide. "Welcome to Cubbon Paints! I thought we could enjoy the scenery and paint something to remember each other by?" He held up the shoulder bag. "I brought supplies for all of us."

Harsha blinked. *Was this a dream?* Sasha seemed to have had the same thought as she shot Harsha a funny look. Harsha's real boyfriends had never put this much thought into a surprise outing with mutual friends, let alone a friend of Harsha's they'd only met one day prior. "This looks fun," Sasha finally said. "You didn't have to plan all this, though. We could have just gone out for lunch."

"I wanted to," Veer said plainly. "I've passed by the event a bunch of times and thought it looked like so much fun." He led the way to an empty spot, spreading a large mat from his shoulder bag on the ground, then took out a large box of oil paints, brushes, and paper and arranged it all on the picnic mat.

They sat down and got on with it, shielding their works of art from one another. Harsha had an eye for photography, but she'd always had trouble with paintbrushes. Sasha wasn't the most creative, either, but she looked like she was having fun—a laugh escaped her lips as she dipped her brush in light brown paint. Knowing her, Harsha was sure Sasha would make a caricature of Veer.

Harsha wasn't sure what to paint. What did she want to remember the most about this trip? Her best friend, of course. She settled on painting Sasha with a large pink heart drawn around her face and cups of coffee around the borders.

An hour later, they unveiled their paintings. Sasha laughed at Harsha's amateur-ish, bare-bones portrait of her but gave her a tight hug anyway. "I'm going to hang this up on my wall back home."

"They'll probably think a seven-year-old painted it," Harsha said, laughing back.

Sasha had, of course, drawn Veer as a bearded man in a barista uniform, a medal around his neck, and captioned it BARISTA OF THE YEAR. "I would have drawn a trophy, but a medal's easier," she said, shrugging.

"It's perfect." Veer grinned, then hesitated as he pushed his own page in front of them. "This one's for Harsha."

At first, she wasn't sure what she was looking at. The painting seemed to be set against the backdrop of a train car, with two stick figures sitting by the window. The only recognizable features were the beard and goofy smile on the man's face, and the woman's long, curly black hair and closed eyes as she slept on the man's shoulder. It took Harsha a moment to remember the train ride from Bandra to Churchgate after the depressing lunch with her family. Was that what this painting depicted?

"This is so cute," she said, running a finger along Veer's painted beard. "Thank you."

He scratched the back of his neck and turned his face away, but not before she caught his wide grin and blush. "I'm glad you like it."

"I love it," she insisted, reaching her fingers forward and taking his hand.

He looked her way at last, his eyes lidded and full of an emotion she couldn't place, but before he could speak, Sasha cleared her throat and stood up. "All this painting has made me hungry. Brunch, anyone?"

They dusted the grass off their clothes, packed up their stuff, and returned to Veer's car. Harsha touched her hand to her heart as she trailed behind Veer and Sasha, who were discussing Sunstag's coffee beans. She couldn't stop thinking about the painting and its implications. Veer could have painted anything he wanted, but he chose to paint a moment that nobody but the two of them would remember. He was making it harder and harder for her to pretend this would only ever be fake . . . and she didn't know if she loved or hated him for it.

Sasha's last day in Bangalore came around sooner than Harsha had anticipated. One moment, they were heading to Cubbon Paints, and the next moment, Sasha was wheeling her suitcase toward the airport's entry gate.

Sasha stopped at the back of the queue and bowed her head. "Well. I guess this is it."

Harsha wiped her nose and wrapped her in a tight embrace. These three days had passed in a flurry, and Harsha wasn't quite ready to let go of her best friend just yet.

But she had to, because Sasha would miss her flight if they waited any longer, and her grad school friends were expecting her in Jaipur.

"I'm only a Zoom call away," Sasha reminded her as they pulled apart, tears flowing down her cheeks too. "I love you, and you'll be fine."

"I'll miss you so much," Harsha whispered. She shut her eyes as more tears formed. "Long-distance best friendships should be outlawed."

"One hundred percent," Sasha said furiously. "And if anything happens between you and Veer at the wedding, you'd better call me right after."

Harsha rolled her eyes. "S, didn't I say that won't happen?"

"You'd be surprised what the magic of weddings can do." Sasha grinned smugly. "I'll text you when I land."

The line moved ahead, so they exchanged one final hug before Sasha entered the airport, and Harsha got into her Uber to head back to the city. She sat back and put on her AirPods. Hopefully, music would distract her from the pain of watching her best friend walk away. Who knew when they'd see each other again? Plane tickets were expensive.

Her phone buzzed.

> **Veer:**
>
> Did you drop Sasha off? Hope you're feeling ok
>
> [photo attached] If not, maybe this will help?

Harsha burst out laughing. He'd sent her an old photograph from his school production of *Little Women*. Front and center onstage, surrounded by other kids, was a young Veer in a wig and a pink dress, playing the role of Amy like his mother had said.

> **Harsha:**
>
> Thank you! This definitely helped 😄

She caught the eye of the Uber driver in the mirror and bit the inside of her cheek, trying to suppress her giddy laughter. Veer Kannan had gone above and beyond for her in his role as her fake boyfriend. She only wished the wedding wouldn't change that. Wouldn't change them.

Two days to go.

"Every time someone steps up and says who they are,
the world becomes a better, more interesting place."
—Raymond Holt, *Brooklyn Nine-Nine*

Veer got emotional when he video called his brother. They hadn't spoken on the phone since the Mumbai trip, and although so much had happened after—including everything with Harsha—Veer didn't know how to express any of it in words.

So all Veer said was "I miss you," trying to blink back his tears. He sat on the couch next to Mom, who was eagerly waiting for her turn to talk to her younger son before Veer left for the drive to Nandi Hills.

"I miss you both so much," Arjun said, his voice hoarse, as his eyes shone.

Veer brought the phone in closer to Mom, so she was in the frame too. "So tell us how things are going. How are you doing there?"

"Well, I'm ranking first in class." Arjun grinned, his voice jubilant. "If I keep this up until I graduate, I could get a really great job during placement season."

"Oh," Mom said, putting a hand to her lips, "this is amazing! We're so proud of you, Arjun. And we love you!"

"There's something else," he said, pausing for a second. His eyes darted back and forth. "I've . . . met someone."

Veer had a weird sense of foreboding, like this was something Arjun had wanted to discuss for a while. That night when they'd last talked on the phone, before Veer cut the conversation short, Arjun must have had something on his mind besides school. Was it this?

Mom and Veer exchanged glances. She grinned and clapped her hands together. "Who is she? What's her name? Can you send us a picture on WhatsApp?"

Arjun froze, his mouth open softly, and Veer thought he knew what was coming.

"Hello? Did the video glitch?" Mom picked up the phone and tapped on the screen to check when Arjun spoke, his shoulders slouching.

"It's not a girl. It's my student mentor, Salman."

"Oh," Veer said, smiling. "Arjun, that's great." But his stomach twisted in knots, because he knew it wasn't *his* approval Arjun was seeking. He turned to Mom, whose face had turned green.

"Mom?" Arjun said weakly.

"Yes, kanna, that's . . . nice. Excuse me, I have to go," Mom said. With her hand back on her mouth, she stood up and went inside her room, slamming the door shut.

"Arjun . . ." Veer leaned forward on the couch, his lip wobbling. "She wasn't expecting it. You know that."

"I was just—" Arjun sighed, clutching a fistful of his hair. "I thought it was better to be honest. Maybe I should have waited. I'm just so excited. He's my first boyfriend, and I'm so happy."

"I'm glad you're happy." Veer hesitated, then said, "I've sort of met someone too. But I don't think she feels the same way. I, uh, haven't told her."

"You should." Arjun's eyes softened. "I only told Salman I liked him a couple of weeks ago. I didn't know if he felt the same way, but he deserved to know, and I trusted him enough."

Veer knew Arjun was an adult now, but it never ceased to amaze him just how mature and compassionate his little brother had become. He nodded, then lied, "Yeah. Maybe I will." The wedding ceremony was tomorrow night, and they were driving down to

Nandi Hills shortly so Harsha could get there early and take instructions from Neha and the original photographer before he left.

He looked at the wall clock. It was nearly five P.M. "I have to run. I love you. Text me soon."

He ended the video call before Arjun could say bye, then got up and knocked on Mom's door. "Mom!" he called out. "Open the door, please."

"Aren't you supposed to pick Harsha up to drive to the wedding?" Mom replied in a strangled voice. "She'll be so upset if you show up late."

Veer paused. Mom had a point, but he didn't want to leave her like this. "Do you want to talk before I leave?"

"No!"

He sighed, pushing away from the door. He wanted to stay and console her, explain to her that Arjun having a boyfriend wouldn't change anything, but he really was running late. As he headed to his own apartment to get dressed, he thought about how to broach his mother's fears after the wedding.

Because Mom was . . . Mom. She was traditional and biased because of how she was raised. Veer hadn't thought of it before, but he could remember her scoffs at movies with gay side characters and her constant assumptions that he and Arjun would have wives.

Arjun had probably kept these moments close to his chest, a reason to hide who he was all this time. "Fuck," Veer mumbled, his eyes damp again. He wished he could call Arjun back; he wished he hadn't hung up on him. But it was more important to drive to the wedding venue, embody District Manager Veer for the final time, and get the last of the payments, for Arjun's sake, if nothing else.

The endgame, as Harsha had said. This was it.

HARSHA WAS TREMBLING AND SHAKING with nervousness up until they pulled into the driveway of the wedding venue in Nandi Hills, at which point the anxiety turned into full-blown panic. It wasn't her old fears about the truth coming to light that bothered her; she trusted Veer and his acting. It was more so the realization that these were the last three nights of the fake relationship . . . and god, she had no idea where things would go from here.

And, of course, there was the added problem of having to work with Neha during her worst bridezilla moments—and find a way to capture only her niceness on camera.

Neha had already told security to let them in. Harsha fiddled with her hair elastic while Veer parked the car in between the fifty or so cars that were already here. As they got out of the car, Veer took her hand in his, and she held on tight, looking around. The venue was breathtakingly beautiful, and at this late evening hour up in the hills, the weather was the perfect balance of cool and comfortable. Stars twinkled up above them, mirroring the fairy lights strung around the rich foliage and dense greenery flanking the parking lot. In the distance, loud music boomed from the sangeet, the beats reminiscent of Bollywood dance numbers.

"Sir, ma'am, please come with me," an attendant said, bowing. They followed him into a smaller cottage that housed the front desk.

"Welcome to Amrutha Rasa," the receptionist said, smiling widely at them. "We're still setting up your room, but please go ahead and enjoy the sangeet festivities in the meantime."

They changed into Indian ethnic clothing in the washroom. Harsha dabbed concealer under her eyes, adjusted the dupatta of her maroon Anarkali suit, and returned to the lobby, where Veer was casually rolling up the sleeves of his cream-colored kurta. She stopped in her tracks, her core clenching. The laidback-man-in-a-formal-suit look had always turned her on, but, gosh, seeing Veer's muscular frame in a well-fitting kurta did something to her.

He noticed her and grinned. "You look great," he said. "Got your camera?"

"Oh, right." Harsha let out a soft whoosh of breath and took her camera out of her tote bag. She wouldn't be capturing anything tonight, but she wanted to make sure her camera settings were in line with the current photographer's style. If the wedding album looked too different from one day to the next, people would notice.

They left the rest of their luggage by the front desk and were directed to the large outdoor venue where all four nights of the wedding would be hosted. A dark ebony signboard with the words NEHA WEDS ROHAN on it was nailed to the top of the archway they walked under as they headed toward the source of the fast-paced music.

Given Uncle Madhu's position in Bollywood, the wedding guest list was surely at least two thousand people, considering how most Indian weddings were focused more on building clout by inviting friends and family of the parents rather than the bride or groom, but the sangeet looked a lot more intimate—relatively speaking, at least, with seating for about two hundred people only. A couple she didn't recognize were up onstage, dancing to a recent Bollywood song; in the front row sat Neha and Rohan.

"Let's go," Harsha said, tightening her hold on Veer's hand. As they approached, Neha noticed them. She wore a glittering saree that started out purple at her chest and then gradually lightened to pink and orange shades. Sweat beaded her forehead; she had probably finished her big couple's dance with Rohan already. "Hi!" Neha squealed, enveloping Harsha in a tight hug.

Harsha turned her body slightly so as to avoid damaging the camera. "Hey," she said when they broke apart. "The place looks beautiful."

"Doesn't it?" Neha gave Veer a polite smile and turned right back to Harsha. "Glad you made it on time. The photographer—his name is Milan—is over there with the videography team, who are thankfully staying put. I need the perfect wedding video, you know?" She pushed a strand of hair from her face and rolled her eyes. "Make sure to talk to Milan before he leaves so he can show you the ropes?"

Harsha hadn't ever done wedding photography before, but Neha's patronizing tone made her grit her teeth anyway. "Got it," she said.

"And tomorrow you'll need to follow me and Rohan around all

day until the wedding at six P.M." Neha smiled broadly. "I want tons of behind-the-scenes photos!"

"Cool," Harsha replied. "Guess I'll get to it."

"Have fun!" her cousin replied, blowing her an air kiss while Rohan just gave her and Veer a polite nod from where he was sitting, then returned his eyes to his phone screen.

Harsha went to speak with Milan, as Veer trailed behind. She spotted her parents standing near the open bar, Papa downing whiskey while Maa talked to one of her socialite friends. There were quite a few Bollywood celebrities in attendance, the ones who were friends with Uncle Madhu or Aunt Pinky—and Neha, by extension. She snuck a look at Veer, who'd noticed the celebrities too.

Would Veer prefer to socialize with them instead of following Harsha around? It wasn't like he was the photographer on duty, anyway. Maybe if he schmoozed, he could build some industry contacts. "Veer," she said, turning back, "you can enjoy the performances and mingle. You don't have to—"

"Nonsense," he said, putting an arm around her and pressing his lips to her curls. "Every photographer needs an assistant, right?"

She smirked at him. "So you're my assistant now?"

He pulled away to bow his head. "At your service, ma'am."

Harsha couldn't help but laugh, all nervousness gone. She entwined her arm around his, and together, they went over to speak to Milan.

"Thank goodness Neha found a replacement," Milan, a thin man in his forties, said as he continued clicking pictures of the stage from all angles, resting his weight on one knee. "Otherwise it would have been my head on the chopping block."

"Now it's mine," Harsha mumbled under her breath.

The performance ended, and the DJ announced a ten-minute break. Milan straightened, groaning when his back audibly cracked. "All right, let's see that camera," he said to Harsha.

They talked shop for a few minutes. Harsha noticed Veer dutifully standing beside her the whole time Milan was tweaking her camera settings to match his style. If Veer was bored or tired after the long drive, he didn't show it.

"All right, give it up for our next performance!" the DJ yelled, just as Milan finished explaining everything to Harsha and returned to his photographing stance. "Please welcome onstage the mother and father of the bride, Pinky and Madhusudan Godbole!"

Harsha joined the roaring crowd in their applause. Her uncle and aunt slow danced to a Hindi song from the '70s, and Neha stood to scream out cheers and compliments, occasionally busting a move in time with the music herself.

Wow. Harsha's mouth dried. Would she ever get the chance to look forward to a moment like this with her parents on her wedding day?

"You okay?" Veer asked.

It was only when she felt his hand on her wet cheek that she noticed the tears. "Yep," she said, laughing it off. "Just, you know, weddings bring up a lot of emotions."

He nodded, his eyes soft. "You want a drink?"

She hesitated, then nodded. Her parents were still at the bar, but it wasn't like she could avoid them forever. They passed some of her younger cousins on the way, who shrieked, "Harsha didi!," only to be reprimanded by their parents for being too loud. Harsha smiled tightly at them, clutching Veer's hand in a vice-grip until she was forced to let go when he headed to the bar to order for them. Bracing herself, she greeted her parents.

Maa pulled her in for a quick hug and air-kissed both her cheeks. "How was the drive from the city, beta?" she asked, then touched a lock of hair on Harsha's shoulder. "Did you leave the car windows open? Your hair looks frizzier than usual."

Harsha forced herself to smile. "I'll use some leave-in conditioner before the wedding."

Maa pressed a hand to Harsha's shoulder. "Good idea. We must all look our best for this special occasion."

Veer stepped in with Harsha's vodka soda, a bottle of chilled beer in his other hand. She thanked him and took a sip, letting the fizzy alcoholic drink ease her growing anxiety as they faced Papa.

"Mr. District Manager, there you are!" Papa barked. He thumped Veer on the back, his whiskey sloshing in the glass. "Have you been to a wedding like this before? It's an experience in itself, isn't it?"

"It's a lovely place," Veer agreed, sipping his beer. His throat bobbed, and he sidled closer to Harsha. "Thank you for the invitation."

"Of course," Maa started, but Papa interrupted her, chuckling. "You should be thanking Harsha, not us, although it was either you or show up alone."

Harsha coughed, spilling droplets of her drink down her front as the glass nearly slipped from her grasp. She gratefully accepted a tissue from the bartender and dabbed at her top while Veer held her glass for her. "Finger cramp," she mumbled, but Maa had already moved on to talking to some other woman; Papa, however, was still staring at Harsha smugly, like he knew something she didn't.

"So, beta," Papa said once she had disposed of the tissue, "I was surprised you agreed to stand in as the photographer for the wedding. Did you really need the work?"

"Business is good, actually," she said, lifting her chin up. "I did another gig in the past week. I'm just doing a favor for Neha."

The music swelled as Aunt Pinky and Uncle Madhu's romantic performance ended. They bowed, both beaming at the standing ovation they received. Aunt Pinky spotted her and waved excitedly from the stage. Harsha waved back, smiling, then asked Papa, "Are you and Maa dancing?"

Papa scoffed as he finished his drink. "Your mother had her fun onstage with her socialite friends before you arrived. Dancing isn't my thing."

No chance he'll dance at my wedding, then, Harsha thought glumly.

"You're good at dancing, right, Veer?" her father asked, smirking. "I seem to recall you and Harsha on the dance floor at the anniversary party. What a wonderful performance that was."

Performance? Harsha knew Papa didn't mean anything by it—how could he know the truth?—but her stomach churned anyway. She tugged hard on her hair elastic, hoping it would ground her, and it broke with a snap. *Shit.*

Veer must have noticed, because his fingers grazed her wrist, his touch gentle and comforting. His shoulders were tensed, too, but to his credit, he only nodded politely. "Thank you, sir. Harsha," he turned to her, "I'm a little tired from the drive. Shall we get dinner up in our room instead?"

"Of course," she said, putting her drink aside before he even finished his sentence. "See you tomorrow, Papa."

Papa raised his empty glass in lieu of a goodbye and went right back to the bar.

Harsha said a quick thanks to the photographer and told Neha she would see her after breakfast, and then they were on their way. She held up her broken hair elastic. "Farewell, old friend of mine," she said to it, sighing. "We braved some tough times together."

Veer pulled her closer to his side as they walked to the lobby. "And I'll brave the rest of them with you," he said. "But I hope you have a spare?"

She laughed, intertwining their fingers. "Thank you for being here, Veer."

He smiled back. "No place I'd rather be."

Chapter

TWENTY-ONE

"The only conclusion was love."
—Sheldon Cooper, *The Big Bang Theory*

Veer led the way to the elevator, holding the room key in one hand and Harsha's fingers in the other. Nobody was around to watch, but he didn't want to let go, and it seemed like she had the same thought. When they got to the second floor, Harsha took the key from him and opened the door with a beep. "Okay, here we go."

Veer's chest tightened. The hotel room they'd just walked into was massive, with a fully stocked bar, a fifty-inch television, a small living area, and . . . a king-sized bed.

"Uh, shouldn't we have twin beds?" he asked, his voice shaky. He stuck a finger into the collar of his kurta and pulled at it.

"Neha booked the hotel room, remember?" Harsha set her camera on a side table and frowned at him. "I couldn't have made her suspicious."

"Right." He looked at the bed, spacious enough to fit three well-built people, forget the two of them. He'd woken up next to women before, obviously, but he'd never had such strong feelings for any of them. This felt . . . different. Scary different.

Harsha sat down on the bed and sighed softly as she took her heels off. "God, that feels good," she whispered, closing her eyes with a smile. "Heels are the cruelest invention to date."

"Mm-hmm," Veer said, his mind elsewhere. There was a foot's distance between them, and they were still sitting comfortably. They could maintain that same distance while they slept tonight, in the same bed. No, not "could." They would.

Veer would sleep on the very edge of his side of the bed, all clothes on. He'd turn away, put on a fancy hotel eye mask, and ignore the beautiful, funny, kind, *perfect* woman sleeping next to him.

Once they'd ordered some naans and chicken curry from room service, Veer sat back down on the bed—a respectable distance away from her, of course—and asked, "Are you feeling okay?"

She shook her head. "This wedding feels like a nightmare, and my work hasn't even started yet. I don't know how I'll function the next two days."

He wanted to put his hand on hers, but he held back. *No touching tonight,* he told himself, *or you won't be able to stop.* "Your dad's a character, huh?" he said instead. "I don't understand why he's always acting like such an—" He stopped just short of saying the word.

"Asshole?" Harsha tucked her curls behind her ear and laughed softly; the sound made goosebumps sprout along the back of Veer's neck. "I wish I had parents who actually cared about me. Neha has Uncle Madhu and Aunt Pinky, and you have your mom . . ." Her words trailed off. "I shouldn't compare my situation to yours. I'm sorry."

Veer rubbed the back of his head, deliberating, and finally said, "I wanted to tell you this sooner, but with Sasha visiting, I didn't want to bring up something so heavy." He sighed. "That day, after coming back from the airport . . . I looked up my dad online and called him."

"What?" She gasped and wrapped her hand around his. It felt so familiar, so easy, that Veer couldn't bring himself to pull away.

"I hung up as soon as I heard his voice," Veer said. "I didn't know what to say to him, and I wasn't ready to confront my past. And now . . ."

Harsha threaded her fingers through his, her eyes pained.

Veer sighed. "My whole life, I've hated my father. For betraying us by leaving. For not even staying in touch afterward, for never giving me that closure. But the past couple of weeks, I've started to wonder if . . . maybe I don't need it anymore."

"Don't need what?" she asked.

"Closure." Veer sighed. "Why am I chasing after a phantom when I have the best family in the world? Not even just my mom and Arjun, but my friends. And . . . you."

She tucked her arm into his, her head on his shoulder, and whispered, "I'm here for you, Veer. Always. And I'm not going anywhere."

"Me neither," he said, kissing the top of her head, knowing it was the truth. When this deal ended, he wasn't going to let her go. He couldn't. Not when she meant so much to him.

A knock on the door interrupted them. The food had arrived. They dug into the meal eagerly while watching Veer's favorite sitcom, *Schitt's Creek,* laughing and grinning at each other in between bites of chicken curry and naan.

Harsha sat beside him on the bed the whole time, her thigh touching his. The heat traveling down his body and between his legs was unbearable, but try as he might, he couldn't shift away from her. She was like a magnet, drawing him to her over and over, and he had no choice but to give in.

But he needed to summon every ounce of his self-control. They were going to be sharing a bed. He had to think rationally.

Once they finished their meal and placed their used plates outside the door, Harsha announced, "I'm gonna go brush my teeth." She rummaged in her suitcase for her toiletry bag and headed to the bathroom.

Veer put on a faded cartoon T-shirt and sweatpants in the meantime. He wanted to shower—night showers were the best, and there would no doubt be an amazing shower system in this bathroom—

but the best thing to do was go to sleep as quickly as possible and get this night, this wedding, over with.

He picked up his toothbrush, wondering if he could knock and ask her if she was done, when he heard the sound of the water running. He froze, his hand midway to the bathroom door. She was showering. And singing. And naked. She was definitely naked.

"Oh my god," Veer whispered. Was there any way to escape this? How had he been doing this for six weeks now? How had he not realized that he wasn't playing a character anymore?

He wasn't faking being in love with Harsha. He was faking *not* being in love with her. And he couldn't keep faking it for much longer.

He took out his phone and texted his friends. We're sharing a bed and I've just realized I'm falling in love with her

Raunak is typing . . .

Raunak:

Permission to say "I told you so"?

Deepika is typing . . .

Veer:

Scratch that, I've already fallen in love with her

Deepika:

DO NOT complicate things by sleeping with her

Raunak:

Yeah, they're already complicated enough

Deepika is typing . . .

Raunak is typing . . .

Deepika:

Look, just get through this weekend.
Two more days and then you'll be
done with this contract

Raunak:

Agreed, you shouldn't do anything
until after the money stuff is over

The water stopped running.

Gotta go. Chat later

A few minutes later, Harsha came out, smelling like strawberries, her face pink from the hot water. She was wrapped in the hotel bathrobe that practically engulfed her. Veer had never thought he would be jealous of a bathrobe. "Bathroom's all yours," she said.

Veer quietly brushed his teeth, staring at his own reflection and trying to logic his way out of this situation. Maybe he wasn't actually in love with Harsha. He was just caught up in the magic of a fake relationship, the way all those actors sometimes were while filming, and the emotions that came with finally getting closure with his dad. Plus, he hadn't been with anyone in a few months; that must be it.

By the time he went back to the room, Harsha had already put her hair up in a messy bun and tucked herself under the heavy white blanket. What was she wearing to bed? Overalls and five sweaters, Veer hoped. He didn't want to accidentally brush up against her in the middle of the night.

He got into bed too, avoiding her gaze and turning his back to her right away. "Good night," he said, switching off the lights.

"Good night," she whispered. Then she added, "Veer?"

"Hmm?"

"Have you ever thought about marriage?" she asked, her words shaky.

He exhaled softly, then turned toward her. He couldn't really see her; his eyes hadn't adjusted to the dark yet. But the sheets rustled from the other extreme edge of the bed. There was at least a foot's distance between them.

"Not really." Veer gulped. "I've never gotten to that point in any relationship."

"Me neither," Harsha admitted. She shifted a little closer to him; as his night vision returned, her bright eyes and askew hair came into focus. "But I don't know how I'm going to find love now."

"Why?" His voice dropped low. "You're a catch. Anyone would want you."

"It's just—" She laughed and moved closer still. Half a foot's distance. "I know this relationship is fake. But I don't know how a real relationship is going to beat this."

"What about your ex?" Veer asked.

"My parents made me believe I was meant to be with someone like Shashank: a rich, successful Indian guy who my family would approve of. But maybe that's not what I want anymore."

"What do you want, then?"

"I want . . ." Harsha sighed. "I don't know yet."

Veer nodded, forcing himself not to ponder upon the meaning behind her words. *Self-control,* he reminded himself. "Fair enough. Good night, then."

"Can I ask one more question?" she said, a soft smile on her lips.

"Sure."

"Why did you need the money so badly?"

Veer's stomach lurched. "I'm using it to pay my brother's tuition," he said at last. "BII, Delhi."

Harsha's mouth opened in a soft O. "Oh, wow. How's he doing there?"

"Top of his class." He smirked. "I guess I have you to thank for that."

Harsha's hand, cold and small, clasped his in the dark. "That's great. I'll send you the final payment after the wedding. Then, well, I don't know what then."

"We don't need to talk about that now," Veer said.

"Thank you." She let out a shuddering breath. She was crying.

Veer wound his arms around her, tight, and pressed his lips to the top of her hair. How had they gone from a foot away to pressed together in less than two minutes? How had he fallen in love with her in six short weeks? And, most importantly, why hadn't he kissed her yet?

Because she'd paid him to pretend to be the perfect guy with the perfect job he didn't have. Because this was all going to end after the wedding. Veer's shoulders sank at that realization.

So he pulled her closer, letting Harsha put her head back on him. A minute passed in silence, and her chest rose and fell against his body, sleep taking over.

In that moment, Veer felt more at peace than ever in his whole life. Holding Harsha like this, for real and not for "practice"—fuck, it was better than sex.

He really was in love with her. And two days later, he would have to go back to being her favorite barista who teased her about her order, and she'd go out there and meet the real love of her life.

And that would be that.

TWENTY-TWO

"If soulmates do exist, they're not found. They're made."
—Michael, *The Good Place*

Harsha woke up nestled in Veer's embrace, his grip tight, as though he hadn't let go for a second, not even in deep sleep. She let a soft smile curl her lips and opened her eyes, soaking in the rays of sunlight filtering in through the curtains.

Veer's face was mere inches from hers, his mouth slightly open and a line of drool on his pillow. She held back a giggle, her eyes tracing the curve of his jaw, the peek of chest hair visible beneath his T-shirt. Her gaze went back up to his mouth when he snored, and she had the strongest urge to kiss him, at long last.

Do it, a voice echoed in her head that sounded suspiciously like Sasha. She snorted and shook off the impulse, snuggling closer still. They probably had time until her alarm rang at nine A.M. so they wouldn't miss breakfast, after which she had to go capture behind-the-scenes photos of Neha and Rohan getting ready. If this was her last full day with Veer as her fake boyfriend, she was going to make the most of it.

The alarm rang seconds after she closed her eyes, or at least, it felt like that. With a loud groan, Harsha rolled toward her bedside table and turned off the alarm.

Next to her, Veer stirred. He rubbed his eyes and asked, "Did you snooze it?"

"No." She sat up to stretch her arms and legs. "You snooze, you lose. It's healthy to get out of bed right when the alarm rings."

"I wake up to my alarm," Veer said, frowning. "The only difference is, I have four alarms spaced five minutes apart. I get out of bed when the final one rings."

Harsha padded out of bed to the bathroom. "You're a goof." She shut the door and decided the smile stuck to her face would only help her brush her teeth better. Veer knocked and entered after she yelled, "Yeah, come in!"

"Couples who brush together stay together," he joked. He stood next to her and squeezed some toothpaste onto his red brush, which he'd left out in the open without a toothbrush cap. Unhygienic, and yet so typical of him. Harsha's smile widened, but it was camouflaged by the toothbrush sticking out of her mouth.

They brushed in silence. Harsha liked that picture in the mirror before her. As much as she found tall guys attractive, there was something to be said about men who were only a few inches taller than her, like Veer. It was easy to rest her head against his shoulder, easier still for him to kiss her forehead.

She wondered, if all this had never happened, if there never had been a need to find a pretend boyfriend, whether she would have seen Veer in this light without the charade. Would they have grown closer at Sunstag? Would he have asked her out if she was single?

Would she have wanted him to?

Harsha spat out the frothy paste and rinsed her mouth. "I'm going to shower later," she said, not waiting for him to reply as she yanked the door open. "Bathroom's all yours."

"Mm-kay," Veer said just before Harsha closed it behind her. She leaned against the door for a bit, cursing herself for entertaining these thoughts. Because it wasn't just the need for physical intimacy, a warm body next to hers, that had made Harsha snuggle up to him last night.

It was the want for him, specifically.

She heard the shower running, so she changed into jeans and a top and sat on the couch, jiggling her foot and waiting for him to come out. Did he have clothes in there? Was he going to come out with a towel tied around his waist? Harsha let out a breath and faced the other way.

"Hey," Veer said a few minutes later, carrying the scent of aftershave and the hotel body wash into the room. "Just need to change, and then we can head down for breakfast."

"Cool," she answered. Her back was still to him. When the bathroom door closed again, she grabbed her phone and texted Sasha.

Harsha:

> Soooo . . . Veer and I went to bed
> cuddling last night

Sasha didn't reply. Harsha put on her shoes, waiting, but Sasha was probably busy with her friends and their wedding festivities. Goddamn it. The only thing that could ease the churning in Harsha's belly was girl talk with her best friend.

Well . . . maybe pancakes would help too.

AFTER A QUICK BREAKFAST, HARSHA and Veer rushed back to their room so she could get on with her photographer duties before Neha had to remind her to show up. "Are you ready?" came Veer's shout from the bathroom, where Harsha had told him to wait until she was done getting dressed for the ceremony, since she wouldn't have time to spare later in the day.

"Almost!" she yelled back. The pastel mint-green lehenga and gold-lined blouse hugged her curves just right; it was hard to look away from her own reflection. Harsha wasn't vain about how she looked, just confident, but this outfit had the potential to change that. Deepika's mother really was a fashion mastermind when it came to pastel.

"Harsha, you're going to be late!" Veer yelled.

She shifted slightly to look at the back of the blouse, and tried without luck to tie the strings holding it all together. There was a zipper on the side, but she'd need to tie the blouse regardless. "I'm done," she called to him.

Veer stepped out, a hand over his eyes. He was still wearing the faded cartoon T-shirt and gray sweatpants he had gone to bed in, since he didn't need to get ready until later that night. "Can I look?" he asked, and she felt a surge of love—no, anything but that word— *adoration* for him.

"Yeah." She blushed when his jaw dropped, then ushered him closer. "Help me tie the back of the blouse."

"Yes, ma'am."

Harsha turned around, putting her curly hair all on one side, feeling Veer's warm fingers work on the strings. "Is this tight enough?" he asked, and she licked her lips. Her skin tingled where his breath made contact with it.

"Harsha?"

"Yeah, it is," she finally said.

Veer finished tying her blouse up. He put his hands on her shoulder and whispered in her ear, "You look beautiful. You kind of remind me of that green pixie emoji."

She laughed but leaned her head back, closer to his face. "That's a fairy. I'm pretty sure pixies are up to no good."

"Then you're a pixie," he said, smiling into her hair. "My pixie."

The urge to kiss him, which last night and this morning had roused in her, increased to full power. "I'm getting late," she said, stepping out of his grasp. "Let me just check my makeup."

She touched up her red lipstick and put on another coat of mascara, then grabbed her camera from the side table. When she turned to look at Veer, he was smiling at her.

"What?" she asked, smiling back. "Can't stop admiring my stunningness?"

"That's not a word," he said, laughing, "but yes. Exactly that."

Eye contact for longer than three seconds was supposed to be un-comfortable, awkward, and sometimes creepy. But Veer looked into her eyes for a full six seconds before stretching his hand out for her to take, and she felt both butterflies and the overwhelming sense of relief and comfort.

Here was a man who knew more about her than her parents, who stood by her and cheered her on, who made her laugh endlessly, whose mere touch as she took his hand gave her more happiness than three months with her ex.

Was this love?

Veer dropped her off outside Neha's room, giving her a tight hug and reassuring her that she could do this, and do it well. "Thank you," she said, giving his hand one final squeeze before knocking on her cousin's door.

Aunt Pinky, wearing a dressing gown like the others in the room, welcomed her inside. The room was abuzz with frantic energy; a man was working on Neha's curls, a comb behind his ear and a hair dryer resting between his neck and shoulder, while the makeup art-ist dabbed foundation on Neha's face with a thick brush. Her assis-tants worked on the bride's guests, including Maa and Aunt Pinky.

Harsha got to work, clicking photographs and requesting the stylist to change hand positions so she could get a better shot. Neha's eyebrows were knitted together, and the makeup artist had to ask her thrice to keep her face expressionless so she could finish drawing her eyeliner.

Every now and then, one of Neha's friends walked in to announce a new problem: the florist was delayed, the panditji was throwing a tantrum about the direction of the wind and how it wasn't "favor-able" for a wedding, and the bar had run out of Uncle Madhu's fa-vorite whiskey.

"Okay," Neha said each time, exhaling loudly. Clearly, she was in full panic mode but trying not to show it. Harsha didn't blame her; there were a thousand things that could go wrong at any wed-ding, and, inevitably, at least ten of those things would.

Once the hair and makeup were through, Maa and Aunt Pinky helped Neha into her stunning red wedding lehenga. Aunt Pinky sobbed the whole time; the makeup artist's assistant had to touch up her makeup and ask her to please control her emotions. Harsha, too, swallowed back her tears. What a special moment between family . . . and here she was, stuck behind the camera.

"I should head to Rohan's room too," she said in between candid shots, hoping it would give her some respite from the scene before her that she was most definitely an outsider to. "Someone needs to take pictures of him getting ready as well."

Her cousin scowled and muttered something under her breath. Harsha put down the camera.

"What, Neha?"

"I just *assumed* you'd bring an assistant, like a professional would," Neha said.

"Neha—" Aunt Pinky started, holding a hand out.

"I *am* a professional," Harsha countered, grinding her teeth so tightly her jaw popped. "Aren't I doing you a favor here?"

"A *favor*?" Neha laughed aloud. "I'm paying you your full rate, by the way."

"You know for a fact I'm undercharging you compared to that other photographer," she fired back.

"Because he has decades of experience, whereas you don't!" Neha said, standing up. "Forget it. I suppose we have enough pictures of me—the bride! Don't we, Harsha?"

A hush fell over the room. Maa folded her arms, while Neha's friends stared awkwardly at one another. Aunt Pinky stepped in, putting her hands on her daughter's shoulder and sitting her down again. "Beta, it's fine. Madhu's invited some of his cinematography staff. They can handle Rohan's pictures."

Neha opened her mouth to protest, then shut it, instead plastering a fake smile onto her face. "Fine. Call them. Harsha, go on. Do your job."

"Fine," she replied testily. Slowly, the tension in the air dissipated, at least to a certain extent. Harsha wiped a bead of sweat from her forehead and resumed her photography duties, exhaustion seeping into her bones, wishing Veer were there to comfort her. He was more family to her than the people she was actually related to by blood. What did that say about her?

What did that say about them?

TWENTY-THREE

"You know when you fall asleep and you stop breathing?
When you're married, there's always somebody
there to nudge you back to life."
—Raymond Barone, *Everybody Loves Raymond*

The wedding was breathtakingly beautiful. An emotional Bolly-wood wedding song boomed from the speakers as Neha was carried to the altar in a small carriage, shouldered by Uncle Madhu, Papa, and two male cousins. Her skin glowed, and the grin on her face put Harsha's extra-wide one to shame. She wore a gorgeous bridal lehenga that was neither gaudy nor glitzy, but sophisticated and stylish. Renuka Mishra's custom-made designs were no joke. A heavy diamond necklace glittered at Neha's neck, decorated with rubies to match her red lehenga, and a big but thin gold ring circled her small, sharp nose. Harsha followed along in the shadows, click-ing picture after picture but leaving enough space for the videogra-phers to capture the magic too.

She knew theirs was an arranged marriage, but Rohan had genu-ine tears in his eyes as his bride approached him, and Harsha was lucky enough to get the moment on camera. When the panditji handed them orchid garlands to exchange, Rohan whispered some-thing in Neha's ear, which made her giggle for almost half a minute before Uncle Madhu cleared his throat, and she snapped back to re-ality and put the garland around Rohan's neck, blushing.

They really were in love, Harsha realized with a lurch as she looked at them through her lens. Despite her loathing for her cousin, she felt herself well up, a pebble in her throat, during Rohan and Neha's seven rounds around the holy pyre that represented the vows they would make to each other to cement their marriage—and love—as eternal. Guests clapped and threw flower petals at the couple as they made their rounds, after which rose petal confetti dropped from the ceiling.

In the distance, all the way across the room, Harsha locked eyes with Veer, who had a beer in his hand. He looked handsome in a dark gray suit with a mint-green tie he must have bought to match her lehenga. He smiled at her, his eyes crinkling, then took a sip, and she zoomed in on him and clicked a picture before she could stop herself. She couldn't wait to go up to him. It had been hours since she talked to him—and that was far too long.

Finally, when the ceremony ended and dinner was announced, Harsha headed toward Veer, but paused when Aunt Pinky approached her, a kind smile on her face. "I hope you caught all the big moments," she said, touching a hand to the camera strap around Harsha's neck, "but we want you to be present in them too."

"Auntie—"

"Why don't you hand over your duties to Vishal for the rest of the night? He works in the shooting department for one of your uncle's movies."

Harsha tried not to roll her eyes. "If there are so many people with filming experience here, why did Neha even ask me to do this?" she snapped.

"I thought you understood why, Harshu." Aunt Pinky sighed, fiddling with the pallu of her saree. "She wanted you here for longer than just one night, and this was the perfect excuse. We all knew you wouldn't stay otherwise."

"Wait, what?" Her eyebrows shot up. "Why would she want that?"

Aunt Pinky smiled wryly. "Maybe you should ask her that yourself. Have a nice time, beta. I'll ask Vishal to take over for now."

Harsha found Veer at a dinner table. He had already kept a plate-ful of piping hot food ready for her, along with a vodka soda. She accepted the meal gratefully, taking a bite of the delicious tandoori chicken. She was starving. "How did you like the ceremony?" she asked Veer.

He paused, his spoon halfway to his mouth. "It was beautiful," he said finally. "I don't say this about arranged marriages often, but I think Neha and Rohan chose well."

"They chose well indeed," she agreed, smiling at him, and he took her hand and kissed the back of it, as though he, too, knew she wasn't talking about just one happy couple.

"How was your day, by the way?" Veer sipped his beer. "I missed you."

"I missed you too." Harsha tried not to blush. "Neha flipped out on me while she was getting ready. I'm pretty sure there are three or four shots of her bridezilla death glare in my camera roll now."

Veer let out a chuckle. "Well, now she's the happiest woman in this room, so no harm done." A server came by to clear their plates, and he added, "Want to dance?"

Her mind flashed back to that moment they'd shared at the an-niversary party—the almost-kiss—and a humming filled her ears at the thought of touching her lips to his, at long last. God, she wanted that more than anything else. "Yes, please," she said.

Veer led her to the other side of the room, where couples already danced to the orchestral Bollywood music played by the band Uncle Madhu had hired. Harsha swayed to the melody, licking her lips, her arms wound around his neck. "It's such a romantic night," she remarked.

His Adam's apple bobbed, his eyes flitting to her mouth. "Mm-hmm," he said, gulping. "It really is. I can't believe we're here. To-gether."

"You know what's funny?" Harsha tightened her grip on him. "The day we discussed the contract at that café, I thought you hated me. I was scared this plan would flop."

Veer grazed her shoulder with a stray finger, smiling when she shivered. "I never hated you," he said, "and I never will."

She bit the inside of her cheek to keep from smiling as he spun her around. "Not even if I say I've been keeping something from you?"

He pulled her back into his arms, his eyes kind. "Not even then. But what's the secret?"

"I overheard you and Deepika at the boutique that day," she admitted. "You told her the truth, and she said you're . . ." Harsha left the words hanging.

Veer stopped swaying. "You know?"

Harsha nodded. "The weird thing is, despite my obsession with the contract, I didn't really care that you told her the truth, because all I could focus on was her saying you could fall for me."

"Well"—Veer's eyes flicked to her lips—"she wasn't wrong."

A small gasp broke through her teeth. Veer pried her hands from around his shoulders, holding them tightly in his grip. "Let's go back to our room and talk?"

She squeezed his fingers, loving how perfectly he fit with her. "Let's go," she said.

As THEY HEADED TO THEIR room, still hand-in-hand, Veer couldn't stop the strong feeling of déjà vu from sinking in. The last time they'd shared an electric moment like this was when they returned from the anniversary party, and Veer had had to rush to the shower to avoid his impulses.

But now . . . it wasn't just sexual tension hanging in the air between them, thick and all-consuming. It was equal parts heavy and light; it was the perfect alchemy of electric chemistry and unwavering fondness.

It was love.

Harsha unlocked the door with a beep, and once they had their shoes off, they sat down on the bed, facing each other. Her curly hair fell to her waist, bare above the lehenga skirt. God, she was beautiful, and he wondered if she felt the pull between them too. If she couldn't resist it, either.

"So," she said, grinning, "you wanted to talk about something?"

Veer took his hand in hers, kissing the side of her wrist. "Can I start by saying how proud I am of you?"

Harsha interlaced their fingers. "Proud of me?" she laughed. "Why?"

He ran his thumb in a zigzag along her knuckles, noting how her chest rose and fell from that singular movement. "We've talked about your work a few times, but tonight was the first time I saw you in your natural element. When you were taking the photographs as Neha walked up to the altar, I couldn't stop staring at you."

Her cheeks turned scarlet. "You're supposed to look at the bride, not me."

Veer pressed his other hand to her cheek. "You're beautiful, Harsha, but that's not all you are. You're passionate, you're kind, you're brave. And you never stop being those things. How could I ever look away from you? I'm always so in awe of you."

A tear trickled down Harsha's cheek and onto his hand. Veer brushed it aside with his thumb and said, "This week has been a lot, hasn't it?"

"It has." She hesitated, then pulled him into the pillows, half-sitting up, resting her head close to his face. "Can you hold me?"

"Of course," Veer said. He put his arm around her, brushing a lock of her curls away from her eyes as though on autopilot. Maybe because he'd done this a hundred times while they'd practiced, so it was second nature now.

Or maybe because he just couldn't stop himself from doing it, charade or not.

Harsha stared up at him through her lashes and licked her lips. Veer gulped, his mouth dry. That look in her eyes . . . maybe it was just the magic of the wedding in the air tonight.

Or maybe it wasn't.

"Veer?" she whispered. She let that word out in a ragged breath, her fingers clasping his free hand.

"Yeah?" he asked. He forced himself to look away, at his half-open messy suitcase and her closed one; at the bright white comforter underneath them; at their feet, nearly touching.

"Look at me."

His heart pounding, he turned to her. Her eyes were latched on to his, her face blank. She was still holding his hand, and Veer was afraid to let go, afraid he'd wake up and this would all be a dream, that he had never been anything more than her barista, that she was still with her ex.

The thought killed him.

She cupped his face with her hand and touched their foreheads together. "I really want this," she whispered.

"Want what?" he whispered back as his pulse raced.

She trailed a line down his pant leg with her foot, and he shivered in response. "This. Us. Do you too?" she asked.

Veer held his breath. He did. He so fucking did. Because he was in love with her, and this was all he'd wanted for weeks. But why did she want it? Did she love him too?

Harsha leaned closer to peck him on the cheek, and sure, they'd done this countless times before, but god, it set off something inside him that he didn't want to hold in anymore; he simply couldn't.

"I do," he said, crushing her lips with his own. Harsha pulled him in closer, her arms winding around his neck. When his hands grazed her bare waist, she let out a breathy moan and opened her mouth to give him better access.

Veer tasted the vodka on her tongue and moved away, touching his forehead to hers. "Are you sure about this? We've both had a drink—"

She nodded, whispering, "I want you, Veer. I've wanted you long before tonight," she admitted. "So badly."

That was enough confirmation for him. He cradled her face with his left hand, weaving his other hand through those mermaid curls.

"You're so beautiful," he breathed in between kisses. "My beautiful pixie."

Harsha gasped as his fingers undid the strings that held her lehenga blouse together.

"Is this okay?" he asked, resting his hand on her belly.

Harsha pulled the zipper down in response, then sat up and peeled her blouse off. Veer looked at her for a beat, marveling at her breasts, her skin, the pinkness of her face as she breathed in and out heavily, waiting for him to make the next move.

And he did. He tugged his tie over his head, and Harsha helped him take off his jacket and unbutton his shirt. His hands were shaking so bad, whether with anticipation or anxiety, he didn't know.

It was definitely her body lotion that was strawberry-scented, because as Veer trailed his lips down her neck and chest, his hands exploring underneath her skirt, the aroma was so strong he wanted to have her then and there.

But no, he would savor every single second of this moment, every single inch of her body. She was beautiful, she was perfect, and now, finally, she was in his arms. He wouldn't rush a thing.

So he touched her, kissed her, worshipped her, hoping his lips wouldn't let slip the words running through his mind over and over again that he had never imagined telling anyone before.

She unzipped his pants. *I love you*. She tugged at his chest hair and moaned when he bit her lower lip. *I love you*. She looked him in the eyes and smiled. *I love you*.

And finally, after twenty-seven years of living, Veer understood the difference between sex and making love.

Chapter

TWENTY-FOUR

"I thought I had hit rock bottom,
but we managed to find a new sub-basement."
—Mindy Lahiri, *The Mindy Project*

Harsha woke up in Veer's arms for the second morning in a row. Except this time, they were both naked. He was still asleep, drool on his pillow again, one hand on her bare waist and the other supporting his head.

Shit. She touched her hand to his face, her stomach clenching at the memory of his beard raking across her sensitive skin. Harsha exhaled through her teeth. The things Veer had done last night with his hands and his lips and his tongue and his—

Stop. Harsha clenched her fists to keep herself from staying on that train of thought. But then there was everything else—his sweet gestures that showed her he cared; his kind words that told her he not only understood her, he *admired* her.

Harsha's parents had taught her that admiration was only given to those who were rich, successful, and had society's stamp of approval. So, of course, she had neither expected nor received it from her parents.

But Veer knew her, inside and out, with all of her flaws, and he was still in awe of her.

So fuck the risks of making this fake relationship real, Harsha decided. How could they matter, now that she finally knew what it was like to have him, touch him, *love* him?

Harsha hid her face in the fluffy pillow and couldn't help but press her thighs together as memories of last night washed over her. The way he kissed her neck and collarbone as he thrust into her. The words he whispered as his lips made their way down her body ("I've never loved strawberries more."). Or how he pecked her on the nose and stroked her hair as she fell into a deep, dreamless sleep.

Then her thoughts wandered to how it all began, with their first kiss. Hard and fast, as though there were nothing else in the world that mattered to him but them. And then his kisses had grown tender, more and more, like he was cherishing every brush of their lips. His fingers knew how to work magic, and he'd read her moans and sighs *so* well.

Smiling like a fool, Harsha gently rolled away from his grip and grabbed her phone from the bedside table. It was only seven A.M., and she didn't have to get ready to photograph the reception until the afternoon. She had plenty of time to have a mature conversation with Veer about last night and about where they would go from here.

As she was putting her phone back, it buzzed with a text message.

Papa:

> Good morning. Pls meet me in the
> hotel lobby. Have to talk to you

What is this about? Harsha stifled a groan. Was it another opportunity for him to belittle her or poke fun at Veer? Tell her off for handing over her photography responsibilities and actually enjoying herself at her cousin's wedding? He was impossible to please.

Harsha:

> I'm still in bed. See you at breakfast in
> an hour or so?

Papa is typing . . .

Papa is typing . . .

"Morning." Veer had woken up. He stifled a yawn. "Did you sleep well?"

She put her phone aside and nodded, settling back into the bed. "I did."

"Come here." He tugged her back into his arms and kissed her on the forehead. "I don't know if I should say this, but . . . I could really get used to this."

Harsha's heart skipped a beat. "Get used to what?" she asked, holding back her smile.

Veer brushed his lips against hers, sparking something deep in her core. "Us, of course."

"Me too," she admitted. She hooked her leg on top of his and kissed him, running her hands through his hair. Three times last night didn't feel like enough. She wanted more of him. She wanted everything he could give her.

Veer groaned against her mouth. "You're impossible to resist. God, I . . . I can't stop replaying last night in my head."

Harsha smiled in between kisses, then rested her head on his shoulder. "Veer?"

"Yeah?"

"Should we talk about where we're going from here? Now that we're"—she gulped—"now that the contract is over?"

He tilted her chin up so their eyes met. His gaze was soft, sweet, kind. Full of love.

Just like him.

"There's no question in my mind of what I want with you, no matter how hard it'll be to figure out," he said. "I knew it before, but last night taught me just how much I—"

Harsha's phone buzzed thrice. She reached for it to put it on silent mode when her father's next set of messages caught her eye.

This is urgent

Pls meet me asap

It's about your secondary account

The phone slipped from Harsha's hands onto the comforter. She held her breath, rereading the third message. It's about your secondary account. What about it? Did—did Papa know? No, no, no way in hell—

"Is everything okay?" Veer asked, planting a kiss on her shoulder.

"I—um—reception emergency," she said, standing up with her phone in her hand. She put on the first set of clothes she could find in her suitcase; her hands trembled when she shimmied into her jeans. "I'll be back soon."

"Harsha—" Veer sat up, but she headed out of the room before he could stop her.

She took a series of deep breaths in the elevator, promising herself that this was about something else, not the money she was paying Veer. Maybe Papa wanted her signature on some bank documents, or this was just an excuse for him to tell her off about last night's fight with Neha.

Papa was sitting on one of the plush velvety chairs in the hotel lobby, his gaze fixed straight ahead at a potted indoor plant. He was rotating his phone around in his hand, seemingly deep in thought, with a thin folder resting on his lap. He didn't stand when she walked in; he only gestured for her to take the chair opposite him.

"Hey." Harsha sat down and wiped her shaky, sweaty hands on her jeans. "What did you want to talk about?"

Papa unlocked his phone screen and showed it to her. "This."

Blood drained from Harsha's face at the sight of the secondary account's bank balance, depleted after the previous two payments to Veer. How did—how could Papa have access to it? "What is this?" she asked, feigning confusion.

Her father rolled his eyes. "Did you think I wouldn't find out that you were siphoning off money from our joint secondary account?"

"Joint account?" she exclaimed. "I thought it was *my*—"

"You thought wrong," he said, scrolling through his phone. "You've transferred large sums of money—my money—to the same person, twice. Veer Kannan."

Panic rose in Harsha's throat, tasting like bile. "He was having money troubles," she lied. "He's going to pay me back."

Wordlessly, Papa took out a photograph from the file and gave it to her. It was a picture of Veer behind the counter at Sunstag. He stood front and center in his barista uniform, busy brewing coffee, his eyes on the cup in his hand.

Harsha looked at the photo again. "Who took this?"

"I had someone pay a discreet visit to Sunstag," Papa said casually, as though he were talking about the weather. "It was eye-opening, to say the least." He took the photograph back from her and sighed. "You've disappointed us greatly, Harsha, for months now."

"I think you have the wrong expectations of me," she fired back. "All you care about is how I make you look, not how I want to feel: independent and capable of making my own decisions."

Papa nodded. "I agree. You should be living life on your own terms. Which is why I'm closing the account and blocking your access to it."

"What?" she whisper-yelled. "Papa, I need—"

He stood up and put one hand on her shoulder. "You need space from us. Understood. We won't bother you or Veer again."

Before she could react, he walked out of the lobby and back to the elevator. Harsha sat on the couch, gripping the armrest with both hands as her body shook with silent sobs. Papa wasn't serious, right? She grabbed her phone and tried logging in to the secondary bank account, but after three error messages, she gave up and let the tears win.

The final sum was due today. What now? How could she tell Veer she didn't have enough in her own account to pay him?

What if this changed the way he felt about her?

Because she knew now that she loved him—that she wanted to be with him, no matter the odds stacked against them. She wanted to make it work. She would do anything to make it work.

But she was helpless without the money, buried in the hole she had dug for herself, and there was no longer any guarantee Veer would pull her out of it.

VEER SAT AT THE EDGE of the bed, his fingers interlocked in his lap. Nearly an hour had gone by since Harsha ran out in a rush. Nothing had gone wrong last night, as far as he knew . . .

She hadn't replied to Veer's confused texts yet. He had brushed his teeth, put on some clothes, and done push-ups on the floor to pass the time. She'd been gone a while, and they only had a few hours before she had to get ready to photograph the reception this afternoon.

When his phone vibrated with a call, he jumped, scrambling to answer it. But it said Ibrahim. Veer frowned. Why was he randomly getting a call from Ibrahim? "Hey," he said, answering the call, "it's nice to hear from you."

"Where are you, man? Bangalore?" Ibrahim said. Voices sounded in the background; he was probably on set for another movie. His career was going places, for sure.

Veer shuffled his feet. Now wasn't the time for a friendly call; his attention was elsewhere. "I'm a few hours away from the city for a wedding. Can we catch up later? I've had a crazy night—"

"It's going to get crazier," Ibrahim said. Veer could hear the grin in his voice. "Did you know Kunal Jowar's filming a queer sitcom in Bangalore? Netflix picked it up. I had to back out of one of the secondary roles last-minute because I got a better job in Mumbai."

"Okay . . . ?"

"So I recommended you, sent them a tape I still had from our acting school days, and they loved it."

Veer's knees gave way; he sat back down on the bed. "I—you what?!"

"You've got yourself a final audition today," Ibrahim said smugly. "They'll email you the script soon. You can make it, right?"

"When is it?" he said, the words soft compared to the loud thumping of his heart.

"It's at noon today. I know it's super short notice, but I don't want you to miss out on this opportunity, Veer. Promise me you'll take it."

"I . . ." Veer clutched his chest with a trembling hand. This was the best news he'd heard in months. Only four hours until the possibility of resuming his acting career not with a fizzle, but with a bang. A role in Kunal fucking Jowar's sitcom! His life had finally come full circle.

And just as soon as the joy came, it faded. His veins filled with ice-cold water. He'd screw this up. He was sure. He hadn't ever had a successful audition since the failed sitcom. Not even a callback. He wondered why they even short-listed him. Sure, he was proud of his tapes from his acting school days, but his résumé was subpar at best. Nothing but sheer dumb luck—and Ibrahim's enthusiasm—could have made this happen.

"I can't," he said, and Ibrahim audibly sucked in a breath. "I'm going to fuck it up."

"Like hell you are," Ibrahim said, chuckling. "And listen, I recommended you, so if you're a no-show, that affects my standing with Kunal."

"You're right." Veer smiled softly. "I have to do this."

"Good luck, man—and let me know how it goes!" He hung up.

Veer pressed his palms into his eyes. Shit, shit, shit. This felt like a dream, but it was actually happening. He let out a giddy whoop and continued pacing around the room. *Harsha, get here now,* he pleaded. She was the first person he wanted to share this news with. God, she'd be ecstatic for him. She would probably kiss him. And then he would tell her he loved her. For real this time, while looking into her beautiful gray eyes.

The door opened with a soft click. "Finally!" Veer exclaimed, racing out of the bedroom toward the living area of the suite. "Harsha, you won't believe—" His words disappeared into thin air at the sight of Harsha's crumpled, red face. "What . . . what's wrong?"

She fell into his arms, unraveling into loud sobs. "I'm sorry," she said in between hiccups. "I'm so sorry."

He pressed her into his chest and wound his arms around her tighter. "What happened, Pixie?" he asked.

Harsha's cries only worsened with the nickname, drenching his shirt with her tears. He stroked her hair and whispered quiet words of reassurance until she surfaced. She wiped her nose with a trembling hand and motioned for him to sit down on the plush couch. He thought she would join him, but she took a seat across from him on a chair.

This . . . was not looking good to Veer.

"We have a problem," she started, interlocking her fingers. "My dad knows."

A roaring sounded in Veer's ears. "What—what do you mean? What does he know?"

Harsha sniffled. "That you're a barista. That I've been paying you."

Veer jerked up from the couch onto his feet as his world came crashing down. He opened his mouth, attempting to speak, but no words escaped him. "What does this mean?" he whispered finally.

A tear splashed down her cheek as she shook her head, and that told him everything before she voiced it. "He's revoked my access to the secondary account. I . . . I can't pay you the final amount."

"That's not possible." He grabbed his hair. Images swam in his mind of what would happen now. Arjun would be called to the dean's office. He'd find out the truth about his lying, unethical brother. And his MBA degree would no longer be reality. "No. No. No. Harsha"—he stared down at her with pained eyes—"tell me you're joking."

She stood up too. Her knees shook, or maybe it was Veer's vision getting more and more unsteady by the second. "I don't know what to do, Veer." Harsha choked out another sob. "I need you to tell me this doesn't change anything between—"

"Oh my god." Veer clawed at the panic swirling in his chest. No. He had to stay calm and figure this out. "What am I going to do now? Arjun's tuition—if I don't pay the final amount by Monday, he'll be kicked out of school."

Harsha stood up, reaching for him, but he pushed away from her. "Veer—"

"If I fail at this, like I've failed at everything else so far, I'll let down the most important people in my life, not just myself." He sank to his knees, crying, as reality sank in.

She crouched down beside him, her hand on his shoulder. Her touch was cool as always, but for the first time ever, it couldn't soothe Veer. "Give me some time," she said. "I'll try to figure something out."

He licked his dry lips. He didn't have time. Not with the college's deadline, and not with the looming audition. If he didn't leave now, he wouldn't have enough time to make it home and go through the script. "I'm sorry, Harsha, but I have to go."

"W-what?"

"I got an audition for this afternoon, and I can't miss it. I . . . I need that opportunity, now more than ever." He grabbed his things from the bathroom and the bedroom, while Harsha trailed after him. As he shoved his toiletries and shoes into the suitcase, she said, "I know we need to talk about last night, but . . ."

He couldn't think about anything except his brother's impending expulsion. The roaring in his ears was too loud, the breaking of his heart too painful. So all he said was "I meant all of it, I swear, but I can't think about that right now. I need to make it home on time."

When he dragged his suitcase closer to the door, Harsha strode forward, blocking his path, her arms folded over her chest. Her eyes were red-rimmed. "Was this just about the money?"

"It was never about the money," Veer said, pushing past her. "I'm sorry, Harsha, but I have to go fix this, for my family's sake. I don't

have a backup plan like you—and I don't blame you for not under-
standing."

"Veer—"

"I'll talk to you soon. I promise." He opened the door and walked
out of the hotel room, stifling his urge to look back at the only
woman he'd ever loved as her sniffles echoed in the silence of the
hallway.

"You are perched on the precipice of a dream come true, and
you can jump knowing, possibly for the first time ever,
that you can achieve anything to which you put your mind."
—Moira Rose, *Schitt's Creek*

Harsha sat on the tiled floor of the suite's bathroom, crying into her
knees for the first half hour after Veer left. The next hour, she paced
around the hotel room, trying to come up with a plan.

How could things have gone from picture-perfect to devastating
in a matter of hours? This morning, she'd woken up deciding to dive
headfirst into love and let her heart win, like Sasha had said. But
now? Their relationship was more complicated than ever, with the
broken promise of money hanging between them.

She had to get her hands on the remaining amount, but how? She
had a couple of gigs lined up, but the next one wasn't for a week,
Neha had already paid her in full, and her past gigs hadn't earned her
enough to cover the final payment.

She called Sasha, hoping for advice, and thankfully, after a ten-
minute cry session, her best friend had an idea ready for her. "Well,
when I'm short on cash, I try to sell off something of mine," Sasha
said. "Do you have anything you could part with easily?"

"I might . . ." Harsha's eyes fell on her Gucci tote bag, and she
swallowed. *Well, there's an idea.* "Thanks, S. I'll talk to you soon."

Within minutes, Harsha had created an account on eBay and put the bag up for sale. She refreshed her email over and over, tears still streaming down her face, hoping she would find an interested buyer before Monday.

It was only when an agitated Neha called, reminding Harsha that it was time for the pre-reception wedding shoot, that she washed her face, grabbed her camera, and went down to the lobby.

She would have to figure out another way to get back to Bangalore after the reception, but it was fine; for the first time, she had no desire to go back to the place she now knew was home. She'd lived in Mumbai and Berkeley longer than anywhere else, but they had never felt like home—no city or town truly had until Veer made Bangalore her happy place. She'd thought the fake relationship was the line that fixed the before/after of her life, but it was right now: the gut-wrenching realization that the love she thought Veer reciprocated for her wasn't enough for them to make it. That he didn't hesitate before leaving once she told him she couldn't pay him. That he hadn't even stopped to kiss her or tell her he loved her, choosing instead to walk away from her. That if she didn't fix this, she might lose him forever.

"Sorry I'm late!" Harsha said, putting on her best fake-cheery voice as she approached the outdoor venue where Rohan and Neha, dressed in matching royal blue wedding outfits, stood waiting. They frowned when they saw her.

"Have you been crying?" Rohan asked, then bit his lip when Neha elbowed him.

"I'm fine!" Harsha exclaimed despite knowing it was futile. If her new cousin-in-law, who'd barely said twenty words to her this whole time, could tell something was off, then she was clearly not as good an actor as she'd thought.

Neha sized her up. "Let's get this over with quickly. You're going to need a lot of time—and makeup—to look presentable for the reception."

Harsha tried not to make a face at her cousin and instead focused the lens of her camera. Neha and Rohan did some fake-candid poses for her, including the classic "bride throws her head back mid-laugh while the groom looks at her with love in his eyes" and the ever-popular "they're seconds away from kissing but not really kissing because, well, it's an Indian wedding."

Half an hour later, Aunt Pinky approached. "Neha, your father needs you. Is the shoot done?"

Neha looked to Harsha, who nodded. "Rohan, let's go."

They thanked her and headed toward the lobby. Harsha, meanwhile, opened her phone and refreshed her eBay notifications, which were blank. *Shit.* Now that there was nothing to distract her, her eyes misted again.

"I'll see you at the reception, Auntie," she said, starting to walk away.

"Wait." Aunt Pinky grabbed her by the arm. "Can I join you in your room? I think we need to talk." At Harsha's confused look, she added, "About Veer."

Harsha's belly churned. Papa must have told Aunt Pinky the truth. How many people had he told? Did it even matter?

Once they got to her room, Aunt Pinky sat down on the bed and patted the comforter. "Sit. We have a lot to discuss."

Harsha joined her reluctantly, wiping her sweaty palms on the front of her jeans. "Does Neha know too?"

Aunt Pinky nodded. "Your father told us an hour ago. Just when I thought there wouldn't be any drama at an Indian wedding for once . . . tell me this, beta"—she took Harsha's hand in hers—"what were you thinking, hiring Veer to . . ." She exhaled. "I can't even say it. What a preposterous idea. How is your life so chaotic, Harshu?"

If it had been any other day, Harsha would have laughed. "I wish I knew. I'd just gotten dumped, Neha saw him with me and assumed he was my boyfriend, and I just . . . went along with it. I didn't feel like I had any other choice."

Aunt Pinky's eyes shone. "You always have a choice. You're a Godbole."

Veer's words echoed in her mind: *I don't blame you for not under-standing*. He was right. No matter how much she ran away from her family, her roots, and her generational wealth, she would always be a Godbole. Her last name alone could make things happen for her, if she allowed it.

"Where is Veer now?" Aunt Pinky frowned as she looked around at the room. "Did he leave?"

Harsha rehashed the events of the morning to her aunt. Aunt Pinky sat back, processing everything, then said, "So you didn't pay him yet?"

"I don't have the money," Harsha whispered. She jutted her head toward her Gucci bag, lying on top of her suitcase. "I put my tote bag up on eBay an hour ago. Hopefully, I find a buyer before Monday—that's the deadline for his brother's tuition fees."

Aunt Pinky got up and picked up the tote bag. "May I?" she asked.

"Uh . . . sure?"

She inspected the bag, running her fingers along the beige canvas and the Gucci logo, then picked it up and slung it over a shoulder. "I like it," she declared. "How much are you selling it for?"

Wait . . . what? Harsha stayed in place, gripping the edges of the bed. "Auntie, you don't need to buy a secondhand bag, you can af-ford—"

Smiling, Aunt Pinky put the bag down and leaned over Harsha, her hands on her shoulders. "You will never forget your roots, Har-sha. But I won't forget mine, either." She pulled back, folding her arms across her chest. "I was a hairstylist at a small salon in Juhu before I met your uncle. I could barely afford an unbranded second-hand tote bag, forget this."

Harsha nodded. She hesitated, then showed Aunt Pinky the eBay listing. "The original price of the bag is close to the amount of money I owe Veer, so that's what I'm charging."

"What a coincidence." Aunt Pinky smiled softly. "It's funny how destiny works, huh?"

"Bullshit." Harsha scoffed. "Destiny screwed me over the minute Neha walked into that bar after I got dumped. If I could turn back time and undo everything, I would."

"I wouldn't agree," she replied. "You and Veer fell for each other because of that coincidence. How can you regret that?"

Harsha waved her hand in front of her face, staving off more tears. "I'm scared that's over, Auntie. After I send him the payment, I doubt he'll want anything more to do with me."

Aunt Pinky shook her head. Clearly, she was still Team Veer. "All right, Harshu. I'm going to purchase that bag from you." She pinched her on the cheek, smiling. "But in return, I want you to talk to Neha and patch things up with her. She leaves for her honeymoon this evening, and I don't want her to go to France without having had a chat with you about, well, everything. That fight from yesterday is still weighing on her, and I'm sure this Veer situation is too."

Harsha swallowed her anxiety and nodded. "You're right. I'll talk to her after the reception."

"Good idea. I'll see you there." Aunt Pinky headed to the door.

"Wait," Harsha said, walking up to her aunt. "I just want to say . . . thank you, Auntie, for everything." She held her in a tight embrace, her body sinking with relief when Aunt Pinky hugged her back. "I will never let you down again."

"No." Aunt Pinky cupped her face in her hands. "Never let *yourself* down again."

Harsha smiled through the tears streaming down her cheeks. "I promise."

VEER REFUSED TO LET HIMSELF cry throughout the drive back home. Harsha never texted him or called to check in, and maybe that was for the best. It gave him space to mull over the events that had transpired since last night.

Now he was gripped with the unsurmountable fear that the final payment would never come, Arjun would lose his admission, and Veer would be resented by his family forever.

In an attempt to distract himself, Veer went through the script for the upcoming audition every time he stopped at a toll booth or in traffic. The sitcom followed a group of friends who'd started their own tech business in Bangalore—India's Silicon Valley—and the main characters were two queer women in a secret friends-with-benefits relationship that would later turn into true feelings. The dialogue was cheeky and well-written, while the characters were hilariously lifelike.

After Veer parked outside his apartment, he took his suitcase out of the trunk and stood in front of the building, staring mutely at the unit below his. The living room window was open, as was Arjun's bedroom window. Mom's silhouette showed through the thin curtains; she was dusting his study table and chair with a feathery cleaning brush.

Forget the audition, he told himself, deciding at the last moment that he couldn't be alone. *Fix this first.*

He got out of the lift one floor below his unit, preparing himself. "Mom, I'm back," he yelled as he unlocked the door with his spare key, wheeling his suitcase inside.

Mom scurried out of his brother's room, still holding the fluffy cleaning brush. "Veer! Tell me about everything that happened at the wedding!"

Veer sat down on the couch, and Mom followed suit, tapping his knee impatiently. "Did you and Harsha have a nice time? Did she look beautiful?"

"The wedding—Harsha—" He locked eyes with his mother and burst into tears, unable to hold his emotions back any longer.

"Veer!" Mom gasped and took her son in her arms. "Kanna, what happened?"

He couldn't speak a word amid his sobs; instead, he fell into Mom's lap and cried. The entirety of last night and this morning played on a loop in his head: that perfect first kiss and their night together, the morning pillow talk, and the final moment that had destroyed everything he'd worked so hard toward—not just for Arjun, but for a future with Harsha.

After a minute or so, Mom grabbed his shoulders and forced him up. "Veer." She studied him. "Did you and Harsha have a fight?"

Slowly, he nodded.

"What happened? She broke up with you?"

"It's worse than that," Veer blurted out softly.

"Tell me everything," Mom said, and he did. From start to finish: the fake dating contract, falling for Harsha, the audition news, and his failure.

"Arjun's future is in jeopardy," Veer blubbered, the tears flowing down his cheeks. "And the worst part is," he sighed, "I never even got to tell Harsha I love her, that it isn't just about the money—"

"I know, my baby." Mom wiped his tears and sniffled too. "But you have to tell her."

"Mom." Veer let out an anguished sigh. "Would she believe me after the way I walked out on her?"

"That girl loves you, it's obvious to me. She'll understand."

"I don't know, Mom . . ." During the drive back home, Veer had thought of a million ways to confess his feelings—from the grandest of Bollywoodesque gestures to a simple three-word text. But now, with tensions running so high, Harsha could think he was trying to smooth things over only for the money.

And besides, with less than five days until the tuition deadline, he couldn't think about his feelings for her right now. Not with his family depending on him.

"Look at me." Mom tugged on his elbow. "Even if she says no, it'll be the closure you need." She thought for a minute, then slid her wedding ring off her finger. "I don't need this anymore. You should give it to Harsha, when you're ready. Give it a new story."

"Mom—" Veer started, but she put the ring in his hand and closed his fist around it. She looked away and breathed shakily.

"It's about time I told you what happened with your father."

Veer gulped, waiting.

"He cheated, Veer. He fell in love, got some other woman pregnant, asked me for a divorce. And I . . . refused." A tear fell down her cheek. "I was terrified. Divorce is a stigma in my generation, and it's always worse for the woman. But he ran out on us anyway, sent divorce papers in the mail, and that was that."

"Why didn't you ever tell us this before?" Veer asked, his mouth dry.

She sighed. "I didn't have the courage to admit how hurt I was. It seemed easier to ignore it altogether. I'm sorry, that was wrong of me, and if you want to get back in touch with him, you should. He's still your father."

Veer opened his fist, looking at the simple diamond-and-gold ring inside. Mom smiled weakly, her eyes on the ring in his hand. "The truth is, sometimes, love fades. I hurt every day knowing I had to break something as sacred as my marriage."

"This is his fault," Veer said, placing the ring in between them. "I don't want anything from him, but Arjun should be able to decide that for himself."

"Veer," she said, "you can't hate him for a mistake he made twelve years ago. I wasn't the best wife, and he wasn't the best husband. And . . ." She sighed. "Maybe I'm not the best mother, either."

"Are you talking about everything with Arjun?" Veer asked, and his mother responded with a fresh stream of tears.

"Mom . . ." Veer's heart broke at how pained his mother looked. "He's gay. And that's okay. He's the same Arjun we love, and if you give him a chance, you'll love his boyfriend too."

A tear fell from Mom's eyes, and she gulped. Her hands came to rest on her knees, and she said with an exhale, "I'll—I'll try my best."

"You're the best parent," Veer said firmly. He hugged her, pressing his lips to the top of her frail head. "And don't let anyone tell you differently."

When they pulled apart, Mom caressed his cheek and said, "Tell Harsha you love her. Give her the ring, and ask her to marry you."

"It's too soon for that," he said, looking at the small diamond-studded ring. "We're not in the eighties anymore. But . . . maybe I could sell it and pay off the remaining tuition?"

Mom's hands flew to her mouth. "Are you crazy? Don't you dare sell that! It belongs to your future wife."

"But Arjun—"

"Veer," she said, smiling, "I have your father's alimony stowed in a savings account that I've never touched. I was going to use it for both of your weddings. We'll be okay for now. And after that, we'll figure it out."

Veer pocketed the ring. "Thanks, Mom. I'm sorry if I disappointed you."

She smiled at him through tear-stained eyes. "I might be hard on you sometimes, but it's only because I want you to stop compromising on your dreams. Choose Harsha. Choose acting. Choose yourself, kanna."

He nodded. "Maybe the audition will work out. It's in an hour."

Mom planted a kiss on his forehead. "My baby. God always shows his grace in the most unexpected ways. You're going to get the job."

He stood up and hugged his mother. She was so short and delicate compared to him—but stronger than he could ever hope to be. "I love you, Mom."

"Love you too, kanna." She tugged on his cheek. "Don't be late. I believe in you; we all do. Just make sure to believe in yourself."

"Thanks, Mom," he said, smiling. "I will."

AN HOUR LATER, VEER SAT in the waiting room of the casting studio with three other actors, his foot uncontrollably jiggling. Mom's admission that she had access to alimony to pay Arjun's tuition had put him at ease financially. He could, very safely, chase his dreams and make it in the film industry.

If he got this role. Which sounded impossible, because when had luck ever worked out for him before? Everything he had achieved had been through sheer hard work, while this opportunity just fell into his lap. Maybe this was his one rare shot at fame. His stomach churned. What if he screwed this up?

He checked his phone to pass the time. His boss at Sunstag had texted asking if he was back yet and whether he could take the eight P.M. shift tonight. He sent back Sure, I'll be there, knowing the extra money wouldn't hurt. Deepika and Mom had sent him "best of luck" texts, while Raunak had said, A casting studio is the breeding ground for hot chicks. Go forth and get laid, my man. Veer chuckled dryly. Right now, getting laid was the last thing on his mind. Especially when there was so much left unresolved in his last interaction with Harsha. She hadn't texted him since, and he wasn't surprised. He had walked out on her with barely a warning. But he couldn't think about that right now—one thing at a time.

One by one, the actors went in for their auditions. Veer was third in line. He stepped inside the room and greeted the three casting directors awaiting him.

"All right, Veer," the female director said, scanning his résumé. "This is Alia." She gestured to the lead actress, who Veer knew as one of Bollywood's most popular actresses. This sitcom clearly had pull, despite being set in Bangalore and not Mumbai. He licked his dry lips, suddenly nervous.

"Let's see it," another director said.

Veer closed his eyes, took a deep breath, and exhaled.

And then he was Raghav Rathore, the heroine's brother. The room quieted to a hush as he and Alia delivered their lines. She was a terrific actress, and even Veer had to admit their rapport was undeniably great. The cherry on top was that she, too, joined in on the claps when they were done acting.

"That was good. Very good." The directors exchanged glances, and then nodded toward the door. "We'll let you know in a few minutes. Thank you, Veer."

"Good job." Alia smiled at him, and he left the room, hoping they hadn't noticed the sweat stains under his arms. He freshened up in the bathroom and walked back to the waiting room just as the final actor took his seat after his audition.

The four actors sat in silence, each of them green and sickly, until the door opened and a male casting director came out. He looked at them one by one, then smiled at Veer. "Veer, come on in. The rest of you, thank you so much. We have your files on record, and we'll reach out if there are any other roles to fill."

A buzzing of sorts filled Veer's ears. *If there are any other roles to fill* . . . implying the role of the brother had been filled. And he was the only one asked to stay. Did that mean—

"Veer," the director said, shaking his hand, "filming starts later this week, so we have a bit of a time crunch. I know you have a full-time job, but for this role, you'd have to take at least a few months off. That's our only concern. Are you in?"

Veer bit his lip to keep from whooping with happiness. "I'm in."

TWENTY-SIX

"If you're not scared, then you're not taking a chance.
And if you're not taking a chance, then what
the hell are you doing anyway?"
—Ted Mosby, *How I Met Your Mother*

Veer went straight to his mother's apartment. He unlocked the door with his spare key and walked inside, exhaling loudly.

Mom muted the television and raced over to him, grabbing his hands. "Veer! What happened? How did it go?"

He looked away, rubbing his forehead, trying to heighten the suspense as his mother paled. Then, when he couldn't hold it in any longer, he squeezed her fingers and said, "I GOT IT!"

Mom screamed, cupping his face. "Oh my god! My prayers worked! Tell me all about it! Wait, let's call Arjun too."

Veer video called his brother, who picked up immediately and said, "I'm studying for an exam with Salman, can we talk later—" He paused when he saw Mom's and Veer's matching grins. "Wait, what's going on?"

Veer took a deep breath, then said, "Guess who's going to be a secondary actor in Kunal Jowar's new Netflix sitcom?"

Arjun gasped, then jumped up and down, pumping the air with his other fist. "Holy fu— I mean, wow! That's fantastic! How did this happen?"

"I thought you were studying," Veer said, laughing.

"This has been a long time coming for you," Arjun declared, sitting down at his desk again. "Schoolwork can wait."

Veer gave his mom and brother a full play-by-play of the audition, pausing every now and then to hear their reactions. Mom gasped when she heard the lead actress's name. "Get me her autograph!" she exclaimed.

"Or invite her home to try Mom's chicken. I bet she'd love it," Arjun said, which made Mom scream with excitement.

Finally, over half an hour later, and after a much-needed virtual dance party, Arjun's eyes flitted to somewhere above the phone. "Okay, I'm officially behind on studying," he announced. "Let's catch up soon?"

"Of course," Veer said. He started to hang up when Mom stopped him.

"Kanna," she said into the phone, "is your . . . friend still there? Salman?"

Arjun shifted in place, pulling on the front of his shirt. "Um, yes. He is."

Mom smiled softly. "Tell him I say hello."

"I . . . I will," he replied, shock registering on his face. "Bye, guys."

Veer ended the call and gave his mother a hug. "Thank you for coming around."

She nodded against his cheek and patted his back. "He's my son."

He grinned, then stood up. His phone buzzed three times: his banking app. Frowning, he checked his phone, then gasped. "Shit," he whispered.

"What is it?" Mom asked, peering at the screen with him.

Someone had just deposited a hundred and seventy thousand rupees—the final amount—in his account. Judging by the notification, it was from Harsha's personal account.

"Return it," Mom said, waving her hand. "We have the alimony."

Veer hesitated. "Let me talk to Harsha first." He kissed his mother on the cheek and went upstairs to his apartment. Harsha didn't pick up the phone, so he sat down on his couch and texted her: I've received the amount. Thank you so much and I'm so sorry for leaving like I did.

He waited a few minutes, but she was still offline. Maybe her phone was on silent. Veer sighed, then decided he couldn't wait around for her to reply. He needed to do something—maybe not a grand gesture, but a meaningful one. He combed through his camera app until he found the photo he was looking for, then he opened Instagram, grinning.

HARSHA SAT IN ONE OF the pouf chairs in the lobby, dressed in casual clothes again now that the reception had wound down, as she edited the wedding photos. Neha was supposed to be on her way to meet her here before she left for the honeymoon.

Biting her lip, Harsha clicked over to the next photo, which was from the ceremony. Neha and Rohan looked beautiful in the moonlight, and their love for each other was palpable even through the pictures, their faces aglow as they walked around the holy fire. She tinkered with the contrast and the brightness, thinking back to the other photographer's style.

The next picture was a candid one from the reception. Rohan stood tall, his arm around a grinning Neha, as Uncle Madhu laughed at something Aunt Pinky was saying beside him. What a beautiful family they made. Harsha knew now that she would never have a wedding like this with her parents by her side—because she didn't want them there anymore.

Her family wasn't necessarily who she shared DNA with. It was who stuck around, in both the good times and bad, even if they were going through their own battles.

Harsha played with her backup hair elastic, her thoughts drifting to Veer. He had texted her just as she got to the lobby, but she didn't know what to say to him. He was right; she would always have influence and connections no matter how "independent" she wanted to be—and she didn't know what she could say to him after the difficult situation she had put him in this morning. Her shame wouldn't let her.

"Hey."

Harsha turned and nodded at Neha. "Sit with me? I'm editing the photos."

Neha was dressed in a comfortable T-shirt and pajama shorts. Her hair was wet and her face was free of makeup. She must have just taken a shower. She took the seat next to Harsha's and peered at the screen. "That's a nice picture," she said, then took control of the laptop without asking. "Can I see the rest?"

"Go ahead," Harsha said, knowing Neha didn't need her permission.

Neha swiped through the gallery, mumbling to herself and going back and forth between photos. She paused at a picture where her face was drawn in a fierce scowl. Chuckling, Neha asked, "Is this from our argument?"

Harsha tried not to laugh too. "It is."

Neha continued clicking through the pictures until she got to one of Veer sipping his beer and looking right at the camera. Harsha's belly swooped at how handsome he looked in that suit. "I'm sorry, Neha," she said.

"For what?"

Harsha put a gentle hand on Neha's arm. "For lying to all of you for so long about Veer, and for . . . well, for stealing your thunder, if the truth did that in any way."

Neha laughed derisively. "Don't worry, it's only my folks and yours who know. Besides, maybe this is karma for me wearing the same color as you at your sweet sixteenth."

"So you did do that on purpose?" Harsha exclaimed, then huffed out a breath. "Never mind. That's not important anymore."

"I know I was being mean that day, when I first met Veer," she admitted, "but I was just so angry seeing you there with your boy-friend, so carefree after changing your plans last-minute. I mean, you moved to Bangalore and didn't even text me. You looked like you had the perfect life . . . without us."

Harsha almost burst out laughing. Neha—with the fancy UN job who married the rich surgeon and had only love from her family—was saying this? "Excuse me?" she said. "My life is any-thing but perfect."

"I respect you a lot, Harshu," Neha said. The nickname made Harsha's heart clench. Neha hadn't called her that since they were kids. She exhaled, staring at the intricate mural painted over their heads in the lobby. "You've always done things your way. You trav-eled the world—with *my* mother!—instead of going to college right away. You turned a hobby into a career, and you're so good at it. And you found someone who loves you, on your own terms."

"But—"

Neha held out a hand, her diamond ring glinting sharply. "Let me finish. I, on the other hand, got my college degree, found a respectable job that I'll have to quit because my new family wants to turn me into a socialite—oh, and my husband works twenty-hour shifts at the hos-pital, so I'll be stuck going to parties with my mother-in-law who secretly hates me. All this while I'll watch from the sidelines as you and my mom become besties. How does that sound?"

"Oh." Harsha bit her lip. "I . . . I didn't know about any of this."

They sat in silence for a minute, until Harsha's laptop screen faded to black. Her throat tightened. She had never considered that Neha's dislike of her stemmed from insecurity. In her eyes, Neha had always been the ideal daughter.

"I'm sorry," Harsha repeated. "For what it's worth, I've envied you my whole life too."

Neha wiped a tear with a shaky finger. "We could have been sis-ters. Instead, we've been enemies."

Harsha deliberated saying it, then decided she might as well: "Well, we're still young. Maybe we can be . . . friends. If not sisters just yet."

"I'd like that." Neha reached for a hug, and they held each other tight, both shaking with sobs. When they pulled apart, Neha asked, "So what are you going to do about Veer? Mom told me he left?"

Harsha rubbed her wet nose. "I don't know. If it weren't for Aunt Pinky bailing me out, I would have ruined his brother's future." She sighed.

Neha shot her an admonishing look. "Are you fucking kidding me?"

She jerked her head back. "What?"

"That man loves you." Neha swept some hair off her shoulder. "It was obvious to me since the anniversary party. Even Rohan doesn't look at me like that."

"Like what?"

Neha smiled sadly. "Like he can't believe you exist and he gets to hold you in his arms."

Harsha clutched the arms of the chair tightly. "It all started because he needed the money—"

"So?" Neha raised an eyebrow at her. "He might have done this"—she gestured to the room they were in—"for whatever financial reasons, but he fell in love with you along the way."

"I just can't—"

"You can't," Neha said slowly, "or you're just scared of what comes next?" As Harsha opened her mouth, Neha went on. "And sure, your fears are valid. Our families are fucked up. And this is a weird way to start a relationship. But so what? If you love him, and he loves you, why can't you at least try to make a real relationship work?"

"Neha—"

"Why are you letting your parents win a fight they shouldn't even be part of?"

Harsha closed her mouth. She didn't want to admit it, but Neha had sparked a small, hopeful flame inside of her.

"Go back home," Neha said, getting up, "and tell him how you feel. I promise he'll say it back. If he doesn't, I'll buy you another bag. A better one this time."

That got a laugh out of Harsha. She stood up too, shutting the lid of her laptop. "I have my eye on a Dior tote bag," she said. "It'll cost you a fortune."

"Don't count on it," Neha fired back, "because you're going to have your big rom-com moment. And I hate to admit it, but you deserve it."

After giving Neha another tight hug, Harsha went back to her room, packing her things and wheeling her suitcase to the exit, where Uncle Madhu had thankfully arranged for a car to drive her back to Bangalore.

As she sat in the back seat, mulling over Neha's words, she noticed a new Instagram notification. She'd been tagged in a photo. Frowning, she opened the app.

"Wow," she breathed. It was a selfie Veer had clicked in the Mumbai local train, exactly like the picture he'd painted for her during their Saturday spent with Sasha. Veer's stretched lips were pressed to her curly hair, mirroring her soft, sleepy smile. Until this very moment, Harsha hadn't realized people could smile in their sleep. Or was it only because she was resting on his shoulder that she had looked so safe and secure? Sunlight streamed from the open window onto their faces, highlighting the honey undertones in Veer's warm brown eyes that were fixed on her.

There was no caption under the photo. Her fingers clicked the Like icon before she even realized it.

Seconds later, Veer sent her another text, though she hadn't replied to the earlier ones: Meet me at Sunstag when you're back? I'll be locking up tonight.

Smiling, Harsha texted back, See you soon, her fingers jittery with her eagerness. She would do it. She would storm into Sunstag and tell him she loved him in front of the entire café, all risks and lies forgotten. It would either be the big rom-com gesture Neha had talked about . . . or the biggest mistake of her life.

She couldn't wait to find out.

"Not enough for me? You are everything."
—Jim Halpert, *The Office*

Harsha exited the car with her suitcase and headed toward Sunstag, her chest heaving. She'd gone there straight from Nandi Hills. With most of the guests leaving around the same time for Bangalore— some heading home, others to the airport—the drive had taken four hours instead of the usual two, and her phone battery had conveniently died midway through the journey.

Now it was past eleven P.M., which was when Sunstag closed for the day, but the lights were still on, so hopefully Veer was still here. She couldn't last another moment without dying of anticipation. She wanted to see Veer, but more than that, she needed to tell him she loved him.

She slammed her hands on the doors, groaning when they didn't budge. *Fuck.* Had she lost her chance? Was Veer gone? She knocked a few times, trying to peer through the doors into the back of the café, but she couldn't see anyone.

"Goddamn it," she mumbled. The car that had dropped her off had already left; it looked like she would have to hail an auto rickshaw instead.

As she started to leave, the doors behind her unlocked with a click, and a soft voice said, "Harsha?"

Her heart leaped to her throat at the sound of that voice. His voice.

"Veer," she whispered. Slowly, she turned and walked in through the open doors of the now fully lit café, stopping a few inches short of him. "How—how are you?"

He scratched his beard with a trembling hand. "I was in the back, finishing up the dishes. I'm glad you came."

"I told you I would," she said, setting her spare tote bag off to the side. "I came here straight from the wedding venue, but my phone gave up on me. Veer, I'm so sorry for everything. I didn't mean to put you through so much shit—"

"Harsha—"

She shushed him and went on, "Starting with the whole fake relationship and tolerating my horrid father, to the money scare . . . you didn't deserve any of that. Do you forgive me?"

His eyes moved back and forth, going from her curly hair to her hands, clasped tight. Finally, after the most suspenseful pause in history, he said, "No."

Harsha hung her head, her eyes prickling with tears. "I understand," she said. "In any case, I'm—"

"I don't forgive you," he interrupted her, taking her hand, "because you have nothing to apologize for. You held up your end of the deal in the end. Sure, it was an anxiety-inducing few hours, but it worked out. Besides"—he cracked a grin—"I got the job I auditioned for."

Harsha clapped a hand to her mouth to hold back a scream. "Veer, that's amazing, I'm so proud of you!" Her eyes locked with his, and she thought back to that moment at the bar, six weeks ago, when she had kissed his hand for the very first time to fool Neha. God. She'd lived what felt like a thousand lifetimes since then.

And all of them had been with Veer.

"What are you thinking, Harsha?" he said.

She licked her lips, trying not to think about the way he'd moaned her name into her mouth countless times the night they slept together, and said, "You said you were in awe of me."

"I am." He shrugged, a lazy smile on his face. "I always will be."

"You know, Veer"—Harsha stepped closer so her sneakers touched his boots—"my whole life, men have liked me, desired me, picked me, and I thought that was enough for love. But . . ."

"But . . . ?"

"Those men never cherished me. They never chose me when things went wrong. Instead, they found reasons to walk away. And when you left our hotel room, I thought you were done with this. With us." Harsha let out a shaky breath. "I was so scared."

Veer threaded his fingers through her curls. "Impossible. You've had a hold on me since the day you walked into Sunstag, wearing that dress with birds on it . . . and I hope you'll never let go."

"I'm not scared anymore," she admitted, "because I realized that you cherished me even when I wasn't yours to have. This relationship was fake, Veer, but your kindness never was."

"No," Veer said, shaking his head, "nothing about this was fake. Not my kindness, not our chemistry, not my love for you."

Love. Harsha's heart did a somersault as she tilted her face up, so close yet so far from him. "Are you gonna say it properly, or should I?" she teased.

Veer smirked, then did something she hadn't expected him to—he picked her up, his arms tightening around her waist, and sat her down on the café counter, coming to stand between her legs. "I love you, Harsha."

She pulled him in, grazing her lips along that beard she remembered all too well against her skin. "I love you, Veer. And I'm yours, if you'll have me."

"You're mine, then." Veer touched his forehead to hers. His lips were an inch away, his minty breath washing over her. "But what about your family?" he asked. "And the money? And—"

She silenced him with a kiss, and the world faded into oblivion.

All of today, the memory of his soft lips, his tongue against hers, and his hands around her bare waist had tormented her. But now, it was all happening in reality, in glorious technicolor, while bright yellow lights shone upon them and soft jazz music played from the speakers at the very café where they'd met for the first time. Almost like they were the lead actors in a Bollywood movie, finding their way to each other at long last.

"We'll figure it out," she said, pulling away. "Together."

He cupped her face with one warm hand. "Together," he agreed, sighing. "Can we start over—a blank slate? Forget everything that happened until now and go on an actual first date?"

Harsha considered it, biting the inside of her cheek. "No," she said. "I'm capable of a lot of things, Veer, but hitting the reset button on how much I love you? That'll never happen."

Veer kissed her, his hand moving to the back of her head as he weaved his fingers into her curls and smiled against her mouth. "God, I love you."

They held each other for a few minutes, kissing in between tears and laughs, then Veer pecked her on the forehead. "It's late. Let me drop you home." When he turned to the side to pick up her stuff, his forehead crinkled at the cheap tote bag she'd bought from the gift shop at the wedding venue. "What happened to the Gucci bag?"

"I sold it. To Aunt Pinky. That's how I paid you."

He smiled. "You sold it? For me?"

She ducked her head as her face flushed. "Yes. I realized it didn't have nearly as much sentimental value as I thought."

"Thank you," Veer said softly. He opened the door, and once he had locked up, they walked to his car, holding hands.

"So, where do we go for our first real date?" Harsha asked, swinging their arms together.

Veer exhaled, his grip tightening on her hand. "I'll treat you well, Harsha. I'll return every single rupee you paid me. Once I can, of course." He kissed the back of her wrist. "I promise."

"No," she said, stopping in her tracks and facing him. "Veer, I don't want dates at a gourmet restaurant with you. I don't want a perfect happily-ever-after ending."

He frowned. "Then what do you want?"

"I want benne masala dosa and filter coffee from CTR and vanilla ice cream with strawberry syrup at my place. I want a love—and a life—that we can build together."

Veer's mouth pulled up into the cute grin that, Harsha hoped, she would kiss for the rest of her life. He jutted his head toward his car, which was parked up ahead. "Then I know exactly where to take you."

She giggled. People had always told her she had a wider-than-wide smile, but the joy bursting out of her chest made her jaw hurt as her lips stretched with pure bliss. "Let's go, then," she said.

"Aaaand . . . CUT!" THE ASSISTANT DIRECTOR screamed. "Good job. That's a wrap for today, guys. See you all tomorrow."

Veer stood up from the desk he had been resting against and blushed at the soft claps echoing from around the studio. Alia, who played his sister and co-founder at the tech start-up where the story was set, smiled at him. "You did great." She seemed to have sensed his nervousness during their first take early this morning, and she had been reassuring him of his performance the whole time. He had lucked out with the best co-stars, who were all excited to be a part of a sitcom that India's queer youth desperately needed.

He said bye to the people on set, including the other actors and the crew, then left the building. Thankfully, the details of filming were still hush-hush, and shooting had started at four A.M., so there were no paparazzi crowding the street outside. Then again, they wouldn't have given Veer a second glance anyway. He wasn't famous—but someday, he could be.

Grinning, he headed to his car to drive to Sunstag. He had decided to quit his job for the foreseeable future, but Harsha was still a regular customer there, and he had promised to join her for a coffee after his first day on set.

"Good morning," he said merrily as he walked through the doors, enjoying the tinkling of the wind chimes above him.

Deepika and Raunak looked up at him with broad smiles. "How did it go?" Raunak asked, rushing to him from behind the cash register, despite a customer waiting. Deepika tutted loudly and took the customer's order, though she was still smiling.

"Amazing," Veer replied. "Is Harsha here?"

Raunak grinned. "She's upstairs, waiting for you." Now that it was a real relationship, Veer's friends had excitedly accepted Harsha as the newest addition to their bar hangouts. She had won their hearts like she'd won his.

Veer took the stairs two at a time to get to his girlfriend's usual table. Her back was to him, and she was, like always, deep into her laptop as she edited photos, probably from the engagement photo shoot she'd done yesterday. Multiple guests from Neha's wedding had emailed her with inquiries, and now she was booked out for the next month and a half. Veer had never been prouder.

"Hello from your local Netflix actor," he said as he bent to kiss her shoulder.

She jumped, pulling her AirPods out. She pecked him on the lips from where she was sitting, then grinned when he joined her. "So?" she asked, her eyes wider than plates. "How did my celebrity boyfriend's first day go? Was Kunal Jowar there?"

Veer tried not to laugh, though he felt his lips twitch. "He's the director."

"I know that." Harsha swatted his shoulder eagerly. "Did you at least get a selfie with him, for my sake? Gosh, he makes the best movies!"

He took her hand and pressed a kiss to it. "Drop by the studio sometime; you can take a selfie with him yourself."

She gasped, her other hand flying to her mouth. "Oh my god, I would love that. Look at us both living our dreams. Who would have thought, five months ago, that we'd make such a power cou-ple?"

"Not me," Veer said, laughing, "although I did enjoy flirting with you."

"I still can't believe you remembered I wore that bird dress that first day—you know, it's still lying in my closet somewhere."

Veer's eyes widened, and he scooted his chair closer to hers. "Could you wear it tonight?"

"Only if you promise to take it off."

He leaned in and kissed her, tasting the vanilla on her tongue as her mouth parted for him.

Harsha shoved him away, giggling. "I have to work! Don't dis-tract me with your kissing and your forearms."

He grinned, pulling her in for another kiss. "Oh, Harsha God-bole, that's one promise I'll *never* keep."

Epilogue

"If you're in love with her, that's all that matters.
Because love is the only real force out there."
—Raghav Rathore, *Pyaar Ke Khatir*

One year later

Veer stepped out of the car, hand in hand with Harsha, as the screams and shouts of fans, the camera shutters of the paparazzi, and the romantic music booming from the speakers greeted them at the premiere of Kunal Jowar's first-ever sitcom.

"I think I might go blind," Harsha whispered, shielding her eyes. "How do people do this again and again?"

"I hope we'll get used to it soon," Veer said, laughing.

She smiled and sidled closer to him. "For you, I could get used to anything—even chocolate ice cream."

Veer nearly floated off the ground at those words. Five months ago, he had landed his fourth acting job and was now making enough to have fully paid Harsha back for his brother's tuition. Mom had offered to chip in using her alimony checks to pay the fees for Arjun's second year of his MBA, and Veer had readily agreed.

"Show us the ring, Harsha!" one of the reporters screamed. Not long after the sitcom's promotional events began, Bangalore paparazzi made the connection that Veer's girlfriend was Madhusudan Godbole's niece, which brought their relationship—and Harsha—

back into the limelight. She awkwardly flashed the small, simple diamond-and-gold ring at the cameras in answer. "For a photographer, I sure have no idea what to do with my hands," she mumbled to Veer. He pecked her on the forehead, chuckling.

Once they were both in a good position financially, Veer and Harsha had decided to rent a bigger, better apartment in Bangalore together—and after making that decision, there had been no doubt in Veer's mind that he wanted to spend the rest of his life with her.

He'd popped the question during Harsha's final night living alone, when they were packing up her things and bidding goodbye to that musty one-bedroom unit. Veer got down on one knee in front of her tiny couch and held out his mother's wedding ring for Harsha to accept.

She screamed and tackled him, getting cherry-red lipstick all over his face, then pulled away to ask, "Why . . . here?"

He'd simply smiled and slid the ring over her finger. "Because the day I came over to fix the faulty tap in your bathroom was the day I started to get to know the real you. And I never want to stop, Pixie."

Now, at the premiere, someone from the paparazzi yelled, "Veer, look here!" so he put an arm around his fiancée and posed for the cameras. He could tell Harsha was nervous because she was playing with the hair elastic that, he'd come to accept, would always be on her wrist.

"You okay?" he whispered in her ear, grinning when he noticed goosebumps sprout along her neck. A year together, and his breath on her skin still had that effect on her.

"Better than ever," she admitted, blushing. "Selfie? Sasha would want to see this."

"Yep," Veer said. He pressed their cheeks together and made a winky-face, and Harsha laughed and clicked the picture. A year ago, Veer never would have believed the uptight, rich customer at Sunstag would be the love of his life, and not at all like his first impression of her.

But that was what he loved about their relationship: It was always growing, and he was always learning new things about her. Like how she couldn't watch horror movies without getting nightmares, which was why Veer had promised never to act in one, not even for a million dollars. Or that she had a ten-step shower routine that took well over an hour every day. Their first week living together, Veer had protested, but when Harsha agreed to stick to her signature strawberry-scented products for all of eternity, he decided it was worth it.

Despite his acting career taking off, he still hung out with his barista friends a few times every month. Deepika had been made the new store manager, as she'd hoped for, while Raunak had done the most unexpected thing—fallen in love.

Lights flashed as Harsha and Veer walked the red carpet. "I can't imagine doing this three more times next year," she mumbled, awkwardly posing for the cameras, and he laughed. He was in the process of filming his next three projects: in one film, set in Mumbai, he was the jealous ex-boyfriend; in another, he was a nosy neighbor; and in the limited series, he was the goofy best friend.

His time would come. Soon, he wouldn't just be standing in the sidelines on movie or TV show posters, he'd be front and center, the hero in a big-budget project where he'd pretend to romance Bollywood's biggest and best actresses.

Kunal Jowar walked up behind them and took Harsha's hand to kiss—eliciting a near-swoon from her—and said, "Harsha, you look more beautiful each time I see you! Such a lovely couple. Veer, you never told me how the two of you met."

"If you knew," Veer said, chuckling, "you'd turn it into a blockbuster movie."

"All the more reason to tell me." Kunal winked. He slapped Veer on the back, adding, "See you inside."

Harsha squealed as he left, and Veer planted a kiss on her head. He knew he had a lot to look forward to: magazine interviews, critical acclaim, raving fans . . . he couldn't wait.

"Let's see how well you can act outside of our charade," Harsha said, nearly dragging him inside the screening room. "I can't believe you didn't give me any spoilers."

"I have other ways to spoil you," he said, which made her giggle. They found their seats, and as the lights went out and the screening of the pilot began, Veer took Harsha's hand in his, a smile on his face from ear to ear.

Yes, he had a lot to look forward to. But what he looked forward to the most was a whole lifetime of real-dating Harsha Godbole.

Acknowledgments

Wow. Here I am again, typing out words on the acknowledgments page. I guess this is proof I'm publishing a book for the second time. I don't know—it sounds kinda fake? But I'm grateful all the same.

No, scratch that—I'm not just grateful, I'm proud. Of myself. Of my journey. Of the dream I kept alive in my chest all these years that I would make a living writing happy, romantic books.

There are a lot of people who've helped me get here, but it's my agent and fiercest advocate, Rachel Beck, who I need to thank before anybody else. Rachel, at the time I'm writing this, we've been a team for two years, and you've sold four of my books to Penguin Random House. Four! Are we superstars, or what?

Thank you to my editor, Mae Martinez, for being the perfect combination of critic and cheerleader that my writing needs. Your editorial eye is as sharp as your heart is kind, which is exactly the sort of editor I would want every author to have.

I'm lucky to have the team at Dell Books/Penguin Random House by my side: Taylor Noel, Vanessa Duque, and Katie Horn from marketing and publicity, Jennifer Rodriguez in production, and Alexis Flynn, who designed the text. Thank you too, to copy editor Liz Carbonell, and proofreaders Lisa Grimenstein and Amy Harned. A special mention to Shauna Summers and Kim Hovey, who have rooted for me since I was a baby author at Dell!

I thought I struck gold with the cover of my last book, but I am once again floored by the beautiful collaboration between my illustrator, Sudeepti Tucker, and Dell's cover designer, Belina Huey, for this book.

After my debut novel *Match Me If You Can* came out, I was a burnt-out, anxious, imposter syndrome-y mess, and my loved ones got me through the worst of it. The biggest thank-you goes to my besties Darshita Agarwal, Amrutha Raja, and Sambhram Puranik, who patiently dealt with my panic attacks and what-if spirals and celebrated my successes louder than I ever could. How lucky am I to call you my favorite people?

Thank you also to my closest friends both in the publishing world and in real life: Ananya Devarajan, Kalie Holford, Anahita Karthik, Noreen Nanja, Aishwarya Tandon, Ishita Paul, Anirudh GP, Krishna Betai, Deeraj Ramchandani, Melly Sutjitro, Kathryn Harris, Stephanie Downey, Shannon O'Brien, Manasa Kannan, Ajmal Amsu, Aastha Sharma, Sourjya Ghosh, and many other people I'm probably forgetting.

Following your dreams is challenging in a million different ways, but my family lightens my load every single day. Appa, you are and have always been my number one supporter and biggest fan, whether it's telling your co-workers to buy my books or hyping me up before launch events. Amma, I love brainstorming book ideas with you and telling you all the juicy publishing gossip. And Kavya, although I know you aren't one for big emotions (after all, I'm the ugly crier in the family), I appreciate your quiet support of my journey all the same. I thank the Universe every day that you three are my family.

And finally, dear reader—thank you for once again giving me and my books a chance. I hope that, just like the main characters of *Can't Help Faking in Love,* you'll trust yourself and let the right person into your life when they make themselves known, no matter the odds and the risks. Because you deserve a cinema-worthy love story too.

PHOTO: © SANTHOSH NARENDRAN

SWATI HEGDE is the author of *Can't Help Faking in Love* and *Match Me If You Can*. She is also a freelance editor, mindset coach, and self-proclaimed coffee shop enthusiast who lives in Bangalore, India, and can often be found at the nearest café with a hot mug of tea or singing her favorite songs off-key at karaoke night. She looks forward to a long career bringing Indian stories and voices to light.

swatihegde.com
Instagram: @swatihegdeauthor
X: @SwatiHWrites